THE ANGEL
STONE

THE ANGEL
STONE

A NOVEL

Juliet Dark

BALLANTINE BOOKS TRADE PAPERBACKS

NEW YORK

The Angel Stone is a work of fiction. Names, characters, places, and incidents are the products of the author's imagination or are used fictitiously. Any resemblance to actual events, locales, or persons, living or dead, is entirely coincidental.

A Ballantine Books Trade Paperback Original

Published in the United States by Ballantine Books, an imprint of The Random House Publishing Group, a division of Random House, Inc., New York.

BALLANTINE and the HOUSE colophon are registered trademarks of Random House, Inc.

ISBN 978-0-345-53339-5
eBook ISBN 978-0-345-53340-1

Printed in the United States of America on acid-free paper

www.ballantinebooks.com

2 4 6 8 9 7 5 3 1

Book design by Caroline Cunningham

For Linda Marrow,
eloquent editor and dear friend

ACKNOWLEDGMENTS

I was lucky enough to be teaching a class in fairy tales at the State University of New York at New Paltz while working on this book. I'd like to thank my students there for their insights and observations that helped fuel this book.

As always I am grateful to my first readers: Gary Feinberg, Juliet Harrison, Lauren Lipton, Wendy Rossi, Cathy Seilhan, Scott Silverman, and Nora Slonimsky. Nor could I venture into the lands of Faerie without the constant love and support of my family: Lee, Nora, and Maggie.

Thanks to Robin Rue and Beth Miller at Writers House, to Dana Isaacson and Lisa Barnes at Random House, and Gillian Green at Ebury for opening a door for Callie's adventures in Faerie and beyond. I would especially like to thank Linda Marrow, whose editorial wisdom and constant friendship have given a home to my imagination for all these many years.

THE ANGEL
STONE

CHAPTER ONE

"Do *you* believe in fairy tales, Professor McFay?"

I turned to the young man who had asked the question, searching his bland and innocent face for traces of sarcasm or derision. I'd just finished going over the syllabus for my Introduction to Fairy Tales class and had asked the class to write a short essay on their favorite childhood fairy tale. When I asked if there were any questions, I'd gotten the usual: "How long does it have to be?" "Can I use the personal pronoun?" (Who, I always wondered, had ever told them not to?) and "Can I borrow a pen?" I wasn't expecting an inquiry on my personal beliefs on the existence of fairies, though the young man looked harmless enough. Like so many of the new freshman class, he was tall, blond, and athletically fit in his snug Alpha Delta Chi T-shirt. He had the face of an angel— but that, I had learned recently, wasn't necessarily a good sign.

I looked down at my roster to remind myself of the student's name. "Good question, Mr. Sinclair. What I *believe* is that fairy tales are culturally important, provide an essential outlet for a child's imagination, and by studying them we gain a critical understanding of Western literature. I believe very much in the value of fairy tales."

"But do you believe that the things that happen in fairy tales really can happen?" he persisted. "That pumpkins turn into carriages and frogs turn into princes? Do you believe in fairies?"

The kid was definitely a plant. What eighteen-year-old would ask that question with a straight face? Of course, it would be easiest just to say that I didn't believe in fairies, but somehow I couldn't. I'd feel as if I were killing Tinker Bell.

"I believe, Mr. Sinclair, that if I spend any more time on your question I'll be shortchanging the class of their thirty-five minutes allotted by the English department to complete the diagnostic essay," I said. "Why don't we put your question off to another day?"

Adam Sinclair merely smiled and shrugged, then picked up his pen and began to write, as did the twenty-three other young people in the class. I breathed a sigh of relief and picked up the extra copies of the syllabus I'd handed out. As I shuffled the papers, I noticed that my hands were shaking. Sinclair's question had disturbed me; maybe it was a mistake to teach this class. I'd thought at first it was a tamer choice than my usual "Sex Lives of Demon Lovers" or "Kick-Ass Vampire Slayers" classes, but I was beginning to wonder if teaching a class on fairy tales at the *new* Fairwick College wasn't akin to running up a red flag.

I retreated behind the podium and made myself look busy. Usually I wrote along with my students to model the assignment, but when I picked up my pen and asked myself what my favorite fairy tale was, I nearly laughed out loud. Then I started to scribble furiously.

There once was a young woman who came to a town where fairies and witches lived together. She moved into an old house covered with honeysuckle vines. The house was inhabited by a prince who had been turned into a demon by the Fairy Queen; he was cursed to a demon fate until someone loved him. The woman almost fell in love with him, but when she realized he was a demon, she sent him away. He returned in disguise, and, although she didn't recognize him, she fell in love with him at the exact moment he was slain by an evil monster.

A drop splatted on my paper, smearing the ink. I quickly wiped the tear away and glanced up, hoping no one had noticed. Most of my students were hard at work, their heads bent over their blue books—all except for Nicky Ballard, who was watching me with concern. I smiled at Nicky and mouthed, "Allergies."

I looked back down at my paper and reread what I had written. *What a sad fairy tale,* I thought. *The heroine fails twice— shouldn't she get a third chance?* But there wasn't going to be another chance. I crumpled up the paper and tossed it in the garbage can.

"Time's up," I said, then checked the clock and saw there were ten minutes left to the class. *Crap.* The last thing I felt like doing right now was leading a discussion. Adam Sinclair might start in again, asking if I believed in fairies. "Would anyone like to read their essay aloud?" I asked, without much hope of getting a volunteer. But then Nicky Ballard—bless her—raised her hand.

I called on the raven-haired sophomore and she began to read.

"The story I loved when I was little was called Tam Lin . . ."

I almost stopped her. Although it had been my favorite fairy tale when I was a child, it was the last story I wanted to hear right now. My parents had often told it to me, and after they died, I imagined a fairytale prince had come to tell me the story. Except it turned out he wasn't really imaginary.

"I love Tam Lin," Nicky continued, "because the heroine, Jennet Carter, doesn't listen to what other people tell her. Everyone tells her not to go to the Greenwood, an enchanted forest filled with boggles and haunts, but she goes because the ruins of her family's castle, Carterhaugh, are there, and she's determined to reclaim it."

Ah, I thought, no wonder Nicky liked this story. The Ballards had once been rich and powerful but had fallen on hard times. In fact, they had been cursed. Generations of Ballard women had squandered their beauty and intelligence on alcohol, drugs, and teenage pregnancies. Nicky would have gone down the same road, but I'd discovered last spring that it was my family who had cursed hers. I was able to lift the curse, but Nicky still lived in a decaying mansion with her ailing grandmother and alcoholic mother. No doubt she dreamed of reclaiming her family's honor as Jennet Carter did.

"So she goes through the enchanted Greenwood to Carterhaugh and meets Tam Lin, a handsome young man, who tells her he was kidnapped by the Fairy Queen seven years ago and tonight, on Halloween, the fairies are going to pay their tithe to hell by sacrificing him. Then he tells her how she can save him."

At least Jennet received clear instructions, I thought enviously. But then, Jennet didn't waste time worrying about whether or not she really loved Tam Lin. Not like some people I knew . . .

"She goes to the crossroads at midnight and waits for the fairy host. They ride by on horses decked out in gold and silver, with goblins and bogeys leering and shrieking, but Jennet doesn't run. She stands fast until she sees Tam Lin, wearing only one glove—"

"Like Michael Jackson," someone sniggered. Nicky glared at the interruption but kept on going. *Good girl*, I thought. She'd grown up a lot during her summer abroad.

"—and one hand bare, the sign he'd told Jennet to watch for. She pulled him down from his horse and he immediately turned into a fierce lion, but Jennet wouldn't let him go. He'd told her the Fairy Queen would make him change shape. Next he turned into a writhing snake—"

"Oooh . . ." a girl began, but Nicky and I both glared her into silence.

"Still Jennet held fast to her Tam Lin. Next he became a burning brand, but Jennet didn't let go. When he was again Tam Lin, she wrapped him in her green mantle. The Fairy Queen was really pissed."

A few students laughed, but I didn't check them. They were with Nicky now. Even though it was time to go, they weren't collecting their books or texting on their phones. The story had caught their attention.

" 'If I had known you would leave me for a human girl,' the Fairy Queen said, 'I would have plucked out your eyes and heart and replaced them with eyes and heart of wood.' But Jennet held fast to Tam Lin, and there was nothing the Fairy Queen could do. She rode away to fairyland, and Jennet and Tam Lin married and lived in Carterhaugh in the enchanted Greenwood. I like this story because it's the girl who saves the boy and also . . ." Nicky paused, swallowed, and looked up at me. "Because it shows that sometimes you have to believe in someone even if they look like a monster. Because people can change."

There was a murmur of assent from a couple of upperclassmen, and one girl, Flonia Rugova, who had roomed with Nicky last year, reached over and squeezed her hand. I imagined Flonia knew, as I did, that Nicky's mother, Jaycee Ballard, had joined A.A. and was trying to sober up. "Absolutely," Flonia said. "People can change."

"That was lovely, Nicky," I said. "I think Nicky has answered Adam's question for me. That's the kind of fairy tale I believe in, Mr. Sinclair. The kind that gives us the courage to persevere through hardship and fight for what we believe in. Think about Nicky's story while you're reading the Bettelheim chapter for the next class."

With only ten minutes to make it to their next class, most of the students took off in a panicked stampede. But Nicky lingered behind and fell into step beside me as I left Fraser Hall.

"I don't want you to be late for your next class, Nicky. You know the new administration has a zero-tolerance policy on tardiness."

"I'm free next period," Nicky said. "What's up with all the new rules, anyway? Fairwick College is totally changed."

I sighed. "I know. It's the new administration. They have a rather different . . . um . . . pedagogical philosophy."

"No kidding! We've got curfews! And mandatory dorm meetings. I get, like, twenty emails a day from campus security—and those new security guards are downright creepy." Nicky lowered her voice as we passed one of the new guards, a short, broad-shouldered man in a green jumpsuit. He leered at Nicky in an unsavory manner. "I don't mean to be mean, but they look like *trolls*."

Now that Nicky mentioned it, they did indeed. I wondered . . . "Stay away from them," I told her. "If you have a problem, call me or Professor Delmarco or Professor Lilly."

"Thank God you guys are still here, but so many of my favorite teachers are gone. I was going to take Stones for Poets with Professor Van der Aart, but he's gone on a sabbatical. Now I have to take two required science classes *and* a class on Milton."

I let out an involuntary groan. I'd barely been able to get

through *Paradise Lost* in grad school; the new requirement for the entire student body to read it seemed crazy. "Some of the faculty are trying to . . . er . . . *persuade* the administration to change their policies. We're meeting this evening to go over our . . . er . . . strategies."

"I'm sure you're doing everything you can, Professor McFay. I don't mean to complain. It's just that everything is so different now—even the students. Like that Adam Sinclair and his frat brothers. I mean, one of the things I liked about Fairwick was that it didn't have a big Greek life like the state schools. But this new fraternity . . . well, look at this flyer I got in my mailbox this morning."

Nicky took out a piece of bright magenta paper and unfolded it. Beneath three large Greek letters—Alpha, Delta, Chi—was a crude drawing of a muscular man in a toga. *Hey, ladies!* the speech bubble by his head announced. *It's never too early to try out your Halloween costumes. Whether you're going this year as a slutty vampire, a slutty cat, or just a total slut, we invite you . . .*

"*Ew*," I said, taking the offensive page from her. "That's gross—and completely inappropriate. I'm on my way to the dean's office right now with a list of complaints. I'll add this invitation to them."

Nicky shrugged. "Don't get yourself in trouble over it. No one I know is going. It's just that those Alphas act like they own the campus—"

Nicky's next words were drowned out by the pealing of bells. Loud, obnoxious bells ringing the quarter hour. "And that's another thing," she yelled over the clanging. "Those bells! They wake us up at the crack of dawn!"

"It's on my list," I told Nicky, offering her a wan smile. We'd reached Main Hall. The Gothic gray stone exterior had always given me a sense of calm and stability, but now that it housed the new dean it felt like a brooding, unassailable castle right out of *Dracula*.

"I feel better knowing you're doing something," Nicky said. "But I didn't follow you only to complain. I wanted to talk to you about my research paper."

"Let me guess, you want to do it on Tam Lin."

"Well, not exactly. You see, the thing is, I'm actually feeling a little . . . well, *disenchanted* with fairy tales these days."

"Oh," I said, unable to hide my disappointment. "You're not dropping the class, are you?"

"Oh, no! You're my favorite teacher, Professor! It's just . . . well, when I was in Scotland this summer I came across this collection of fairy tales and ballads that were collected by a woman folklorist named Mary McGowan—there's a ballad in it that's a sort of variation on Tam Lin. I wrote about it in my essay, but I didn't read that part in class. Anyway, I thought it was interesting that the stories were collected by a woman folklorist and I'd like to find out more about her . . . like what made her interested in folktales and how she came to write about them. I thought it would be interesting to write about a real person instead of just writing about fairy tales."

"Hmm . . . I've never heard of her. It sounds like a fascinating topic, Nicky. Of course you can write about that. I look forward to seeing what you dig up."

"Thanks, Professor. And I hope you don't mind what I said about fairy tales. I know they're your thing."

"It's perfectly all right, Nicky," I told her as I turned to go into Main Hall. "There are days lately when I wish I had specialized in something a little more practical."

CHAPTER TWO

I paused for a moment outside the door to the dean's office to collect myself. The conversation with Nicky had unnerved me a bit. It was one thing to watch my college taken over by evil forces and another to see the effects of that takeover on the students I cared most about. The students had no way of knowing why the college was so different. They didn't know that the Grove—a club for ultra-conservative witches, to which my grandmother happened to belong—had conspired to close the door to Faerie with a mysterious all-male British club that turned out to be run by nephilim. I hadn't even known about nephilim a couple of months ago. My specialty was fairy tales, not Bible studies. Truthfully, I'd never had much interest in angels, fallen or not. They always seemed much less interesting to me than fairies, pixies, elves, and goblins.

But the nephilim weren't even fallen angels, as much as they liked to think they were. According to Soheila Lilly, they were elves who had been kicked out of Faerie because they couldn't keep their hands off human women. For hundreds of years they had nursed their resentment of the fey—and the human witches who aligned themselves with the fey—and conspired with the Grove to close the door to Faerie. Once the fairies—and a number of humans, including Dean Elizabeth Book, who had gone to Faerie with her partner, Diana Hart—were gone, the nephilim had free rein to take over Fairwick. Duncan Laird, their leader, had taken over as dean. I wondered if Liz would have left if she had known what would happen to her beloved college. She would be furious to see the changes that had been made . . .

"Are you going to come in, Professor McFay?" A voice came from behind the door. "Or stand out there in the hall all day?"

I'd forgotten the nephilim had such good ears . . .

I opened the door.

. . . and such big teeth.

Duncan Laird, DMA (Doctor of Magical Arts) Oxford, wizard of the Ninth Order, and nephilim, sat behind a large desk, grinning. Even from across the room, those teeth looked too white and shiny, reminding me of the long, sharp fangs he'd revealed when he'd been unmasked and assumed his true shape. I glanced at his hands, folded over a thick folder on top of the desk. They were smooth and manicured, giving no hint of the claws with which he'd nearly slashed my throat—nor was there any sign of the wings that he could extend at will. As I crossed the room, though, I could sense a disturbance in the air, a fluttering . . . I studied the wall behind Duncan, but all I saw were an array of framed diplomas. Perhaps the sound was my heart pounding with fear.

"Have a seat, Professor McFay. I won't bite."

"You tried to rip my throat out," I reminded him as I sat on the edge of a leather chair in front of the desk.

Laird pursed his lips and made a tutting sound, as if recalling some minor social faux pas. "Oh, Callie," he said, leaning forward, "if I had *tried* to rip your throat out, you wouldn't be here right now. I only needed a drop of your blood mixed with the blood of your beloved incubus to close the door. Of course I never intended to harm you."

"You killed Bill," I said.

"An incubus who had been preying on you!" he exclaimed, spreading his hands out in a gesture of appeasement. The motion had the fluid grace of wings opening, and once again I had the impression of invisible wings beating the air. Was that part of the nephilim's power? I wondered. Did they use their wings to move and affect the air around them? "Do you really believe you two had a future together?"

"I loved him," I answered. "He had just become human."

Duncan shook his head. He looked down, noticed the folder on the desk—which I saw was actually a thick envelope with many foreign stamps affixed to it—and turned to put it in the file cabinet behind his desk. "Ah, that was unfortunate timing, then. I had no idea you felt that way about Handyman Bill."

"That was only the incarnation he took," I said defensively. Then, realizing I'd sounded snobbish, I added, "Not that I wouldn't love a handyman if he was as kind and good-hearted as Bill Carey." I blinked back tears, determined not to reveal weakness in front of Duncan Laird. I'd worked out why my incubus lover, who'd materialized once as a hunky poetry teacher, had chosen to come to me the second time as a taciturn handyman. He'd inadvertently knocked my own handyman, Brock, from the roof when he arrived from Faerie, so he'd taken the shape I needed most. It had also given him the opportunity to fix some things he'd broken during his incubus rages. In the two months since Bill had died, I'd had ample time to notice all the little things he'd fixed in the house and to appreciate a man who fixed things rather than broke them.

Duncan Laird canted his head to one side and studied me with sharp blue eyes. I felt a fizzle of electricity at his gaze. It was a sensation I'd mistaken for attraction when I first met him, but now, although I could recognize in the abstract that he was handsome, I knew the sparks between us were warning signs. Still, when he purred, "Is that what you *really* need most, dear Callie?" I felt a flash of heat course through my body. The nephilim, I'd learned through intensive research these last two months, produced their own Aelvesgold—the magical elixir of Faerie—and could transmit it through the air as an aphrodisiac. Over the millennia, they'd used their powers to seduce human women. I suspected that some of our new freshman class might be the offspring of such unions. Which reminded me . . .

"What I *really* need right now," I said, slapping the magenta flyer on the desk, "is a campus where women aren't denigrated and exploited. This flyer is lewd and insulting. I can only imagine what will happen to any hapless girl fool enough to go to this thing. What are you going to do about it?" I demanded, glad to have a channel for the heat in my body.

Duncan Laird picked up the flyer and examined it, his face grave. If his lip had so much as twitched, I would have accused him of sanctioning the fraternity's misogynistic language, but his expression remained suitably serious. When he looked up at me, a crease had appeared between his eyebrows.

"You're absolutely right. This is unacceptable. I'll talk to the president of Alpha Delta Chi immediately and demand he issue an apology to the female student body."

"Okay . . ." I said tentatively, thrown off guard by his compliance. "And what about the party?"

"I'll send security to monitor it," he said. "I don't want anything going wrong there any more than you do, Callie. Especially when it's so close to your house."

"That has nothing to do with it," I snapped, although of course it did. It had broken my heart to see frat boys move in to the Hart Brake Inn, not only because the inn was across the street from where I lived but because it profaned the memory of my dear friend Diana Hart. "Why not cancel the party as a consequence of this offensive flyer?"

"That would be an overreaction and initiate a chain of bad feeling throughout the campus. Better that the new students learn to play by the rules and assimilate into the campus culture."

"If anything does go wrong . . ."

"You have my assurance that nothing will." He learned forward and smiled. I heard that rustling again and felt a sizzle in my veins. I summoned all my power to resist the pull of Duncan Laird's charisma. "I would like us to be friends, Callie—"

I snorted.

"—but if that's not possible, can we not be congenial colleagues? I welcome your input and suggestions and will be happy to work with you for the good of the college. Isn't that what we both want?"

The sizzle in my veins chilled as I realized what Laird was proposing. I could prevent harm to the students if I collaborated with the administration. And, in truth, wasn't that why I had stayed at Fairwick? After the door to Faerie had closed, with most of my friends trapped behind it, I considered leaving. The academic job market wasn't in great shape, but I could have gone back to the city, kicked out my subletter, and taken adjunct jobs until I got something better. I could have turned my back on Fairwick and the world of fairies and witches and returned to the life I'd left only a year ago. But then there was Bill's last note to me.

There's another door.

If there was another door to Faerie and there was any chance of freeing my friends—and any remote chance that Bill was still alive there—I absolutely had to stay in Fairwick and look for that door.

"We don't want the same things at all," I said. "I want you out of here and my college back."

Duncan smiled—or maybe he was baring his teeth. "Fair enough, Professor McFay. I appreciate your honesty. Now, if you'll just give me the diagnostic essays your class did this morning—"

"No," I replied.

"No?"

"No. I'll read them and respond to them."

"Didn't you get the memo specifying that all English faculty were to hand in their students' essays for review by the administration?"

"Yes, I got that memo and the ninety-six other memos your office has issued in the last week, but I have no intention of handing over my students' papers. If you persist in the request, I'll go to the MLA and complain. Fairwick College won't be as useful to you if you lose your accreditation."

Duncan's smile vanished. His jaw tightened. I thought I heard teeth grinding and invisible wings beating. "You might be surprised at how the MLA would respond to your complaints. We have friends there. I think you'll find we have friends"—he smiled, but this time without showing his teeth—"everywhere." He splayed his hands out in the air again. "But

I believe in picking my battles. Keep your papers. I'm sure I'll have ample opportunity to get to know each and every one of your students."

He held his hands higher. The gesture would have seemed conciliatory but for the shadow they threw on the wall. It resembled nothing so much as giant wings spreading over the room.

CHAPTER THREE

I walked briskly across campus, pouring my anger—and fear—into pumping muscles. It was a beautiful early-September day, cerulean-blue sky, a hint of autumn in the air, a touch of color in the ancient trees: the perfect day to showcase a Northeast college. The old brick buildings basked in a warm, mellow glow, and the faces of the students I passed reflected that same tint in tanned skin, toned bodies, and the white even teeth of privileged youth. It was everything I loved about academia, but everywhere I looked there were signs of darkness lurking below the Arcadian idyll.

Those magenta Alpha Delta Chi flyers were spread over the quad like a virulent mold, the green-jumpsuited security men were arrayed across the campus like an invading army, and those noxious bells were pealing again, driving all rational thought out of one's head. (Soheila thought they might be a form of brainwashing.) The most glaring atrocity, though, was the one I saw first thing every morning and the one I saw now as I came out of the southeast gate onto Elm Street. Directly across from my house was the lovely old Victorian that was formerly called the Hart Brake Inn. Nailed onto the gingerbread molding above the porch were three giant Greek letters painted a garish gold: Alpha, Delta, Chi. On the porch where Diana had served afternoon tea, bare-chested boys slumped in an assortment of lawn chairs and old broken-down couches, drinking beer and smoking pot—or at least I had thought it was pot at first. The miasma issuing from the house smelled like ashes and cloves, leading me to wonder if young nephilim smoked church incense.

Because that's what these frat boys undoubtedly were—nephilim, or perhaps the spawn of nephilim.

Two of them, wearing nothing but skimpy gym shorts and flip-flops, were stringing party lights along the porch railing. I recognized Adam Sinclair from class as he looked up and saw me. He whispered something to the other boy, who looked my way and laughed.

Great, now I'd become the butt of frat-boy humor. Adam waved at me. Not wanting to look like the cranky old lady neighbor I suddenly felt like, I waved back.

"Prof," Adam yelled. "Wanna come to our party tonight?"

I held up the magenta invitation and smiled tightly. "I don't think I have the right costume, boys."

Adam grinned. "You could come as a fairy."

At least he hadn't suggested I come as a slutty fairy. "I'll be busy grading your papers," I replied. "Hopefully the noise won't put me in a bad mood."

"No worries, Prof. We'll keep it down to a dull roar. If we're keeping you up, though, come on over."

"You never know," I said, a thought occurring to me. "I might just do that."

Several of the boys hooted at that and, as I turned around and walked across the street to Honeysuckle House, I was conscious of many sets of male eyes on my back—or probably a little lower. I was glad I'd worn a demure knee-length skirt for the first day of classes, but still I had to concentrate on not swishing my hips. And if I felt reduced to a sex object by these boys, how must my female students feel?

Stepping onto my porch, I met another pair of accusing eyes. In the fanlight above my door, a face set in stained glass stared dolefully at me. I'd come to recognize my demon lover in those green eyes and full lips. An altercation two months ago had cracked the glass below one green eye, making it look as if the figure were shedding a single tear. Each time I saw it now, I thought of my demon lover. Sometimes I thought of him as the creature made of moonlight and shadow who had made love to me in my dreams. Sometimes I remembered Liam Doyle, the broody Irish poet who had shared my bed last winter until I banished him to the Borderlands, but mostly I pined for Bill Carey. The kind brown-eyed handyman had fixed my house and tended to the damaged pieces inside me. I'd discovered that my parents had warded me in my childhood to hide my powers from my grandmother—and then died before they could remove those wards. The wards had not only restricted my powers, they'd kept me from being able to love. Bill's love for me—proved by throwing himself in front of Duncan Laird and taking a lethal blow meant for me—had broken the last of those wards. I'd recognized him and realized I loved him at the same moment his blood flowed onto the threshold of the door to Faerie—closing that door forever.

Gazing up into the green glass eyes, I asked the question I asked every time I looked into them: "Are you really gone?"

And always the same silence for an answer.

I sighed and opened the door. The big old Victorian house seemed to return my sigh in sympathy as floorboards creaked and curtains huffed at the windows. But it was only the breeze

I'd let in. When I closed the door, the house settled down into its hundred-year silence.

Broken by a diminutive squeak.

I looked down and saw a tiny gray field mouse, white patch on his chest, sitting at my feet. I crouched down and held out my hand.

"Hey, Ralph, have you got a message for me?"

Not that Ralph could talk, even though he was a magical doormouse imbued with a spark of the sacred fire of Muspelheim by his maker, Brock. Still, he could type on laptops and was excellent at carrying messages. He was carrying one now inside the tiny silk pouch he wore around his neck (I'd sewn it from a jewelry pouch). I tipped the pouch over and a tiny origami crane fell out—flapping its paper wings and taking a spin around the foyer.

A message from Soheila, then, I thought, cheered by the crane's antics, despite my foul mood. I held out my hand and waited for the paper creature to alight. Experience had taught me it was fruitless to chase the little messengers. After a couple of spins around the foyer, it glided gracefully into my palm and obligingly unfolded itself.

Mission Fallen Angel in effect. Meet below Main tonight when the damned bells toll midnight.

I laughed at the dramatic wording. Soheila may have folded the message, but it was written in Frank Delmarco's handwriting, and the flair for the dramatic was pure Frank, who, it turned out, loved the Hardy Boys and French Resistance movies. I'd accused him more than once of enjoying the nephilim occupation a bit too much.

I read the message one more time and made sure I had it memorized. Then I tossed the paper into the air and cried, *"Flagyr!"* The paper burst into flames. The ashes formed themselves into tiny gray cranes as they drifted down to the ground.

"I think," I remarked to Ralph as he batted at one of the sooty cranes, "that Soheila has a little too much time on her hands these days."

I had a few hours to kill before meeting Frank and Soheila, so I made myself a pot of tea and a fried-egg sandwich for dinner, settling down on the library couch with a stack of student papers to grade. As much as I liked teaching, I'd already learned that a stack of student papers got heavier and thicker the longer they went unread. Especially handwritten ones. Sheesh! I remembered my college professors railing about my generation's handwriting, but this new crop of freshmen wrote as if they'd penned their essays while driving down a dirt road. I'd seen Linear B tablets that were easier to decipher. Staring at the scrawling lines made me more fatigued than I already was. I was relieved when I got to Nicky's essay, written in neat dark ink (one of the Cinderella essays had been written in a glitter gel pen) and serviceable syntax. I read through her retelling of Tam Lin again and saw that she'd written another whole page about the variation she'd discovered in Scotland, a ballad called William Duffy.

I'd never heard of it. I considered looking it up in Sir Walter Scott's *Minstrelsy of the Scottish Border,* but that was on the top shelf and I was warm and cozy on the couch. I snuggled down deeper into the cushions, pulled the afghan over my legs, and settled into the tale, delighted to be in the hands of an able storyteller.

The story begins with a young man named William Duffy, who goes to the enchanted Greenwood one Halloween night and falls in love with a fairy. They lie together in the Green-

wood, and the fairy—who's some kind of guardian of the door to Faerie—forgets to lead her people safely through the door.

I looked up from the paper, stunned by this detail. Last year, when the incubus had first appeared to me, I'd begun to have dreams in which I was leading a troop of fairies through a meadow, but I'd abandoned them to go into the woods with a handsome young man. Later, when I learned that I was descended from a line of fairy doorkeepers, I'd wondered if my dream was a vestigial memory of my ancestor. Now I wondered if the William Duffy story was about my ancestor. I read on.

Because the doorkeeper failed to bring her people to the door, many of her kind faded and perished. The Fairy Queen appeared and exacted a punishment for the two lovers. She banished the doorkeeper to the human world and took William Duffy to Faerie as her prisoner. The doorkeeper begged the Fairy Queen for a chance to save William, and the queen agreed. "In seven years, the host will ride out on All Hallows' Eve with William. If you pull him down from his horse and hold on to him—even as he transforms into frightful shapes—he will be free. But if you fail to claim him, he will be sacrificed as the tithe we must pay to hell."

The doorkeeper vows to save him. In token of her promise, she unpins a brooch from her dress. She breaks apart the brooch and hands half to William.

"Keep this as a token of my love," she said. "My heart will be halved until we are together again."

The Fairy Queen whisked William Duffy off to Faerie. Seven years later he rode out with the host, searching the Greenwood for his beloved to save him, but the woods were blasted as though by lightning and there was no sign of the doorkeeper.

"Ah," the Fairy Queen told William, "she has forsaken you. Mayhap she has been destroyed by demons. When she broke her brooch in half, she halved her power. Foolish girl! I should give you as tithe to the demons of hell, but I am not heartless. Because of the love you bore one of our kind, I will let you dwell in Faerie instead. True, you will become a demon, but if ever you are loved again, you will become human."

I put down Nicky's paper on the coffee table, feeling tired and sad. My incubus had been made through the foolishness of my own ancestor! I didn't have the heart to write comments and correct grammar anymore. I closed my eyes and pictured the Greenwood where the fairy doorkeeper and William Duffy lay together. I pictured a soft bed of emerald-green moss and wild heather, dappled with leaf shadow and sunlight filtered through ancient beech trees, and a young man who looked like Bill . . .

"You've come back for me," he said, pulling me down beside him. In the dappled leaf shadow, his face was the face of the man in the stained-glass fanlight, then Liam's, then Bill's. Then he was some new combination of the three. My Greenwood lover, William Duffy.

"I never went away," I told him, kneeling beside him on the heather bed but unwilling to let him pull me down beside him. "It's you who went away. That monster killed you. I watched him slash your throat, and then you vanished. I thought you were dead."

He lifted his hand to my face and brushed away a tear. "Not dead. Only trapped in Faerie, waiting for your return."

"But the door is gone. I don't know where there's another."

He shook his head and laughed—a musical sound that riffled the leaves in the beech trees and made my skin tingle. "How can you not know where the door is? The door is here." I looked around us at the Greenwood and saw we were in a valley. Above us a castle loomed, its ruined walls guarded by gruesome stone gargoyles. A broken stone archway, also carved with gargoyles, stood on one side of the glade.

"But where—" I began to ask, but his arms were around me and he was pulling me down to the forest floor. His lips found mine and I forgot my questions. What mattered was that we were together and I could feel his warm hands touching me, peeling away my petticoat and long skirt, my tartan cloak—why was I wearing so many clothes?—and laying me down on the soft heather bed. He plucked a sprig of heather and brushed it along the line of my jaw, releasing its heady perfume into the air. He drew the flower lightly down my throat. I trembled at its touch . . . like velvet lips . . . and then I felt his lips on my skin, planting kisses on each breast, his teeth like the scratch of rough grass as he drew his tongue down to my navel and slipped his fingers between my legs. I cried out and arched my hips and reached for him, digging my heels into the velvet moss. I wrapped my hands into his hair and pulled his face to mine and kissed his mouth. He tasted like wild heather and peat smoke. His skin felt like furred moss and, where it was tenderest, flower petals. I drew him into me, feeling as though I were pulling it all inside me—the dappled sunlight, the mossy bed, the scent of heather. As it all burst, his green-gold eyes locked on mine and he said, "See, you knew where the hallow door was all along."

I woke up on the couch in the darkened library, my fingers digging into the velvet cushions, my body pulsing with the force of the dream.

It was just a dream.

The reality of that crashed over me. I hadn't found my way into Faerie, and the man in my dream hadn't been Liam or Bill or my demon lover. He was William Duffy, the hero of Nicky's ballad, summoned by a sex-deprived teacher falling asleep while grading papers.

Well, *that* was embarrassing.

I unwound myself from the tangled afghan—remembering the prickly wool of the tartan mantle I'd worn in the dream— and sat up, trying to shake off the fog of sleep. On the mantel above the fireplace, a clock chimed the hour. It was eleven o'clock. I'd slept the whole evening away, but at least I hadn't overslept my meeting with Frank and Soheila. I got up, the afghan falling to the floor. Something else fluttered to the floor—a scrap of paper. I hoped I hadn't been shredding my student papers in my sleep. That might be hard to explain. But when I bent down to pick up the scrap, I found it wasn't paper at all. It was a sprig of heather.

CHAPTER FOUR

I tucked the heather sprig between the pages of Scott's *Scottish Minstrelsy*, where I had searched in vain for a ballad called William Duffy or any mention of a hallow door. At last, afraid I'd be late, I went upstairs, took a shower to wake myself up, and dressed in black jeans, a black turtleneck, and sturdy black work boots. I combed my long red hair back and braided it and tucked it under a black beret. Frank had given me the beret. I felt a little silly wearing it, but it hid my hair—and perhaps made me look a bit like Simone Signoret in *Army of Shadows*.

I packed a small black backpack with flashlight, compass, spell book, and Ralph. Then I crept out the back door and headed into the woods.

A hundred and twenty years ago, when Silas LaMotte had built a house for his wife, he named it Honeysuckle House after her favorite flower and planted honeysuckle shrubs all around it because she loved the scent. But his wife had died a few months after they moved into the house, and in the years that Silas's daughter, Dahlia LaMotte, lived there, she'd been too busy writing her romance novels to worry much about the gardens. She let the shrubs go wild. Fed by the primal magic coming from the door to Faerie, they spread into the woods, growing into a dense, twisting bramble that perfumed the whole town in summer.

Or at least it had. When the door to Faerie was closed, the woods were blighted. Flowers died on the vine, and now their leaves hung yellowed and dry, like scorched paper. The bare branches resembled bones in the moonlight. Ducking under a low arch, I felt as if I were passing through the skeletal jaws of an extinct sea monster . . .

At least, I hoped extinct. The bare limbs creaked and moaned around me, and the dry leaves chattered like gnashing teeth hungry to devour me. *Your fault, your fault,* I imagined the shrubs muttering. I'd been unable to stop the nephilim from closing the door, and now the woods were dying. I was almost relieved when I came to the cave.

Almost.

The cave still freaked me out a bit. The entrance was a narrow cleft between boulders. I had to take Ralph out of my backpack so I wouldn't crush him. He scurried into the narrow opening before me. I followed, turning sideways and pressing my back against damp stone and feeling my way with fingertips along the slimy rock—there just wasn't room to hold a flashlight—until I found the notch that signaled the . . .

Drop. As usual, I missed it and plunged headfirst into the cave, landing on my knees in the dark. For a moment, as I scrabbled in my bag for my flashlight, I thought I heard a scraping sound, but when I fumbled the light on, the shadows shrank back too quickly for me to make out their shapes. Only Ralph remained, crouched by my side, his eyes big in the beam of my flashlight.

"It's okay," I said, trying to reassure myself as I aimed the flashlight around the tunnel. "They're probably just bats." I counted to a hundred. When I was sure nothing was coming, I turned and followed Ralph into the tunnel that led to the campus. As dirt floor gave way to tile, and stone walls to cement, I breathed easier—or as easy as I would ever breathe twenty feet underground.

When I reached the first crossing, I stopped and took out my compass and map. The map was hand-drawn by Soheila. She'd been in the tunnels before 1959, which was when a senior named Dolores Maynard had disappeared in them. Liz had them closed then, so that no students would stray into them again. She'd had all traces of them erased from campus maps and memory of them expunged from the memories of all mortal students and faculty. A wealth of campus lore had persisted about the tunnels, though. As Soheila had explained to me, no spell could entirely destroy a memory. Erasing a memory from the conscious mind simply drove it deeper into the subconscious, where it became lore, which, it turned out, was how most urban legends got their start.

Since she was not mortal, Soheila remembered the tunnels, and she had suggested we use them to move about the campus, unobserved by the nephilim. The map was sketchy and incomplete (by her own admission, Soheila and her succubi sisters had lousy senses of direction), and every time I ventured into the tunnels I worried that I would stray into one of the unmapped sections and vanish like poor Dolores Maynard.

Who, I had learned last spring, had evaporated into steam and taken up residence in the heating pipes.

I shook that thought away and concentrated on the map. Soheila's note had said to meet her beneath Main Hall. I traced out the most direct route, trying to choose tunnels I'd been in before, but I hadn't traveled this far in the tunnel system yet. I'd gone only as far as Fraser, where there was an entrance to the tunnels through Soheila's office closet. But Main was on the far north side of campus, and some of the tunnels leading there were sketched in with dotted lines—Soheila's code for *unexplored*. In one of them, Frank had scrawled *Here be dragons!* next to a cartoon of a ferocious fire-breathing beast.

Very funny, I thought, taking the tunnel to my right. It was narrower than the one I'd been in and lined with wide steel pipes that were covered with rust and peeling paint. Previous tunnel explorers had left their marks on the walls: a long-nosed *Leroy was here*, several hearts with initials, and a scrawled *Help me! My English teacher has read too much Poe and buried me alive behind this wall!*

I followed the twisting route until I heard voices. I stopped and listened.

"I'm just saying he didn't seem so bad. The man was a Jets fan, after all," a man's voice, which I recognized as Frank Delmarco's, said.

"He wasn't even a man," replied a lilting female voice that could only belong to Soheila Lilly. "He was an incubus, and it's in his nature—*our* nature—to be pleasing. He probably told you he was a Jets fan to win you over."

"Nah, I can always tell a real fan. Besides, he had no reason to win me over. And when we were on our way to the door that morning, he told me something . . ."

I held my breath, eager to hear what Bill—clearly whom Frank was talking about—had told Frank. They'd gone together to find a way of unmasking Duncan Laird on the morning of the summer solstice, but then Bill had stepped between Duncan and me and taken the lethal blow meant for me.

"He said that if anything happened to him, I should tell Cal—"

"I don't want to know," Soheila cut Frank off. "Whatever protestations of love he made—however real they might have seemed—make no difference. He's gone. Callie needs to get over him."

"But that's just it. He may not really be gone. He said . . ."

In my eagerness to hear what Frank said next, I stepped forward—and tripped. My flashlight clattered to the ground.

"What's that?" I heard Soheila cry.

"It must be Callie."

"Frank, don't. You don't know it's her . . ."

But Frank was already barreling down the tunnel, like one of his beloved football players, ready to tackle an unknown foe. You had to love Frank—but if he was keeping Bill's last message from me, I was going to throttle it out of him.

"I'm fine, Frank," I said, scrambling to my feet and shining the flashlight at him. In black turtleneck, jeans, and beret, he looked like a special-ops agent. "I just fell."

"Jeez, McFay, could you be a little more careful?" he huffed. "You scared Soheila."

I heard a musical laugh behind Frank as Soheila came into view. If anyone could make urban guerrilla camouflage look chic, it was Soheila Lilly. She was wearing tight black leggings, which clung to her every curve, tucked into tall lace-up boots. Her silk turtleneck was just a shade off black—aubergine, I thought, although it was hard to tell in this light—and worn under a black leather jacket. Her abundant dark hair fell in luxuriant waves around her face, and the beret Frank had given her was tilted to a rakish angle. Whatever she wore, Soheila emanated a seductive charm. Whenever she laughed, the air around her rippled with the scent of cardamom and cloves, reminding me that she had once been a wind spirit, before the desires of humans had shaped her into a beautiful woman. For thousands of years she had fed on those desires, becoming a succubus who needed the human life force to survive, until she had fallen in love with a human, whose returned love had made her partly human. When Angus Fraser died, Soheila had sworn off feeding on humans, using Aelvesgold to maintain her life force. But now that she was cut off from her source of Aelvesgold, she would inevitably grow weaker. I noticed that even though it was warm in the tunnels, she looked as if she was freezing. Still, she smiled as she said, "I think Frank was just looking for an excuse to come to your rescue, Callie."

Frank scowled, an expression so habitual that he had vertical lines etched on his forehead. Those furrows had deepened over the last two months, as he'd watched his college fall into the hands of evil creatures. He carried an extra burden of guilt, I knew. Frank had worked as an undercover operative for the internal-affairs division of IMP—the Institute for Magical Professionals—preparing a report for them on unorthodox otherworldly activities at Fairwick. But Frank hadn't known that his report would be used by the Grove to coerce IMP into going along with the closing of the door to Faerie. Or that once the door was closed and most of our fey colleagues were gone, the nephilim would be able to take over the college. I knew Frank wouldn't rest until he banished the nephilim and got our friends back, which was why, I was pretty sure, he'd been so quick to come to my rescue right now, *not,* as Soheila was hinting, that he was sweet on me. My suspicions were confirmed by the glance he gave Soheila under lowered brows.

"I'm pretty sure McFay can take care of herself," he said. "She's more powerful than the two of us put together."

Soheila looked from Frank to me and then back at Frank again. "You're right. Callie is growing very powerful." She gave the two of us a smile that turned the stale tunnel air into a sultry desert breeze laden with spices, then turned on her heel and walked briskly away, tossing over her shoulder. "It's time we put that power to use."

Frank and I followed side by side—as Soheila had planned. She was always trying to arrange for us to be alone together. Since Soheila had renounced human contact, she wouldn't allow herself to admit her feelings for Frank, and she also thought my attachment to the incubus was unhealthy. In her view, that made Frank and me the perfect match.

"What's up?" I asked Frank.

"Soheila thinks that Duncan Laird was contacted today by the Seraphim Club in London. White Eagle, our informant in the mailroom—"

"You mean Earl?" I asked.

"Shh. The code names are to protect the network, McFay. *White Eagle* tells us that Laird received a package today from London."

"I saw it!" I said. "He had a package on his desk when I was in his office. It had foreign stamps on it. He put it in his file cabinet when he saw me looking at it."

"Good work, McFay. Soheila thinks it may have information about the nephilim's plans. Now we just need to get into the office. That's where you come in. Someone has to break through the wards—and who better than a doorkeeper?"

"I'll do my best," I assured him as we joined Soheila at the foot of a flight of stairs. She sat on the bottom step, holding Ralph in her hand. They appeared to be having a conversation.

"Ralph is going to go upstairs and make sure the building is clear. If he sees a security guard, he'll distract him."

"Are you sure that's safe?" I asked. "Those guys are scary. Nicky said today that they look like trolls."

"Trows, actually," Frank said.

"A species of troll from the Orkney Islands," Soheila explained. "They've made a compact with the nephilim in exchange for a supply of Aelvesgold. It's very disappointing. The trows may not be the brightest of the fey, but they were essentially harmless creatures until the nephilim got ahold of them. Once they've pledged allegiance to a master, they're unfailingly loyal. They haven't a shred of initiative, though, and they're not quick on their feet. Ralph should have no trouble staying ahead of them, will you, my brave little soldier?"

Ralph squeaked and fluffed out his fur, preening under Soheila's praise. Apparently, magical doormice were not immune to succubi charm. She carried Ralph up the stairs, inched open the door at the top, and crouched down to let him through the crack. I knelt beside Soheila on the darkened stairwell, peering past her into the dim lobby of Main. I could make out a guard sitting on a chair, tipped back, eating Cheetos, and listening to a baseball game on a small portable radio.

"A Red Sox fan," Frank muttered. "Figures!"

The guard was so mesmerized by the game that he didn't see Ralph creeping across the floor until he was practically under his feet. Ralph sat up and squeaked.

"Oi!" The guard shouted, narrowly missing Ralph as he tipped forward in his chair and spilled his bag of Cheetos on the floor. Ralph dodged under his legs and ran a circle around the guard, who spun trying to keep up with him and then toppled dizzily over to one side. Soheila giggled at the sight, but I was too worried for Ralph's safety to enjoy the spectacle. The trow might have been slow, but he was huge. One misstep and Ralph was mouse soup. But Ralph nimbly evaded the lumbering guard and took off across the floor away from us, with the guard in hot pursuit. We could hear his footsteps pounding toward the opposite side of the building.

"Come on," Frank said, clamping Soheila on the shoulder. "Let's go."

A tremor passed through Soheila at Frank's touch. She pretended to need something from her backpack while Frank took the lead. Glancing at her, I saw a flush of crimson in her cheeks. She looked up at me, her eyes wide, her pupils dilated. "Hurry!" she commanded, expelling a gust of air that nearly knocked me over. I wanted to comfort her, but I knew that the last thing she wanted right now was to be touched by a human, so I followed Frank through the dimly lit lobby of Main Hall, past bulletin boards where the magenta Alpha flyers glowed in the dark with a malevolent radioactive sheen. Soheila caught up with us on the stairs. At the top, Frank held us back with a restraining arm while he checked that the hall was clear, then motioned for us to follow, backs against the wall, to the dean's office. When we reached it, Soheila stepped in front of Frank and held her hand over the doorknob.

"It's warded," she said. "One touch and it will send an alarm signal to Duncan Laird."

"Then we won't touch it," I said. I raised both hands and focused my attention on the door. As a doorkeeper, I could dissolve wards. Ironically, it was Duncan Laird who had commenced my education in wards this past summer. Since then I'd been studying Wheelock's *Spellcraft* and had learned how to open warded doors. The trick was to fit the opening spell between the wards, like a skeleton key slipping into a lock.

"*Adulterina clavis,*" I murmured, sending the words into the spaces between the intricate labyrinth of wards Duncan had erected. I felt the words still tethered to me, navigating around the wards. Something clicked . . . and the door swung open.

"Brava, Callie!" Soheila whispered. "That was a very sophisticated spell."

"Yeah," Frank agreed, entering the office. "What was it? It sounded like *adulterous key*."

"It's a Latin expression for a skeleton key," I said, beaming with pride.

"Well, if you don't get tenure, you've got a brilliant future as a cat burglar ahead of you."

Soheila tsked. "Of course Callie will get tenure—once we expel the nephilim, that is."

"We'll all be out of a job if we don't get rid of them," Frank said, looking around at the array of diplomas that hung over Laird's desk. "Sheesh, this guy's got more degrees than a thermometer."

Soheila giggled. "That's terrible, Frank."

"Yeah, but you laughed, didn't you?"

I was glad to see Frank and Soheila kidding around. I left them studying Duncan's academic degrees and addressed myself to the filing cabinet where I had seen him put the foreign package. It was warded, as well, but far less elaborately than the door. I easily maneuvered an opening spell around the wards and opened the second drawer from the top. The package was stuck between two folders labeled in Greek letters.

"What's with all the Greek?" I asked as I pulled out the package.

"It's the preferred language of the nephilim," Soheila replied, turning away from the framed diplomas to look at the documents I'd removed from the package. I'd studied Greek in college but never taken to it as well as to Latin. My Greek teacher was a crazy man with a pointy beard, who used to slam the Liddell and Scott lexicon on his desk if we mistranslated a passage of Homer. I passed the documents on to Soheila. "It's rumored that one of Alexander the Great's generals was a nephilim and that he used Alexander's conquests to spread the rule of the nephilim."

"We think they then held key positions in the Roman Empire," Frank added, joining us at the desk. "And in the Roman Catholic Church after that. I think I may have had a few as priests when I was in Catholic school."

"But I thought the nephilim were descended from elves, not angels."

"They were," Soheila replied, "but the nephilim weren't happy with that origin story, so they created the story that they were descended from angels. They believed that when their fathers mated with human women, they created monsters, which the fathers then turned their backs on—the way God turns his back on the fallen angels. They say that when the last elf died, he shed a tear for his children and the tear turned into a stone."

"The angel stone," Frank said. "I thought that was just a story."

Soheila laughed, a melodious sound that rustled the papers spread out on the desk. "What else do we have but stories? The angel stone is the one token that has power over the nephilim. I've heard that the witch hunts were finally stopped by using the angel stone."

"It's true that the witch hunts were the last we'd heard of the nephilim," Frank said. "We thought they'd died out."

"But clearly they simply went into hiding," Soheila said. She held up a handful of papers from the desk. "There are reports here from heads of government and financial institutions. They're everywhere. These are letters congratulating Duncan Laird on his takeover of Fairwick. They were planning this for years."

"But why Fairwick?" I asked. "Why would a little Northeast liberal arts college be so important to them?"

"Because we had the last door," Soheila answered. "The nephilim knew that the fey would stop them from taking their next step."

"Their next step?" I asked. But Frank and Soheila were too engaged in reading the papers to answer right away. If only my Greek were better, I thought, picking up one of the indecipherable pages. But then I recalled one of Wheelock's translation spells.

"*Convertere,*" I said. Instantly, the words on the page resolved into English. The letter was from the president of a Swiss bank, assuring Duncan Laird that he had full support for Project NextGen.

"What's this Project NextGen?" I asked.

Soheila looked up from the page she was reading. All the color had drained out of her face. Her amber-brown eyes had turned a sickly yellow. "I believe they are planning to use Fairwick students for breeding."

CHAPTER FIVE

"That's . . . that's . . ." I stuttered, unable to come up with the words to describe my disgust. Frank had no such trouble.

"Loathsome, despicable, and subhuman."

"Savages!" Soheila hissed, her breath singeing the corners of the papers. I'd felt her breath warm the air, but I'd never before seen it *burn*. "We must alert the witch communities and remaining fey about what the nephilim are planning."

"But who can we trust?" Frank asked, scowling. "The nephilim are using their Aelvesgold to bribe fey and witch alike. It's not just the trows. The fenoderee and the pixies have signed oaths of allegiance to the nephilim." Frank held up two documents with heavy wax seals affixed to them.

"We must do something," Soheila insisted. "We can't stand by and let these evil bastards prey on innocent young women."

"As long as the nephilim have the only source of Aelvesgold, we won't be able to trust anyone who depends on the stuff—" A look from Soheila cut him off. "I don't mean you, of course."

"How do you know, Frank? How do you know I won't

turn you both in to Duncan Laird for a bit of Aelvesgold?" Soheila asked bitterly. "I need it as much as any creature of the otherworld."

"I trust you because I know you," Frank said, looking into her eyes. His hand moved toward hers but she snatched it away, sparks flying from her fingertips. Soheila's eyes glittered like gold coins, and Frank looked away, embarrassed. "And McFay's too young to have developed a dependency, right, McFay?"

"Oh, yeah, right," I said, guiltily recalling my brief flirtation with Aelvesgold two months ago, especially a brief interlude in Faerie when Liam had used the elixir to enhance our lovemaking. I had other, less pleasant memories of the substance. Although it increased magical power and sexual prowess, it also brought nightmares and strange delusions. I'd almost drowned in my bathtub once after using the stuff. I hadn't touched it since, but I'd caught myself thinking about it once or twice. Now, though, at the thought of the nephilim preying on my students, my blood was racing and my skin prickling without any need for Aelvesgold.

"But many witches have grown dependent on it," Soheila said. "We've lost two of the circle in Fairwick."

"Two?" I asked. I knew about Ann Chase, a longtime member of the Fairwick witches' circle and respected member of the community. She had been bribed by Duncan Laird to vouch for him as my tutor. She claimed that she'd thought he was my incubus, but we learned later that she'd known all along that he was a nephilim. Ann had a daughter with Down syndrome, whose all-too-short life span had been prolonged with Aelvesgold. The nephilim had promised to give her enough Aelvesgold to live forever. "Who else has defected?"

"Lester Hanks," Soheila replied. "I saw him performing at Fair Grounds last night. He had enough Aelvesgold in him to light up a city, and he sang and played like Kenny Rogers. The Aelvesgold is giving him a chance to realize his wildest dreams. How long before everyone in the circle defects?"

"We should call a circle to discuss Aelvesgold use," I said. "If everyone understood the side effects—"

"Yeah, that worked so well keeping kids off drugs," Frank cut me off. "What we need is to find the other door, the one Bill told you about in his note. It's not in any one place. Bill told me something that morning . . ." He paused at a warning glance from Soheila. "He told me that there's a door to Faerie that you, and only you, could open anywhere—but also that opening it would put you in great danger. See . . ." He turned back to Soheila. "That's what I meant about him being a good guy. Even if he was an incubus, he was capable of selfless love."

I swallowed the sob I felt rising in my throat. "Did he say anything else about this door?"

"Only what it was called," Frank said. "He said it was known as the hallow door."

"That's a myth," Soheila said.

I stifled a laugh. "You're a myth, Soheila. Everything I've encountered since I came to Fairwick is a myth or fairy tale. I've heard something about a hallow door"—I didn't want to say that I'd heard about it in a dream, because then I'd have to admit I'd started having dreams about my demon lover again—"um . . . in an old Scottish ballad." That was half true. The dream figure who'd told me about it had come out of a Scottish ballad.

"Then why don't you research it?" Soheila said, in an unusually clipped tone that produced a noticeable chill in the air. "I'm going to find out more about what the nephilim are planning. What about you, Frank? Why don't you help Callie with her research."

"McFay knows her way around a Scottish ballad. I've still got contacts in IMP who may be able to help."

"Good. In the meantime, I'll do some research on the angel stone, and we should all keep a vigilant eye on our female students—"

"The frat party!" I cried. "I tried to get Duncan to cancel it, but he refused. It's the perfect setup for preying on girls."

"Not if I have anything to say about it," Frank growled. "Let's get over there."

"Excellent idea," Soheila said briskly, sweeping the papers on the desk into a neat stack with a spell that reordered them as we'd found them. When the pages had slid themselves into their envelope, she returned the package to the filing cabinet and closed the drawer with a gusty shove. "You two go to the party. We'd better leave now. We can't expect Ralph to keep that security guard busy forever."

Soheila led the way out of the office to the back stairs. Frank followed, trying to catch up to her, but when he saw that she was determined not to talk to him, he fell back next to me.

"What did I say?" he asked, an unaccustomed look of confusion on his face.

"That part about an incubus being capable of selfless love. Soheila doesn't believe it. She thinks her kind will always take advantage of a human. It's why—"

Frank cut me off by holding up his hand. We'd reached the lobby. A great lumpy-looking figure was sprawled across the floor in front of the janitor's closet—our entrance to the tunnels. I stepped closer and saw that it was the security guard. For a moment I thought that Ralph had somehow killed him, but then I heard him snoring. Ralph was sitting beside his

head, cleaning fluorescent Cheetos crumbs out of his whis-
kers.

"Wow, you exhausted him!" I said, crouching down and
holding out my hand for Ralph. "You must be tired, too."

Ralph yawned, climbed into my hand, curled up, and
promptly fell asleep. I tucked him into my backpack.

"Did he have to pass out right in front of our entrance to
the tunnels?" Frank asked.

"It doesn't matter," Soheila responded. "It's late enough that
we should be able to find our ways back across the campus. I'm
going to the library to look up matters related to the angel
stone. You and Callie go to the Alpha party, and then you
should make sure Callie gets home safely. If Callie *is* the only
one who can open this hallow door, then she's in grave danger
from the nephilim. You have to protect *her* as well as the students." She gave Frank a look to impress upon him the gravity
of this responsibility, but it was so full of longing that the air
between them literally steamed up. She quickly turned and fled
through the back door of Main, trailing fog behind her.

"Sheesh, McFay, I will never understand women. Come on,
let's get to the Alpha House before Soheila unleashes a hurricane on us."

We followed Soheila out the back door—onto a campus
wreathed in mist. It might have been a natural weather front,
but I was betting that Soheila's conflicting emotions for Frank
had collided to form the fog bank. At least it provided cover
for us as we walked toward the southeast gate and I summoned up the nerve to ask Frank if Bill had said anything else
that morning the door closed.

"I'm sorry I didn't say anything earlier. I thought maybe it
would be better if you forgot him if he's really gone."

"But he told you about a door that only I could open."

"He said you had the power to open something called the

hallow door but that doing it might kill you. He wanted me to promise to keep you from trying to open it."

"And did you promise?" I peered through the fog at Frank. With his beret pulled low over his eyes, it was hard to make out his expression.

"I told him you were too stubborn to listen to anyone. He laughed and said he'd noticed that, but he thought that if anyone could talk some sense into you it would be me. After all, I'd talked you into letting me look down your shirt to check for vampire bites."

I blushed at the memory. "Liam was furious when he came upon us that day. Was Bill?"

"Bill looked like he still wouldn't mind clocking me one about that, but he was more concerned that I watch out for you. So I told him I would."

"I'm not the one who needs watching out for right now," I said, pointing at the Alpha Delta Chi house, which glowed like a malevolent Christmas tree. Pounding music, raucous shouts, and high-pitched giggles drifted toward us on the fog. "I can't believe that any of our female students were stupid enough to go to this thing."

"Let's have a closer look," Frank said.

In the fog, we sneaked around the garage and into the backyard. There was a two-story gazebo; its top floor would afford us a good view of the party. In Diana's time, the gazebo had been covered with climbing roses and night-blooming jasmine that scented the inn. Now the roses hung dead on their vines, and the gazebo smelled like beer and that noxious clove incense that permeated everything the Alphas touched.

"I'm getting an uncomfortable flashback to my days as an altar boy," Frank whispered as we climbed up into the second story of the gazebo. "Stop me if I start confessing."

I started to laugh at the notion of Frank as an altar boy, but my amusement was cut short by the crack of a gunshot, followed by a high-pitched female shriek. Frank pulled back a handful of dead vines and we looked into the yard. Adam Sinclair, in a flowing toga and nothing else—I could tell from the way the house light shone through the flimsy fabric—was standing in the middle of the backyard, aiming a pistol at the fence. A throng of young women dressed in skimpy costumes stood around him. Toga-clad boys and more girls in skimpy costumes sat on the back porch, egging him on.

"Do Bambi next!" one of the girls, dressed in a slutty-vampire costume, shrieked.

I looked toward the fence and breathed out a sigh of relief when I saw there wasn't a live deer, but, still, what I saw was macabre enough. Arranged across the top of Diana's white picket fence was her beloved collection of ceramic figurines: deer, rabbits, foxes, and an entire family of red-capped gnomes.

"Bambi it is," Adam said, cocking the trigger of the gun.

There was a sharp crack, and a ceramic deer exploded in plaster dust. Slutty Vampire and her friend Slutty Nurse shrieked with laughter, but a girl in a Little Red Riding Hood outfit didn't. I thought I recognized her from my Intro to Fairy Tales class.

"I *liked* Bambi," she said. "This is stupid." She downed the rest of her beer, burped, and started weaving her way toward the back gate. One of the toga-clad boys detached himself from the crowd and followed.

"Uh-oh," I said. I switched sides so I could keep track of Red Riding Hood, who was walking now in the narrow alley between the garage and the gazebo. She'd reached the gate but was having trouble working the clasp.

"Let me help you with that," said the boy who had followed her, coming up behind her.

"Thankth," she slurred.

The boy reached his arm around her as if to open the latch but instead grabbed her by the shoulders and pushed himself against her, pinning her against the gate.

"Hey!" she cried. "Get off!"

"I'm going down there," I said, turning to Frank, but he was gone, already in the alley. He tapped the frat boy on the shoulder. When the boy turned, Frank punched him in the face and he slumped to the ground. I hurried down into the alley, not sure whose rescue I was coming to—Frank's or the repellent Alpha's. I wanted to wallop the frat boy myself but didn't think it would help either of our professional careers if we murdered him.

Frank was going in for a second punch when I reached him. I grabbed his arm. "Whoa there, Delmarco. I don't think this one is going to be bothering anyone else tonight."

Frank glared at me, but he pulled back his arm. "Yeah, but what about the others?"

"I have an idea. I thought of it earlier today."

I rummaged in my backpack and drew out a round pomander ball and Ralph, who was, amazingly, still asleep.

"Aw." Red Riding Hood, who had barely reacted to Frank pummeling her attacker, revived herself to coo at Ralph. "A little mouse! He's adorable!"

"He's got a job to do. Wake up, Ralph!" I poked his fat, Cheetos-filled belly. Ralph yawned and stretched, evoking another chorus of oohs and ahs from Red, and looked up at me expectantly. "Take this into the yard," I said, holding the pomander ball up by its ribbon. It had originally been a Christmas gift from Diana. She had filled it with potpourri. I had filled it with something else. "Then drop it and run—and be careful. They're taking potshots at ceramic animals."

Ralph took the ribbon in his mouth and jumped onto the fence. He ran along the top railing. When he vanished into the yard, I motioned for Frank and Red to follow me into the gazebo. We climbed to the top and observed Ralph's progress. He was creeping along the fence.

"I'd have thrown it, but I was afraid the contents might explode," I explained to Frank when Red slumped on the gazebo bench and started snoring.

"Good to know you've been carrying unstable explosives all night, McFay," Frank said. "How are you going to activate it from here?"

"I planted a correlative fuse inside. It's magically connected to this one." I held up half a shoelace—the only thing I could find to use. "I just have to light it when Ralph drops the ball."

I peered into the yard and saw Ralph drop the ball at the feet of Adam Sinclair. He was beginning to run back when Slutty Vampire shrieked, "A mouse! A mouse! A real mouse! Shoot it!"

Adam wheeled around in a circle, one foot crunching the pomander, and spotted Ralph, clearly visible by the white patch on his chest. He lowered the gun and aimed it at Ralph.

I lit the fuse. Just as Adam pulled the trigger, the pomander exploded in a cloud of smoke, throwing him off balance. He fell backward, right into Slutty Vampire and Slutty Nurse. The girls giggled and shrieked at the sudden closeness of a half-naked frat boy, but when the smoke from my pomander reached them, they both pushed him away.

"Ew," Slutty Vampire said, wrinkling her nose. "You're kind of gross."

"Yeah," Slutty Nurse agreed. "When was the last time you showered?"

Both girls rearranged their costumes to cover a few extra

inches of skin. The other girls at the party extricated themselves from the arms of the frat boys, with similar comments on personal hygiene.

Frank wrinkled his nose. "What was that, McFay?"

"An anti-aphrodisiac," I said. "It makes any male within a hundred-yard radius repellent to any female. The Alphas won't be luring any girls to their parties anytime soon."

Red Riding Hood murmured in her sleep, "Boys stink!"

"I'll get Red back to my house," I said. "You'd better go home and take a shower." Frank shot me an accusing look. "I just mean that you'll want to get rid of any traces of the spell. I'm not sure how long it lasts."

"Thanks, McFay. Like I wasn't having a hard enough time in my love life."

We half-carried Red Riding Hood out of the gazebo and across the street to my house. The Alphas were too busy fanning smoke out of their yard to notice us. I took the opportunity to grab a couple of Diana's gnomes off the back fence. I knew she was fond of them and that she'd be devastated to see them serving as target practice—especially since I was pretty sure they were partly sentient.

Frank helped me get Red into my house and then excused himself when she woke up enough to tell him that he reeked. I watched Frank walk down Elm Street toward his downtown apartment, then I got Little Red Riding Hood settled on my library couch, tucking my afghan over her. Asleep, she looked as young and innocent as the girl in the fairy tale. As I turned off the lights in the library, I reflected that the big bad wolves had been smoked out of their house and Red was safe and sound. Kind of a mixed-up fairy tale, but, I would have told Adam Sinclair, the kind I believed in.

CHAPTER SIX

I was in the Greenwood, stretched out on a bed of heather beneath the beech trees. The ruins of the vine-covered stone gate framed one side of the glade; deep, impenetrable woods bordered the other. I had the uneasy feeling there were presences in those woods—*boggles and haunts.*

"Ye never want to stray in there, lass."

I turned to look at the man who lay stretched out beside me. He was wearing slim brown trousers of heavy sueded cotton and a soft white shirt opened to reveal smooth, tawny skin dappled a golden green by the beech light. Sunlight and leaf shadow tangled in his hair. His face was in shadow.

"Bill?" I asked. "Liam?"

He laughed. The sound seemed to shake the leaves in the trees. I felt its vibration deep in my belly.

"Most men would no' like their lover not to ken their name, lass."

"Since when do you have a Scottish accent?" I asked dubiously, squinting through the glare at his face. I saw Liam, then Bill, then my demon lover, and then a young man whose

face was both utterly familiar and startlingly new. "You're William Duffy," I said. "Is that who you were first?"

"First, last—I've been so long in Faerie I hardly ken myself anymore. But you, lass . . ." He touched my face and moved closer, his eyes filling with the emerald light of the Greenwood. "I'd know you anywhere. I've been waiting for you to come and save me." He stroked his hand along my cheek and then down my neck, his touch making me tremble like the leaves in the beech trees. He lowered his head and pressed his lips against my skin. With his head ducked down to the hollow of my throat, I saw the ruined door behind him. The fluted pillars on either side were carved with strange creatures—dragons and griffins, unicorns and gargoyles. Something about the gargoyles struck me as familiar, but I couldn't think why. The things that William was doing with his strong hands and soft lips were distracting me.

"Um . . . William?" I said as he undid a button on my blouse. "Is that the hallow door?"

"Mmmm . . ." he murmured, kissing my breast and sliding himself on top of me. "Don't worry yourself about the door, lass, for you may not open it until All Hallows' Eve."

"But where . . ." I began to ask, but the question turned into a moan as he pushed my skirts up and stroked the tender flesh of my thigh.

"William Duffy," I said, digging my hands into his hair and pulling his head up to look into his green eyes. "How will I ever save you if you don't answer my questions?"

"Ah, lass," he said, pushing himself into me, "the answer is here."

I woke up in a tangle of bedsheets and early-morning sunlight, the scent of heather lingering in the air—and not just its scent. Strewn across the tangled sheets were sprigs of purple heather. "Damn it, William Duffy," I said aloud. "What the hell did you mean, *the answer is here*? Could you be a little more specific?"

A loud thump came from downstairs. Could it be . . .

I jumped out of bed. Maybe when William Duffy said the answer was here, he'd meant *he* was here.

I raced downstairs, smelling coffee in the air the way I would in the mornings when Liam got up early and made us breakfast . . . but instead of finding my dream lover waiting for me, I found a redheaded girl sitting on the library couch. I'd forgotten about Little Red Riding Hood. And that I'd set the coffeemaker on automatic last night.

"Professor McFay?" she asked, rubbing her eyes. "Oh, thank God! I thought I might be at Alpha House, but then I didn't think it would be this neat. What happened?"

"How much do you remember?" I asked, sitting down on a chair and sliding my arms into a cardigan that I'd discarded there. "Miss . . ." I peered at her, willing her name to pop into my head, but it was too early in the semester for me to remember all my new students' names.

"Ruby Day," she said, then with a grimace she added, "Ruby Tues Day. My parents were big into the Rolling Stones. I'm in your Intro to Fairy Tales class, but I don't blame you for not recognizing me in this getup." She looked down at her low-cut frilly blouse and turned as scarlet as her cloak—although, in truth, it wasn't nearly as revealing as the outfits worn by some of the girls she'd been with. "I'm so embarrassed. My suite mates, Jessica and Debbie, talked me into going. I've always loved dressing up for Halloween, and I thought it was a good chance to use my Little Red Riding Hood outfit early. That's the fairy tale I wrote about in your class yesterday." I glanced guiltily at the stack of unread papers on the table. "But I didn't know that the girls would dress up so . . . *sexy* . . . or that the boys would be so aggressive. Oh—" She clamped her hand to her mouth. "I do remember a boy trying to paw me. He didn't . . . I didn't . . ."

"No," I said quickly. "He didn't do anything to you. Frank—I mean Professor Delmarco—had a word with him, and then I brought you here, since you didn't look like you could make it back to the dorm."

Ruby blushed again. "Oh, Professor McFay, I am *so* mortified! I don't usually drink, but the hot apple cider was so delicious and the boys said it had only a teensy bit of rum in it. It was kind of spicy, so I couldn't really taste the alcohol."

"Spicy?" I asked, peering closer at Ruby's eyes. "What kind of spices?"

"Gosh, I don't know. It reminded me of my gran's pumpkin pie. And after I drank one, I wanted more . . . Oh, my, do you think they put that date rape drug in it?"

Ruby's hazel eyes were wide and flecked with gold—which might have been her usual eye color or it may have been traces of Aelvesgold. Was that how the nephilim were going to accomplish Project NextGen? By spiking girls' drinks with Aelvesgold?

"I don't know, Ruby, but I'm going to the dean to complain about their behavior. In the meantime, tell your friends to stay away from the Alphas, and Ruby . . ." I hated having to enspell the girl—she'd been tampered with enough—but I couldn't risk her telling anyone about last night's adventure with Frank at Alpha House. I leaned toward her and injected the gentlest of memory-expunging spells into my next words. "It's important no one knows that Professor Delmarco and I were at Alpha House. Do you understand? *Professor Delmarco and I were never at Alpha House.*"

Ruby blinked. "Sure . . . whatever," she said. "Hey, is that coffee I smell?"

I made breakfast for Ruby, who ate with the appetite of the very young. By the time she left my house—in borrowed jeans and sweatshirt—she didn't look like a girl who'd been out carousing last night. When she was gone, I showered and dressed and then spent the morning grading papers and searching through my folklore books for any references to a hallow door that could be opened only on Halloween. Although I found many references to fairy sightings on Halloween, there was no mention of a particular door.

I walked to campus, enjoying the brisk September weather and the touches of fall color already tinting the trees, until I got on campus and noticed the orange flyers that had replaced the magenta ones—as if the virus had mutated. They were stapled on every bulletin board and lamppost. The Alphas couldn't be throwing another party so soon . . . But when I read the flyer, I saw that no one would be throwing any parties anytime soon.

Attention from the Dean's Office, the flyer read. *Due to an act of vandalism last night at the Alpha Delta Chi House, all social functions and gatherings of more than six are hereby suspended until further notice.*

"Man, that blows!"

I turned toward the voice and recognized Scott Wilder, who had been in one of my classes last year and was in the fairy tales class this year.

"Hey, Scott. When did these go up?"

"Dunno. I just got up. There was an email, too." He grinned. "But I don't have to tell you, Prof. I heard you and Mr. D went all vigilante on the Alpha House and schooled those dudes." He held his hand up, palm out. "High five, Prof! That was epic!"

"Where did you hear all that, Scott?" I asked, gingerly slapping Scott's hand.

Scott rubbed his head. Leaves fell out of his thick dirty-blond hair. Where had Scott been sleeping? I wondered. "Dunno, but everybody's talking about it."

Had my spell on Ruby Day failed? Or had someone else spread the story? But the only other person to witness the event was the Alpha whom Frank had punched, and it seemed unlikely that he would have spread the story of his inglorious trouncing by an over-thirty professor. Puzzled, I headed into Fraser Hall and upstairs, thinking I'd stop by Frank's office, which was down the hall from my mine, and see if he had any ideas about who had leaked the story. When I got to the top of the stairs, though, I saw that my office door was wide open.

I should probably get Frank, I thought, instead of confronting an intruder on my own, but I was already crossing the hall, my skin itching at the violation of my space. I charged into my office, banging the door wide open, and found Duncan Laird standing in front of my desk, looking up at my bookshelves.

"You really do have an interesting collection of folklore here, Professor McFay," he remarked, unperturbed by my dramatic entrance. "But nothing on angels or the Bible. Have you ever considered doing a class on angels?"

"No," I snapped. "How did you get into my office?"

"The same way you got into mine," he replied, turning and smiling blandly. "If you look at your door, you'll find the traces of my skeleton-key spell, just as I found yours."

I touched the lock but saw nothing.

"Use the spell," he suggested.

"*Adulterina clavis,*" I whispered. An image of a skeleton key with an ornately carved bow appeared on the handle—a much more elaborate key than the one I'd used on Duncan's door.

"Really, my dear, don't you recall the lessons on wards I gave you this summer?" He smiled lasciviously. Before I knew that Duncan Laird was a nephilim, I'd thought he might be my incubus, and I'd let him get . . . well, *a little too close*. The memory made my skin crawl. "If you'd paid attention *and* read Wheelock's footnote, you would have learned that the one downfall of the *adulterina clavis* spell is that it leaves a trace of its user—a sort of caller ID, if you will. If you like, I can show you how to block it."

"That won't be necessary," I said, leaning against the doorframe and folding my arms over my chest. "You've made your point. Did you have anything else to say?"

"Yes. I want to apologize for the behavior of the Alpha Delta Chi brothers last night. It's come to my attention that some of them behaved rudely to female students. I've reprimanded them, as you suggested yesterday, and suspended their party privileges for the rest of the semester."

"I saw the flyers," I replied warily. "It sounds like you're prohibiting all parties for the rest of the semester."

"Well, yes, that seemed the most expedient course of action. If I permitted other parties on campus, the Alphas would no doubt cause trouble."

"So expel them," I said. "It's not fair to punish the whole student body because the Alphas can't control themselves."

"It's the safest course of action for now. You do agree that the priority should be keeping the students safe, do you not?" He smiled, showing a lot of white teeth. I shivered, feeling the implied threat behind his words.

"Yes, so why not expel the Alphas?"

Laird's mouth remained stretched in a smile, but his eyes darkened. "That would be premature. They need to learn to assimilate to . . . *college life*. As part of their rehabilitation, I've ordered them to perform community service. And if all goes well, we can reinstate social gatherings in time for a Christmas party."

"Christmas?" I repeated. "What about the Halloween party? It's a Fairwick tradition—"

"A *pagan* tradition," Duncan cut me off, all trace of his smile disappearing. "It's time Fairwick gave those up. I would think that after your experience with monsters and ghouls you'd be the last person to want to celebrate Halloween."

"I have a fondness for candy corn," I replied.

"I'd get over it," he suggested, moving toward the door. "There'll be no Halloween party, and," he added, tapping the lock on my door as he walked past me, "in pursuance of our mutual goal of making the campus safer, I've ordered all the locks to be changed to spell-resistant ones."

When Duncan Laird was gone, I closed the door and sagged against it, my anger and outrage leaving me drained and deflated. I didn't have time to recover, though; I was already late for my class. I'd have to talk to Frank later. I rushed down the stairs and into the lecture hall . . .

. . . where I was greeted by a round of applause.

The last time that happened was when I'd canceled the final after being attacked by a liderc.

When the clapping stopped, I smiled and gave the students a puzzled look. "Gee, I'm excited about today's reading, too, but I really think Bruno Bettelheim deserves the lion's share of the praise."

"No, Professor, that's not why we're clapping," Scott Wilder objected. "It's because you schooled those Alpha dudes. Epic!"

Apparently *epic* was the new *awesome*. I kind of liked it, but still . . .

My eyes flicked guiltily toward Adam Sinclair, who was leaning back in his seat, surrounded by empty desks. His ostracism was no doubt a result of my stink-bomb spell. His eyes were hidden by Ray-Bans.

"Did something happen at your party last night?" I asked innocently, taking out the folder of corrected papers.

"Nah," said Adam. "Some girls got scared because they saw a mouse."

"Ah," I said. "Rodent infestations can be bad around here. That must have been the odor I detected coming from Alpha House this morning."

"No worries," Adam said, showing a lot of white teeth as he smiled. "We've put out traps."

I smiled back at Adam, despite the chill I felt at the implicit threat. I'd have to keep Ralph from going over there.

"Well, if that's all, let's turn our attention to Bruno Bettelheim. What did you think of his assertion that the Little Red Riding Hood story reflects Oedipal conflicts during puberty?"

Nothing galvanized students more than a good sex-symbolism debate. Half of them thought that reading sexual content into their favorite bedtime stories was heresy. The others were delighted to be talking about sex. The lively discussion took their minds off my supposed heroic exploits. Ruby Day took part enthusiastically, declaring that she liked the Little Red Riding Hood in Roald Dahl's version, in which Red takes out a gun and shoots the wolf. Adam Sinclair remained quiet through most of the class period, until it was nearly over, when he said, looking straight at Ruby Day, "Little Red Riding Hood got what she deserved. You don't go walking in the woods alone if you want to avoid wolves."

I was about to say something in response, but Nicky Ballard did it for me.

"You could say that about the wolf, too. If you go around attacking defenseless girls, you can expect payback."

A good note to end class on! I saw that Nicky wanted to hang back to talk to me, but I told her it would have to wait because I needed to go see Professor Delmarco.

"Sure, Prof," she said with a sly smile. "I think it's really great you guys are, like, fighting the man together."

"We're doing no such thing, Nicky!" I said sternly, but she just kept smiling.

I went upstairs to talk to Frank. I found him in his office, feet up on his desk, the sports section of *The New York Times* spread in front of his face.

"Hey," I said without preamble, "did you know that the whole campus knows about our exploits at Alpha House last night and they also think we're a couple?"

Frank lowered the newspaper and looked at me over the rims of his reading glasses. "Let me guess, you tried a memory-expunging spell on Ruby Day?"

"Yeah, how'd you . . . I mean, it had the opposite effect."

"Don't you remember what Soheila said about what happened when Dean Book tried to erase the tunnels from campus memory? It drove the memory into the subconscious, where it became lore. You and I are legends now. Frankly, I would have preferred to have become mythic for my athletic prowess, but being a badass counterrevolutionary's not bad."

"But how are we going to protect the students if Laird knows what we're doing?"

"I've been thinking about that," Frank replied, folding his newspaper. "And as much as I hate going to them, I think we need to enlist the help of the creatures with the most practice in keeping a low profile. It's time we went to the vampires."

CHAPTER SEVEN

Frank was right: the vampires were our best bet for protecting the students from the Alphas. Still, it felt wrong somehow to entrust the welfare of a bunch of young people to bloodsucking creatures of the night—even if they were tenured college professors. Maybe *especially* since they were tenured college professors. Frank assured me, though, that in the eight years he'd been at Fairwick and keeping a close eye on the three Eastern European Studies professors, Anton Volkov, Ivan Klitch, and Rea Demisovski, they had never fed from a student or an unwilling adult. And even though the vampires had secretly joined the Grove, they had not supported closing the door to Faerie. Anton had explained to me that the upyr, the ancestors of the vampires, had originally dwelt in Faerie, but had become so enamored of humans that the Fairy Queen banished them and commanded a witch to curse them to an eternity of darkness and living off human blood. (A story not unlike the nephilim's origin story, it occurred to me now.) Anton had admitted that his kind had taken their anger at the fey out on humans but that a few more-enlightened vampires had come to Fairwick, seeking a different kind of existence.

When the door to Faerie closed, the vampires could not be banished to Faerie, but Anton knew that the nephilim despised his kind. It was only a matter of time before the nephilim drove the vampires out of Fairwick or destroyed them, so the vampires were motivated to help us. Still, I always felt a little uneasy around Anton.

The first meeting of the campus safety committee was called for the end of the week, but when the time came, I sent Frank and Soheila an email saying that I had a migraine and couldn't make it. Let Frank and Soheila handle the vampires, I thought, settling onto my library couch with a stack of books on Scottish folklore. I planned to spend the weekend combing them for any mention of or reference to the hallow door. I found none, but each night, as soon as I closed my eyes, often with a dozen old books of folklore sprawled across my bed, I was back in the Greenwood in the shadow of the ruined door in the arms of this new incarnation of my demon lover, William Duffy. I had the same dream every night for the next two weeks, waking up each morning with a bed full of heather and feeling as if I'd spent the night making love. It was all I could do to keep up with the demands of the new semester—learning my new students' names, getting my classes used to my policies (yes, I really would dock them a grade for late papers; no, it wasn't all right to text in class), and the added responsibility of protecting the female students on campus from the Alphas.

For the most part, my students were polite, well-mannered young people. The biggest challenge was getting them to think outside the box and speak up in class, but they were soon all chiming in. The fairy-tales class worked especially well for the freshmen. They were, after all, venturing out on their own for the first time, leaving the safety of their childhood homes and setting forth into the unknown, much like Little Red Riding Hood heading into the woods for Grandmother's house or Beauty embarking for the Beast's castle. By the end of September, most of them had identified some topic to explore in the term's final research paper. Surprisingly, it was Nicky Ballard, a sophomore and one of my best students, who came to see me with a problem one late September evening at the end of my office hours.

"It turns out there's just not a whole lot written about Mary McGowan."

"I know," I told her. "I've been looking, too."

"Really? To help me with my project?" Nicky beamed as if she wanted to nominate me for Teacher of the Year.

"Well, she sounds fascinating. I've never heard of a seventeenth-century female folklorist." I didn't mention that my interest in her stemmed from the fact she'd recorded the origin story of my demon lover. "Where did you first hear of her?"

"In this book I found in a used-book shop in Edinburgh." Nicky removed a book from her backpack. It was bound in soft burgundy leather, its spine stamped with a pattern of intertwining heather and thistles and the title, *Scottish Ballads of the Borderlands,* and the author's name, Mary McGowan. I turned to the title page and my heart skipped a beat. On the facing page was an engraving of a rustic scene—the ruins of an arched doorway overgrown with thistles and climbing roses. It was the door from my dream. I read the caption beneath the doorway.

The hallow door from the ballad of William Duffy.

"I've read the whole book twice," Nicky was saying, "but I don't know what I should do next."

I tore my eyes away from the illustration and looked back

at the title page; the book had been published by McGowan & Sons, Edinburgh. It was the fifth edition. The first edition had been published in 1670.

"Look, the publisher has the same name as her *and* they published the first edition. Perhaps she was the wife or daughter of the publisher. Why don't you try writing to The Center for the Book in Edinburgh? They might have records about McGowan & Sons that contain information on Mary Mc-Gowan. While you're waiting to hear from them, you should go back to the book. All these other ballads—Tam Lin, The Twa Corbies, Proud Lady Margaret—they're all pretty standard except for William Duffy, which I haven't been able to find anywhere else. Maybe there are details in that ballad that reveal biographical information about Mary McGowan. If you compare it to Tam Lin, which it so closely resembles, and examine the details that are different, you may be able to find out some clues about the author. Here . . ." I held out the book for Nicky regretfully. I liked the feel of the book in my hand, its leather cover smooth and warm to the touch, its pages softly dog-eared, and wanted to conduct my own research into Mary McGowan and her story that had somehow traveled into my dreams. But I couldn't take it away from Nicky when it was the only copy of the William Duffy ballad.

"You can keep it," Nicky said. "I made a copy of the William Duffy ballad and the title page so I could makes notes on it."

"Oh, of course you couldn't write notes in this," I said, stroking my thumb along the smooth beveled curve of the pages. "But are you sure? It's such a beautiful book."

"To tell you the truth, Professor McFay, I bought it for you." I looked up, surprised, and saw that Nicky was blushing. "As a thank-you for helping me get the scholarship to

St. Andrews in the first place. I thought you'd like the ballads and, well, when you read William Duffy you'll see why I thought it was perfect for you."

She smiled slyly, and this time I was the one to blush, as if Nicky somehow knew of my dreamlike dalliances with William Duffy.

Thanking her, I kept the book in my hand as we walked together out of Fraser Hall. I was surprised to see that it was dark already.

"It's getting dark early already and cold!" I shivered in my light corduroy blazer. "It feels like it was summer five minutes ago."

"Winter comes on quickly up here," Nicky said, giving me the rueful look the natives reserved for city people. I noticed she had on a heavy red-and-black-checked fleece jacket. "You should dress warmer," she said.

"Thanks, Mom," I said, rolling my eyes. It made me happy to see Nicky feeling confident enough to hand out advice to her teacher—and I was touched that she would care. A year ago Nicky was nervous and unsure of herself, fearful that she very well might end up like her mother—a teenage mother with a drinking problem—and she would have if I hadn't been able to avert the curse my ancestor had placed on her. "But speaking of motherly advice, I don't think you should walk around the campus by yourself. I'll walk you to your dorm."

"No need, Professor McFay. I already called Night Owl."

"Night Owl?"

"Yeah, didn't you get the email from the new campus safety committee? They brought in a security outfit from town called Night Owl to escort students at night."

I recalled receiving a half a dozen emails from the new committee Frank had formed with the Eastern European

Studies professors, but, caught up in my own concerns, I'd ignored them all. Could the Night Owls be the vampires? But they weren't from town . . .

"Here's my Night Owl now," Nicky said, pointing behind me.

I turned quickly, afraid that one of the vampires would be behind me, but found instead the wide, cheerful face of Mac Stewart. He blushed when he saw me.

"Professor McFay, I didn't know the call was for you. I'd've been here sooner. Where can I escort you? If it's off campus, I can go get my car."

"The call's from Nicky here," I said, glancing at Nicky, whose eyes were flicking between Mac and me with undisguised curiosity. "But it's nice to see you again, Mac. You and your family were so helpful this summer, looking for those missing fishermen."

In truth, the Stewarts, who were an ancient clan of stewards pledged to guard the woods, had helped to apprehend an undine who was seducing fishermen.

"It was the most exciting time of my life!" Mac declared. "That's why I convinced my dad and grandpa to start this security company to watch after people in the town and on the campus. See . . ." He patted the owl emblem stitched on the pocket of his plaid flannel shirt. "I named it after you."

"Huh? I don't get it," Nicky said. "What does an owl have to do with Professor McFay?"

"Um, it's sort of a private joke . . ." I said, glaring at Mac. I'd run into Mac one night when I was patrolling the woods after shapeshifting into an owl. When an undine tried to drown him, I transformed back into a human to save him. Unfortunately, when he woke to see a naked woman with owl feathers in her hair, he decided I was an owl princess and declared his undying love for me. ". . . Um, because I stay up so late . . . um, grading papers, which I have to go do now. You make sure Nicky gets back to her dorm safely, Mac."

"But what about you, Professor?" Nicky objected. "You shouldn't be walking alone on campus, either."

"That's right," Mac eagerly concurred. "Why don't you walk with us to the dorm and then I'll walk you home?"

The last thing I wanted was to be alone with Mac Stewart, but what kind of a role model would I be if I walked around the campus by myself at night when I was urging my students not to?

"It will be my pleasure to escort Professor McFay home."

The voice, silky and urbane, came from the shadows beneath a nearby pine tree. A tall man-shaped figure detached itself and glided forward. It wasn't a man, though; it was Anton Volkov, Eastern European Studies professor and vampire.

"Mr. Stewart." He acknowledged Mac with a nod and a slight quiver of his long patrician nose. Mac tended to smell like chewing tobacco and hay. "Miss Ballard, I enjoyed your paper on *The Master and Margarita*. Such an original take on the devil." And then, turning his glittering eyes on me, he bowed. His blond hair looked silver in the moonlight. "Professor McFay, I've missed your company at our security meetings."

"I've been b-busy with my classes," I stammered.

"Of course. But there are some matters that have come up that you should be aware of. I can catch you up on the walk to your house. Mr. Stewart and Ms. Ballard are right that you shouldn't walk alone after dark. You never know who—or what—may be lurking in the shadows."

Like you, I thought. But he was right that I needed to know what was going on. Giving Mac and Nicky a brave smile, I joined Volkov on the path leading off campus.

"You've been avoiding me," he said as soon as we were out of earshot of Nicky and Mac.

"No! I've been busy with the semester start-up and . . . a research project. I'm trying to find another door to Faerie."

I hoped that mentioning the door to Faerie would distract him and change the subject, but he remained quiet; his face, when I glanced over at him, was as impassive as that of a marble statue. We were walking on the path to the southeast gate, a heavily wooded and isolated spot where I'd once been attacked by a giant winged creature. I shivered at the memory.

Quick as a bird's wings, Volkov's jacket was off and around my shoulders. The silk lining was cool, holding no hint of warmth from its previous wearer, but it soon made me feel warm.

"Okay," I admitted as we reached the gate. "I have been avoiding you. I haven't forgotten our deal." Volkov had given me the name of the witch who had cursed Nicky Ballard's family, and he'd told me he would ask a favor in return. I'd been afraid he would ask for my blood, but he had only requested that I speak to the Grove on behalf of the nocturnals. Then the Grove had turned on Fairwick and I hadn't been able to carry out my end of the bargain. "I know I still owe you . . . a favor."

Volkov stopped past the gate and laid an icy hand on my arm to halt me. Once before he had used his touch to paralyze me, but I didn't feel unable to move this time, just *unwilling*, held by the magnetism of his gaze. "That's why you've been avoiding me?" he asked, his eyes holding mine. "Because you think I will ask for payment in some other kind?" He stroked a finger along my throat, from the base of my jaw to the rise of my clavicle. Although his skin was cold, his touch stirred a sensation of warmth under my skin, as if the blood in my veins were attracted by it, as if my blood were magnetically

drawn to him. He'd said to me once that he would never demand anything of me that I didn't desire, but, if he sensed my
desire, would he take what he wanted without asking?

"I know with the supply of Aelvesgold dwindling in this
world, you must be . . ." I tried to think of a polite way of
saying *hungry*, but he finished the sentence for me even more
alarmingly.

"Starving?"

I nodded.

He smiled. "It's true that when my ancestors were banished
from Faerie and cursed to drink the blood of the creatures we
loved best, some of us tried to use Aelvesgold to stanch our
hunger, but we have learned other ways to control our appe-
tites over the centuries. Other creatures are not so . . . well
equipped with alternatives. That's what I wanted to talk to
you about. We've been finding animals in the woods that have
been savaged and drained of blood as if by some kind of
beast."

"Drained of blood?" I asked, feeling suddenly woozy.
"Could it be one of your kind?"

"No!" he growled, so fiercely I had to keep myself from
bolting. "There are talon marks on the victims. My kind"—he
held up his long, elegant hands and twirled them in the
moonlight—"are monsters in many ways, but we do not have
claws. But something *with* claws is roaming the woods and
feeding on animals. I thought you should know since you live
nearby."

He lifted his eyes to Honeysuckle House and then to the
woods behind it. The moon, just risen above the tips of the
trees, cast long, branching shadows across my back lawn. It
looked as though the woods were advancing on my back door.

"Thank you," I said. "I'll be careful. I've only been going
into the woods to take the tunnels—"

"You might want to reconsider that path," Anton told me. "The blood-drained creatures we've found have been near the entrance to the tunnels, and we've found smears of blood that seem to vanish inside them, as if . . ."

"As if what?" I asked when he paused.

"As if these predators are clinging to the roofs of the tunnels like—"

"Like bats," I finished for him, remembering the stir of wings I often heard when I was inside the tunnel.

"Yes," Anton agreed reluctantly. "Giant bloodsucking bats."

CHAPTER EIGHT

Anton saw me to my door. I thanked him for letting me know about the creatures in the tunnels. "Have you told Frank and Soheila?" I asked.

"Yes. They offered to convey the information to you, but I said I would tell you myself. I wanted to make sure you didn't think that these creatures had anything to do with my kind."

"Liz always said you were a perfect gentleman, and you've behaved like one with me."

He smiled and then leaned down to whisper in my ear. I felt the brush of his lips like cool water on my cheek. "If I didn't know your heart still belonged to another, I might not behave in such a *gentlemanly way*."

Then he was gone, vanished into the night as swiftly as . . . well, as a bat. I shook the image away and went inside my house. Anton had assured me that vampires could not turn into bats. That was a myth. But there were some batlike creatures living in the tunnels and killing animals. I'd have to talk to Frank and Soheila tomorrow about how to protect the campus from them. As if we didn't have enough to worry about . . .

I put on my warmest flannel nightgown and got into bed, but I knew it would be a long time before I could sleep, with the thought of those creatures in the woods, so I opened the old book Nicky had given me. A notecard marked the ballad of William Duffy. I opened it and read the note from Nicky.

A good teacher is a door to other worlds, she had written. *Thanks for opening so many doors for me.*

Feeling grateful for Nicky's kind words, I propped the note-card up on my night table and turned to the ballad of William Duffy. The story was much as Nicky had summarized it, until I reached the part where the fairy girl gave half her brooch to William Duffy as a token that she would return for him. Nicky hadn't described the brooch, but Mary McGowan had.

The brooch was made of two interlocking hearts. Where the two hearts overlapped was a stone. When she broke the brooch in half, the fairy girl kept the half with the stone.

The detail sparked a memory. I got out of bed and rummaged through my jewelry box until I found the silver brooch my mother had given to me. She'd explained that it was an heirloom from my father's family, passed down through the generations, and was called a Luckenbooth brooch after the shop stalls in Edinburgh where they were once sold. Originally the brooch had been shaped with two interlocking hearts, but at some time it had been broken, leaving a loop where the other heart had overlapped. Could this brooch be the one the fairy girl had broken in half?

I went back to the story, searching for another clue, but the rest was much as Nicky had related it. There was, however, an interesting note from the author at the end of the tale.

I heard this story from an old woman in the village of Bal-lydoon, who said that William Duffy was her nephew. She told me that after William disappeared, a strange weeping girl appeared in the village, dressed in rags. The villagers thought

*she'd perhaps been tampered with by reivers in the Green-
wood. A local family took her in and nursed her back to
health, but she always remained peculiar—she talked but little and was afraid to touch iron and would not go to kirk.
Nonetheless, a good man of the village fell in love with her
and married her. She gave birth to a girl the following year. All
might have been well enough, but around that time the witch
hunters came to Ballydoon and sent for her to be brought
before them in the kirk. One of the villagers warned her,
though, and, rather than be taken by these brutes, the peculiar
girl ran into the Greenwood and was never seen again. The
old woman who told me the story said she believed the girl
had tried to escape back into Faerie but was lost because of
the Fairy Queen's curse. She believed this because she never
saw her nephew William again and so she knew the fairy girl
had not been able to save him. The old woman told me that
although the villagers called her Katy, the girl's name was
Cailleach, and she showed me the half brooch she had left
behind for her daughter.*

The hair on the back of my neck stood up. If Mary Mc-
Gowan had walked into the room and whispered the news
that she had found the origin of my kind, I could not have
been more startled. I felt as though she was speaking to me
across the centuries. I turned back to the book, but the next
page was the ballad of the Lass of Lochroyan, which, as far as
I could tell from a quick perusal, was nearly identical to a version that appeared in Scott's *Minstrelsy*. I leafed through the
rest of the book and found a selection of classic ballads from
the Scottish Border Country. In no other ballad had the author added a personal note like the one at the end of William
Duffy.

Frustrated, I closed my eyes, which stung from staring at
the small, faded print of the old book, and tried to work out

what Mary McGowan's note meant for me. I'd guessed that my ancestor had a connection with the incubus, but now I knew for sure. I wondered what had happened to the stone that had once been in the brooch . . .

My head swirling with the details of the story and the hundreds of years between its telling and my birth, I fell into a fitful sleep and a dream as restless as my thoughts.

I was running across a meadow, searching for someone. Following in my footsteps were my fairy companions. We were all in danger. I kept looking back over my shoulder to see if we were being pursued. The woods on either side of the meadow were full of shadows. I heard the skitter of claws scraping bark and the heavy thunk of leathery wings crashing through the branches. I had to open a door into Faerie to save my companions and myself, but how? The air shimmered in front of me and I saw him: William, my Greenwood lover, mounted on a giant white steed. He had come to find me, even though it wasn't yet All Hallows' Eve. And I didn't have the stone! Still, he reached for me. I reached for him but could see my arms fading. I tried to hold on to William's arms, but they passed right through me. I was vanishing into thin air . . .

I awoke, arms flailing, grasping for something solid to hold on to, to keep from fading into nothingness. My hand hit the edge of the night table, hard enough to bring me fully awake and send something skittering across the floor . . . *claws scraping bark . . .*

I jumped to my feet, scanning the predawn shadows of my bedroom for the winged creatures in my dream. But then I saw a glint of silver on the floor beneath the window and padded cautiously over to it, keeping my eyes on the window for winged monsters. I knelt and picked up the silvery object, which turned out to be the Luckenbooth brooch. The half brooch. I traced the heart with my fingers and noticed that along the inside rim of the heart were little bumps. I'd seen them before and always thought they were part of the design, but now, looking more closely at them, I saw that they were prongs that had been worn down by time. Prongs that had once held a stone. I held the brooch up to the window. The milky light of dawn filled the loop inside the heart and glowed there like an opal—like a tear-shaped opal. *An angel's tear.* At some time, my brooch had held the angel stone.

Although it was only five in the morning, I knew I wouldn't be able to sleep anymore. Pulling a warm fleece hoodie over T-shirt and leggings, I slipped the brooch into the pocket to keep it close by me. Then I went downstairs, made coffee, and spent the next few hours searching for more information on the angel stone or the hallow door—and finding nothing. I emailed Frank and Soheila, telling them I'd like to talk to them both later about a research topic for this winter's MLA conference. We'd agreed that MLA would be code for *need to talk.* The code worked.

It was barely light out when I heard a knock at my door and opened it to find Frank, Soheila, and, more surprising, Mac Stewart on my front porch.

"Frank was worried by your email," Soheila said, giving me a meaningful look.

"I was worried, too," Mac said, slapping his flannel-covered chest. "You shouldn't have gone into the woods with that man, Callie. He's a"—Mac lowered his voice and leaned in to whisper—"vampire!"

"I know, Mac," I said, "but he's a perfectly well-behaved one. He wanted to warn me about some blood-drained creatures he's found in the woods . . ." I looked past the porch to the trees on the edge of my property. Even in the morning light, the woods had taken on a menacing look.

"Yes, we need to talk about that, too," said Soheila, "but right now Mac has something he needs to tell you. May we come in?"

"Of course!" I said quickly, embarrassed I'd kept them standing on the porch so long—not that I had anything in particular to hide in my house, but I felt that, with her acute senses, Soheila might pick up some residue of the dreams I'd been having. As I opened the door, I found myself sniffing the air, as if erotic dreams would have a particular scent, but all I smelled was a delicious aroma wafting out of a bag Mac carried.

"Oatcakes!" Mac said. "My mom made them for you!"

"Thank her for me," I said, hoping that Mac's mother hadn't somehow gotten the idea I was a potential wife for Mac. "I'll brew some more coffee to go with them." I steered my guests toward the living room, but they all followed me into the kitchen. Mac sat at the kitchen table and folded his hands in his lap like a boy waiting for his afternoon snack. Soheila went to the cupboard to take out the Franciscan Rose teacups left there last fall by my erstwhile roommate, Phoenix. Frank sat down next to Mac and leaned so far back I was afraid he'd break my spindly kitchen chair. I turned my back on them and busied myself at the coffeemaker and arranging the oatcakes on a plate. The rich buttery smell instantly brought me back to childhood and made me feel calmer. I brought the plate over and Mac eagerly tucked into the warm oatcakes, slathering them with the strawberry jam I'd also provided.

"Just like my nan always served them," Mac mumbled, spewing crumbs.

Soheila and Frank exchanged a look across Mac, as if he were their overgrown child who was refusing to perform for their guests.

"Your nan's culinary preferences are very interesting, but you told us that she had something to tell Callie," Frank said impatiently. He looked up at me. "Mac said you were the only one she could tell."

"That's what Nan told me. She said Callie was the only one she could tell about the hallow door."

"Your nan knows how to find the hallow door?" Now I was the one impatient with Mac. "Why didn't she mention this earlier?"

Poor Mac's eyes widened. I hadn't meant to snap at him, but hours of fruitless search had left me frustrated.

Frank cleared his throat and looked embarrassed. "Mrs. Stewart hasn't been well . . ." he began.

"She fell last summer," Mac said. "Hit her head and broke her hip. She needed surgery, and when she came out of it she wasn't right in the head. She's always been sharp as a tack, but after the surgery she didn't even know me." Mac's voice betrayed the hurt of a favorite grandson. "We thought she'd be senile for the rest of her life, but then yesterday when I was there for my weekly visit she sat up in bed, her old self again, and asked me to send for Cailleach McFay."

"She knew my name? But I've never met her."

"Um . . . I may have mentioned you to her," Frank said. "I went to her the morning of the solstice to ask if she knew any way to unmask a nephilim. She was friends with my grandmother and I knew she had spells for unmasking predators, but it never occurred to me she knew anything about opening a door to Faerie . . ." A terrible look came over Frank's face, and he slapped his hand down on the table. "Damn! It was right after that she had her fall. I must have drawn their attention to her."

"You mean to say that those nephilim creeps hurt my nan?" I'd never seen Mac Stewart look so angry. His bland innocent face turned the color of his flannel shirt, and his bee-stung lips drew back in a grimace.

"But why?" I said. "Just because she knows something about another door . . ."

"She knows more than that," Mac said. "Nan used to tell us stories about how the Stewarts had destroyed evil monsters back in Scotland."

Frank pounded the table again. "I should have protected her!"

"Don't blame yourself, Frank," Soheila said, laying her hand over Frank's.

Instantly I saw a change come over Frank. His anger poured off him like water moving over a rock. He lifted startled eyes to Soheila, and she removed her hand.

"That's right, Mr. Delmarco, it's not your fault. It's those . . . *those bastards!* What kind of monster would pick on a sweet old lady? Well, they'll be sorry they did. She's herself now and is fit to be tied. When my nan gets her temper up—well, you don't want to be on her bad side. I once let my brother Ham fall off a ladder when I was supposed to be watching him, and I couldn't sit for a week."

"Your grandmother sounds like a formidable woman, Mac," I said, repressing a smile at the thought that a good spanking might defeat the nephilim. "But I wouldn't want to put her in more danger by involving her."

"I don't think we have a choice," Soheila said. "All my research into the angel stone indicates it was last seen in Scotland in the seventeenth century."

"That coincides with what I read in the story Nicky gave me." I told them about the ballad of William Duffy and the broken brooch.

"You have half of the brooch?" Frank asked.

I took the piece of jewelry out of my pocket and laid it on the table. The empty tear-shaped loop seemed to shimmer against the white enamel surface. "My mother said it was an heirloom passed down through generations of my father's family," I said.

"Then your ancestors must have once had the stone," Soheila said. "That makes sense. I found a reference that said that only a doorkeeper could wield the power of the stone."

"That's great," I said, "but my mother never mentioned a stone that went with the brooch. I think the fairy girl—my ancestor—must have lost it or had it taken from her . . ." I remembered the moment in the dream when I—or the first Cailleach, I supposed—was running through the meadow. I knew in the dream that she didn't have the stone with her, but I didn't know why not or what had happened to it. "In Mary McGowan's note, she says witch hunters had come to the village—"

"They might have been nephilim," Soheila interrupted. "Many witch hunters were."

"Maybe. But why would she run away if she had something to destroy them?"

"Maybe the stone didn't work without the whole brooch," Frank said. "What was the name of the village?"

"Ballydoon," I said.

"That's where the Stewarts come from!" Mac exclaimed, his features freed from anger with the elasticity of youth. "Callie, that means our people come from the same village. It's like we're fated to . . . meet," Mac finished bashfully. I was afraid he'd been about to say fated to *marry*.

"It might even mean you're related," Frank added teasingly.

Mac's smile vanished. "Related? But that would mean . . ."

"Don't worry," Frank said. "You'd be distant cousins at most—kissing cousins."

I kicked Frank under the table. "Let's focus on learning where the stone is and how to get it. When can I visit your grandmother, Mac?"

"Oh, she's my great-grandmother, at least! No one even knows how old she is. We can't find a birth certificate for her and she says she can't remember the year, although she does say she remembers Calvin Coolidge's inauguration, so I guess she's pretty old. We Stewarts are long-lived." He puffed out his chest, as if he'd come up with a selling point that was sure to convince me to marry him even if we *were* distantly related. "I'll take you there to meet her later. The doctors wanted to have a look at her this morning, so she suggested that we come around teatime."

I couldn't suppress a smile. The woman had been in a state of dementia for three months and now she was ready to conduct a high tea. "Okay. We can all go at four."

Mac's face fell at the inclusion of Frank and Soheila.

"It's better you go yourself, Callie," Soheila said. "Mrs. Stewart asked specifically for you. She won't want a crowd—and she's more likely to tell you about the hallow door since you're a doorkeeper."

"And," Frank added with a mischievous smile, "if she thinks you're her future granddaughter-in-law."

Mac blushed for the third time in ten minutes, and I glared at Frank.

"I'd be delighted to meet your nan," I said to Mac. "Is there anything I can bring her?"

Mac looked down at the pile of crumbs that was all that

was left of the oatcakes. "I don't suppose you know how to make those?" he asked doubtfully. "I forgot that Ma said I was to save some for Nan's tea."

"As a matter of fact, I do."

"Really?" Mac gave me an adoring look, and I realized that if I hadn't had it already, I'd just secured his eternal devotion. Mac said he'd better get his farm chores done then and got up to go.

Soheila and Frank walked with me to the front porch to see him off. As I watched Mac get into his shiny new pickup truck, I thought that I could probably do worse than to marry a man who did all his chores and visited his ancient granny every week at the nursing home even when she didn't remember who he was.

"You'd go crazy in a month," Soheila said, divining my thought.

"Yeah," Frank said, walking ahead to his car. "I don't see you as a farmer's wife, McFay."

Soheila lingered behind for a moment. "But he'd certainly be a better choice than the incubus you're dreaming about," she said in a low whisper.

So she *could* sense my dreams. "But it's not really my incubus," I objected. "He's . . . different."

Soheila exhaled a world-weary sigh that gusted autumn leaves off my porch. "Of course he's *different;* that's why my kind are so seductive. We change with you, shifting ourselves to fit every mood and whim. But remember, Callie, the incubus died in his last incarnation. He can't come back again. You'll never be able to be together in the flesh."

"Then there's no danger in dreaming about him, is there?" I countered, lifting my chin defiantly.

Soheila shook her head, and the leaves in my yard spun into a small whirlwind. "Just because he can't have you in the flesh doesn't mean he won't still try to have you in your dreams. He'll make you unfit for loving anyone else. Don't let him, Callie. Use him to find the door and the stone if you have to, but then let him go. Or someday you'll find you're not able to."

CHAPTER NINE

I spent the afternoon making bannocks. I did, in fact, have a recipe for the traditional Scottish oatcakes, from my father, who had made them for my childhood tea parties when he and my mother weren't off on an archaeological dig. When I was ten, he'd taught me how to make them, explaining how he'd learned from his grandmother, who had learned from her grandmother. Every family had their own recipe, he'd explained, and the McFay bannocks were known as the lightest and sweetest cakes in all of Scotland. As I kneaded the dough, I could almost feel his hands over mine, showing me how it was done. I had to stop to wipe my eyes on the apron I'd put over the nice Sunday visiting clothes I was wearing.

I took off my apron and brushed flour off my plaid wool skirt. Perhaps I was laying it on a bit thick by wearing a Scottish plaid to visit Mrs. Stewart, but I wanted to make a good impression and so had also put on tights, a crisp white blouse, and even the silver Luckenbooth brooch. Pinning on the brooch, I'd remembered something else my mother had told me when she gave it to me. "A McFay is never complete until he—or she—finds the match to this heart. Your father said

that I was his *other heart*." If Soheila was correct and my incubus could never return, would I ever find my *other heart*?

Mac came to the kitchen door just as I was transferring the
hot bannocks into a basket. He was wearing an ill-fitting
sports jacket over a fancier-than-his-everyday plaid shirt (cotton instead of flannel) and dress slacks instead of jeans. When
he saw what I was wearing—and smelled the bannocks—he
burst into a wide smile.

"My nan is going to love you!"

I instantly felt guilty because I'd gone to all this trouble to
get information out of the old lady and not because I wanted
to marry her great-grandson. But at least I'd made Mac happy.
He grinned all the way to Shady Pines, which was a short drive
away, near the edge of the downtown area. I'd passed the non-
descript two-story brick building before without really noticing it. There was a large, shaded patio in front, on which
elderly people often congregated. Today it was festooned with
balloons that said HAPPY BIRTHDAY GRANDMA! A large multi-
generational group was gathered around a tiny elderly woman
wearing a pointed party hat. Mac stopped by on our way in to
wish Mrs. Rappaport a happy birthday and ask how her new
hip was. I stood in my nice plaid skirt, holding my basket of
fragrant bannocks, while the entire Rappaport family scruti-
nized me as a potential fiancée for Mac. By the time we left
here today, the whole town would think we were engaged.

The cheerful exterior and pleasant staff inside couldn't quite
disguise the antiseptic smell of an institution—or the fact that
many of the residents were not as spry or as well attended as
Mrs. Rappaport. We passed a lounge where an elderly group
slumped in front of a television set, their wrinkled faces slack
and colorless. I was aware of eyes tracking us as we passed the
residential rooms, and I felt strangely as I had looking toward
the woods this morning. A woman in a pink tracksuit, mak-

ing her laborious way down the hall with her walker, raised her head as we went by and lifted a shaking hand to stop us.

"Is there something I can do?" I asked her.

"You can get me the hell outta here!" she cried. "There are monsters here!"

"It's okay, Mrs. Goldstein," Mac said in a soothing voice. "I'll call an aide to help you."

"Traitor!" Mrs. Goldstein hissed. "Collaborator!"

Mac only smiled and nodded at Mrs. Goldstein's accusations and pulled me away. "Don't worry about Mrs. Goldstein. She's a Holocaust survivor, and now she thinks she's back in the camps."

"That's horrible!" I said. "The poor woman!"

Mac nodded, but we'd arrived at his nan's room, and he was too busy slicking down his hair and straightening his tie to worry about Mrs. Goldstein's delusions. He took my arm and led me into a comfortable bedroom that included a small sitting area, toward a wizened old lady in a powder-blue velour tracksuit with a plaid wool shawl draped over her shoulders. I recognized the wide Stewart face beneath crisply waved white hair, and she had the same blue eyes, only hers were slightly clouded by cataracts. When she lifted those eyes, though, they fastened on me with a keenness I'd never seen in Mac's face.

"Ah, Cailleach McFay," the old woman said in a surprisingly strong, steady voice. "At last. I've been waiting a long time to see you."

I looked uncertainly at Mac, wondering if Nan hadn't slipped back into dementia. Mac shrugged and looked embarrassed, then said in a loud voice, "You told me to bring her at teatime, remember? And, look, Callie's made you some bannocks."

I put the basket on the table, which was set with a brown

glazed teapot, three flowered teacups, a bowl of brown-sugar cubes, a jug of milk, and little pots of jam and what looked like clotted cream. Mac and I sat down on the two comfortable chairs opposite the couch. He poured tea and filled his grandmother in on the latest news—how the crops had come in, the quantities of jams and pickles put up by his mother and aunts, the purchase of a new tractor, the health and activities of a dozen or so grandchildren and twice again as many farm animals. Mrs. Stewart maintained the regal poise of a queen listening to the assizes, her eyes, the same Wedgwood blue as the teacups, all the while focused on me. When Mac had finished his report on the state of the Stewart clan, he took a gulp of tea and crammed a bannock into his mouth. His eyes widened.

"Why, Callie!" he exclaimed with a full mouth. "These are just like the ones Nan makes. How did you get the recipe? Nan always says it's a family secret!"

"It's how my father made them," I replied. "He said he learned from his grandmother."

"Mmph." Mrs. Stewart made an enigmatic sound. Then, turning to Mac, she said, "Be a dear and go talk to Mrs. Gulliver about putting me into the Friday afternoon bridge game, and don't let her tell you it's full just because Babs Meriweather swooped in and took my seat while I was indisposed. I'm back now."

"Sure, Nan, only I could go after our visit—"

"You'll want to catch her now before she leaves, lad, and this will give the lass and me time for a little girl talk."

"Oh!" Mac said, turning bright red at the thought of what girl talk might entail. He gave me a wary smile and hurried out before he might accidentally overhear some embarrassing female detail.

"Mrs. Stewart—" I began when he had gone.

"Call me Nan, lass. I feel as though I've known you for centuries."

I sighed. "Nan, I know Mac's told you a lot about me, but I hope that hasn't given you the wrong impression about our relationship . . . not that Mac isn't a fine young man."

"Tsk, tsk," Nan Stewart clicked her tongue at me. "I know you're not sweet on my boy, lass—ye could do worse, mind ye, but he's no' the man of your dreams, is he?"

I met those sharp blue eyes. "What do you know about my dreams, Nan?"

She leaned forward, and her thin, arthritic hand grasped mine with surprising force. "That the man who comes in them is as sweet as heathered honey." She sniffed as though she could smell the heather strewn all over my bed after my dreams. "And I know ye willna let go of him, even though ye should. But when do we ever do what we should when it comes to love, eh?" Her eyes clouded, as if a mist had washed over them, and the years fell away from her face. I glimpsed a young woman in front of me, her eyes burning with love. I returned the pressure of her grip on my hand.

"Not often," I replied. "But I want to do what's right for Fairwick. Not for . . . *him,* but to fix things here. I know you've been . . . indisposed, so you may not know that something awful's happening."

"Not know it, lass? Who do ye think *indisposed* me? Those bastards, that's who! They knew I'd never let them take my village, and so they struck me down and scrambled my senses. If I hadn't had the plaid to protect me, they would have killed me."

I guessed that she meant the magic tartan the Stewarts used as a force field, not the plaid shawl around her shoulders.

"The plaid has many powers," she said. "We used it to banish the nephilim in Ballydoon when they tried to round up the old folk and the wisewomen."

She let go of my hands and leaned back against the sofa cushions. Lines of strain had appeared on her face, and I worried that dredging up these painful memories might be too much for her. I held her teacup up to her lips, but she waved it away. "They came to my village many years ago, hunting down the old folk and those who believed in them."

"The old folk? Do you mean . . ."

"You know who I mean, lass. The good people. The fairies. You've got more than a touch of the fey in you. Enough to open the door between worlds. The McFays came from the same village as us Stewarts. It were a McFay who charged the Stewarts with protectin' folks from the wrong sort of sprite— and from those evil winged bastards."

I blinked at the old woman's ferocity.

"They rounded up the last of the fairies and all who sheltered them. Called them witches and burned them at the stake. 'Twas a fairy that drove them out."

"Do you know how she did it?" I asked. "Did she have a stone?"

Nan shook her head, and her keen eyes seemed to grow a little dimmer. "When I think on it, I get a little confused, like. But, aye, I think there was a stone . . . and I think it's still back there."

"Back where?" I asked, beginning to worry that Nan hadn't completely recovered from her dementia.

"In Ballydoon," Nan snapped, as if I were the one whose faculties were in question.

"Ballydoon, Scotland?" I asked. "You want me to go to Scotland?"

Nan sighed. "You'll no' find the stone in Ballydoon *now*.

You have to go through the hallow door and go back to Ballydoon *then*."

"You mean go back to the time of the witch hunts? To the 1600s?"

"Aye, thereabouts. You wear that brooch you've got on now"—she stabbed her finger at the brooch pinned to my blouse—"and the hallow door will take you to the right place."

"But where do I find the hallow door?" I asked.

Nan made an exasperated sound. "Find it? Why, lass, don't you know? You *are* the hallow door."

I opened my mouth but found I had no words. It didn't make sense. How could I *be* a door?

"Did you not know a doorkeeper may become the door? Of course, you need to have made a blood bond with the last door before it closed."

"But I did that," I told her. "I used a heart-binding spell from Wheelock, but then when Bill died"—I took a breath to keep away the sadness that always rose when I thought of that moment—"the door exploded."

"Aye," Nan said, patting my hand. "It was because your heart was broken. Never you worry, lass, it will mend. And ye still have the bond to the door. You'll be able to open a passage anytime, anywhere, but for the first time you'll need to do it on All Hallows' Eve, and you'll need help. You'll need, as that Clinton woman so wisely said, a village."

"A village?"

"Aye. Hallows' Eve is only as powerful as its observance. That's why the nephilim always try to stamp out the old ways wherever they go. You watch: they'll try to keep the town and college from observing Halloween this year."

"They've already prohibited parties," I said.

"See! Next it'll be trick-or-treating and costumes and decorations."

"Do those things really make a difference?" I asked skeptically.

"Yes," she assured me, "they do. But they're not all you'll need. You'll need a witches' circle. At midnight, go to the spot where the door was opened before. They'll try to stop you, mind. You'll need my boys to keep out the nephilim and the circle to focus your power. At the stroke of midnight, you'll become the door."

"But how?" I asked.

"How should I know?" Nan snapped. "You're the doorkeeper—and a witch. Look through your book of spells."

"Okay," I said, wishing Nan could be more specific. "Once I've opened . . . or, er, *become* the door, what then?" I asked. "How can I get rid of the nephilim?"

"Why, find the angel stone, of course," she said. "And bring it back."

"But where exactly—" I began, but I saw a rictus of pain distort Nan's face. I'd exhausted her.

"You'll find it just as ye did before," she said.

"I will," I said, even though I wasn't sure what she meant. Perhaps she was confusing me with my ancestor.

Mac came back then and Nan changed the subject, asking him to tell her all the details of his cousin Isobel's wedding, which she'd had to miss when she was *not herself*. Mac happily obliged, exhibiting a remarkable memory for bridesmaids' dresses and place settings that drove home to me how much the young man was looking forward to his own nuptials. I caught him giving me moon eyes while describing the wedding cake. He talked until we both noticed that Nan had fallen asleep.

"We'd best leave her," Mac said, getting up and tucking the shawl around the old woman's shoulders. "I'll go tell her aide to look in on her."

He went ahead of me as I bent down to pick up the tea tray. I adjusted a stray edge of the shawl and carried the tray down the hall to the kitchen. When I came out, I met Mrs. Goldstein standing in front of the elevator. "You have to help me get out!" she wailed plaintively. "The monsters are back."

"It's all right, Mrs. Goldstein," someone murmured, coming up behind me. I turned and found Adam Sinclair.

"What are you doing here?" I asked.

"It's part of my community service," he said, smiling as he walked past me and put his arm around Mrs. Goldstein's frail, trembling shoulders. Mrs. Goldstein lifted pleading eyes to mine as Adam steered her walker around and guided her back down the hall.

CHAPTER TEN

N an Stewart was right about the nephilim lockdown of Halloween. In the next few weeks, as the leaves changed and the air sharpened and the local stores put out displays of Halloween candy and children's costumes and my neighbors decorated their doorways with jack-o'-lanterns and leering skeletons, my in-box was peppered with emails from our dean, prohibiting Halloween parties on campus. The emails cited incidents at other colleges of razor-spiked apples and rampant vandalism and studies linking campus violence to the watching of horror movies.

My students grumbled and complained, but no one wanted to risk getting summoned to the dean's office. The students who had been called in—for breaking curfew or missing classes—came out cowed and nervous. It seemed that Dean Laird had a way of targeting a student's weakness, whether that meant a call home, a threat to financial aid, or the refusal of a recommendation to law school. Most disturbing, some students formed a group to back up the dean's recommendations—the Committee for Positive Change at Fairwick. Unsurprisingly, it was led by Adam Sinclair, but it also included plenty of other students, even, I was shocked to see, Scott Wilder. When I asked Scott about it, he shrugged and said there was really good food at the meetings, which he needed because the food at the cafeteria was worse than ever this year.

Soheila and I went to the cafeteria one day to make sure that the students weren't being poisoned. We were served a bland assortment of overcooked and oversauced food—chicken à la king with soggy green beans, mayonnaise-drenched lettuce, orange Jell-O, and watered-down fruit punch.

"It's not poisoned," Soheila said, making a face as she sampled the fare, "but it's as though all the flavor and life has been sucked out of the food. The body might be sustained by eating this . . . *swill,* but not the spirit. No wonder they all go to the Alpha House dinners."

When I walked past Alpha House, I could smell the intoxicating aromas wafting out of it. Not only had the Alphas managed to clear out my stink bomb, but they had also erected a layer of wards protecting the house from any of my spells. I watched helplessly as students trooped into the nephilim's stronghold, but I stayed out on my porch—no matter how cold or how late it got—until each and every girl who went into Alpha House came out. I even tried calling up Duncan's office and complaining that they were breaking the no-gathering rule.

"Didn't you read the email? Meetings approved by my office as sanctioned college activities may meet on Tuesdays and Thursdays between the hours of six and ten P.M."

"I guess I missed that one," I said. "Can I get approved to hold student meetings at my house?"

"Of course," he replied magnanimously. "What kind of meeting do you want to hold?"

"I've been thinking of starting a folklore club," I said, making it up on the spot. "To explore local traditions and the folklore of other cultures. We could have food from the different cultures we were studying . . ." As I spooled off more activities, I started to think it was actually a good idea. I must have talked long enough that Duncan Laird got tired of hearing my voice.

"Fine," he said abruptly. "That sounds harmless enough. You have my permission."

I thanked him and got off the phone before he could change his mind. Half an hour later I had sent out emails to all my students, announcing the first meeting of the Fairwick Folklore Society for the following week. First order of business— exploring the folklore and traditions of Halloween.

Once I'd launched the folklore club (Nicky Ballard and Flonia Rugova volunteered to run it), I concentrated on the next order of business—gathering a witches' circle. I'd been introduced to the witches of Fairwick this past summer, but since then Liz Book had gone to Faerie and the circle had disbanded with the defections of Lester Hanks and Ann Chase. These days the closest thing I had to a mentor to teach me how to use my powers was Frank Delmarco. I asked Frank to go with me to talk to the remaining witches in Fairwick who hadn't aligned themselves with the nephilim. We met on a Saturday afternoon in mid-October at Fair Grounds, the town coffee bar. I ordered a pumpkin spice latte and an apple cider donut from Leon Botwin, hipster barista and witch.

"I'm going on break in five minutes," Leon told us as he steamed the milk for my latte and served Frank an austere espresso. "Moondance should be here soon, but Tara called to say that she can't make it."

"Uh-oh," I said. "Do you think she's gone over to the other side?"

"Might have." Leon shook his head as he wiped down the brass fittings of the espresso machine. "Her husband lost his job and she's expecting another kid. And her husband nominated two new members for the Lions Club who looked suspiciously *nephilitic*."

"You belong to the Lions Club?" I asked, more surprised at that than the possibility that the club had been infiltrated by nephilim. In his skinny black jeans, scruffy goatee, and black Converse high-tops, Leon hardly looked the Lions Club type.

"I bought Fair Grounds when Dory Browne had to leave town this summer. It was either that or let it become a Starbucks. Anyway, now that I'm a small-business owner, I thought I should join. The problem is . . ." He looked around to see if anyone was close enough to overhear, suspiciously eyeing an old man examining the chalkboard menu, and then leaned over the counter to whisper, "There were so many empty spots after the summer migration that there are a lot of new members. These two guys that Tara's husband nominated just bought Browne's Realty. They've got that tall Nordic look going on, *and* one of the first things they did was veto the town's Halloween parade."

"But that's a tradition!" I objected. Every year on the afternoon of Halloween, Main Street was closed to traffic and the stores gave out candy to trick-or-treaters. The elementary school organized a costume parade that ended in the town square, where apple cider and donuts were served.

"I hear that Tara has also organized the town PTA to prohibit the elementary school parade. Haven't you seen the buttons?"

"Buttons?"

Leon pointed his scraggly goatee toward a tall gray-haired woman. She was dressed in a long burgundy wool coat and a floppy crocheted hat decorated with a button of a jack-o'-lantern with a line drawn across it.

When she caught me looking at her, she pursed her lips and shook her finger at me. "The new pastor at my church gave a most enlightening talk. Do you know that Halloween was originally a satanic mass and that the ancient druids sacrificed children on their bonfires? Here . . ." She dug into a large crocheted bag and handed me a printed pamphlet entitled "The Devil's Night." "That'll tell you all you need to know. That's all I'm giving if any children come to my door this year. I'll have a nonfat decaf latte, young man, and make sure the milk is fresh."

Frank and I took our coffees to a table while Leon filled the woman's order. As we waited, I noticed a few other people in the café wearing banned-jack-o'-lantern buttons. I was beginning to think the whole town had turned against Halloween when Moondance came in, wearing a black T-shirt proclaiming BLESSED SAMHAIN in orange lettering beneath a witch silhouetted against an enormous orange moon. Since Moondance was not a small woman, the moon loomed large as she approached us. I felt a moment's trepidation. Moondance had been sharply critical of my inclusion in the witches' circle this summer. I was an untrained novice whose erratic energy had thrown off the circle twice, and in the end I hadn't been able to stop the door from closing. I was expecting at the very least a sharp-tongued drubbing, but instead I got a bone-crushing hug.

"Thank the Goddess you haven't gone over to the dark side!" Moondance held me out at arm's length, hands gripped on either forearm, and gave me a shake. Her frizzy orange hair wafted around her head like dried chrysanthemum blooms, and her pale-blue eyes were glassy with unshed tears. "And you . . ." She let me go and turned to Frank. "I knew a Delmarco would never abandon the cause. Your grandmother would be proud of you."

"Yours, too, Moser," Frank said, stepping into Moondance's embrace and thumping her soundly on the back. "Glad to have you on our team."

"I'm afraid it's not much of a team," Leon said, handing Moondance an algae-colored shake as he sat down at our table. "Four is not enough for a circle."

"But we need a circle . . ." I looked around the café to make sure no one was listening, but all the other customers had left. Noticing that, as well, Leon nodded at Moondance.

"Was that an aversion spell?" he asked.

She nodded, her rust-hued hair bobbing cheerfully. "Home-burner spell. The citizens of Fairwick were all suddenly struck with an overwhelming conviction that they'd left something on the stove, forgot to turn off the gas, or didn't leave water out for their cats. We should be able to talk in peace for half an hour. No time to waste, though. Tell me what you need the circle for."

I relayed to Leon and Moondance what Nan Stewart had told me about the hallow door.

"Huh," Leon said, stroking his goatee. "You *are* the door? How metaphysical."

"It's also confusing," I said. "I'm not sure how to 'open myself,' and she says I still need to do it on Halloween."

"That part makes sense," Moondance said. "Samhain is the time of the year when the barriers between worlds, between living and dead, between seen and unseen, are thinnest. The hinge of the year, some Wiccans call it."

"A hinge on which a door may open," Frank said. "Especially if we have a doorkeeper who's made a blood bond to the door."

All three looked at me. "But I can't do it on my own. Nan Stewart says I need a witches' circle in the grove and a wider circle of observance in the village. Halloween, she said, is only as powerful as its observance."

"That's why the nephilim are trying to shut it down," Leon said. "They don't want Callie to open the door."

"Which, I'd say, is reason enough to open it," Moondance said, "but if we're going to summon a circle, I'd like to be clear on why." Her eyes, no longer cloudy with tears, now sharp as tacks, flicked to me. "So far I've heard a lot about the hallow door, Callie, but if you don't mind me saying, how do we know it's not just a way for you to get back together with your incubus boyfriend?"

Frank made a sound that I knew was preparation to launch into my defense, but I held my hand up to stop him. "Fair question," I said. I felt the blood rush to my face at the memory of my erotic dreams. They'd become more urgent as the nights lengthened toward Halloween, as if William Duffy knew he was running out of time. "Nan said that when her village in Scotland was invaded by the nephilim, the doorkeeper was able to use the angel stone to destroy them. And she says the angel stone is still in Ballydoon." I didn't mention that Nan had been a little vague on that point, but Moondance sensed my uncertainty and pounced.

"So we're all supposed to risk our lives on the gamble that you'll find your way back to a seventeenth-century Scottish village and find this stone that *might* destroy the nephilim?"

"Risk your lives? I'm not asking—"

"You are," Leon said. "The nephilim don't want this door opened. They'll try to stop you. The circle's to protect you while you open the door, but the nephilim will try to break through it. If the circle breaks, we'll be at their mercy. We'd need powerful, experienced witches, and I only see three of them here."

I began to object, but he stopped me. "You don't count. You'll be in the center of the circle. We need at least six to make a circle to protect you. Where are we going to find three seasoned witches by Halloween to risk their lives against the nephilim?"

"Right here."

We all looked up, startled by the sound of a woman's voice at the door. We hadn't heard the door open—or the bell on it jangle—but a woman of average height stood silhouetted against the bright glare of sunlight coming in from the street. There were two more figures behind her. Another triad, I thought, which didn't bode well, especially when the first woman stepped forward out of the glare and I recognized her as my grandmother.

CHAPTER ELEVEN

"Adelaide," I said, getting to my feet. I heard the scrape of chairs as Frank, Moondance, and Leon also got up. A crackling tension in the air raised the hair on the back of my neck. My three companions were marshaling their magical powers to stand against my grandmother. I didn't blame them. To the uninitiated, my grandmother might appear to be a harmless Upper East Side matron, with her impeccably cut and dyed chin-length blue-black hair, her knit St. John suit, pearl choker, and no-nonsense handmade Swiss shoes, but anyone with an inkling of witchcraft could sense the power rising off her in waves. She was a venerable witch and leader of the Grove, an ancient federation of anti-fey witches who had joined with the nephilim to close the door to Faerie once and for all. Somehow, she must have gotten wind of our attempts to open the hallow door and had come to prevent it.

Adelaide stepped forward and, sniffing the air, said, "Oh, my, I have a sudden urge to go home and check that I turned off the stove. What a quaint aversion spell! Yours?" she asked, looking straight at Moondance, who bristled like an angry cat

THE ANGEL STONE · 99

under Adelaide's regard. Adelaide lifted her right hand, her heavy gold charm bracelet gleaming in the sunlight. As a child, I'd been fascinated by her charms—the miniature gondola and cuckoo clock with tiny working parts. A miniature fan now winked in the sun as its blades began to move. Instantly I smelled singed copper, leaking gas, and heard the cry of a hundred thirsty house cats—Moondance's spell amplified and turned on us. I was seized with a nameless dread that I'd forgotten something urgent. I stepped forward to push Adelaide aside so I could run home and . . . I didn't know what. I just had to be home. Then Adelaide shook her charm bracelet and a pair of miniature scissors opened and snicked shut. The tension in the air snapped like a sprung rubber band, and my compulsion to go home evaporated.

Adelaide smiled and tilted her head, as she did when I was little and I was expected to kiss her cheek. I felt the same pressure now but resisted it.

"Darling, aren't you going to invite your old grandmother in and get her a cup of tea? I hear you've been visiting the elderly lately."

So she'd heard of my visit to Nan Stewart.

"I suppose your nephilim friends told you that. Did they send you here to punish me? Is that what you've become? A gofer for the nephilim?"

I'd only meant to vent some of my anger at Adelaide. Throughout my childhood and adolescence, she had a knack for making me feel small and inferior. I knew now that part of her attitude toward me stemmed from shame at my father's fey ancestry. Like many anti-fey witches, she believed that a union between witch and fey canceled out both powers. But that didn't excuse the cold, loveless environment in which she'd raised me after my parents died—or her conspiring with the nephilim to destroy my town. I didn't expect, though, to see those feelings of shame and smallness reflected in her own eyes.

"I am not here at their bidding," she said loudly. She lifted her hand to smooth her already immaculate hair, and I noticed that the fingers were bent and knotted. Her arthritis, which had been cured with Aelvesgold, was back.

"What's wrong?" I asked coldly. "Did they cut off your supply of Aelvesgold? Is that why you're here? Well, you're just going to have to use Motrin and Bengay. There's no more Aelvesgold here." That wasn't entirely true. I knew that there was a whole lump of the stuff—an Aelvestone—in the headwaters of the Undine, but that was meant to nourish the undine eggs I'd moved there this summer, and I wasn't about to tell anyone about that. "The nephilim have sucked all remaining traces of it out of Fairwick."

"Yes, they did to us, as well," Adelaide said, her voice tremulous. I peered into her face. My grandmother had looked much the same from my earliest memories on, never seeming to age a bit, yet now her face was creased with a network of fine lines that looked like cracks in a dry desert. She looked as if all the moisture—and life—had been sucked out of the marrow of her bones.

"To all of us," one of the women behind her said, stepping forward. The voice, with its gravelly Australian accent, was familiar. It sounded like that of Jen Davies, a reporter I'd met last fall when she exposed my roommate Phoenix's fraudulent memoir and who, I'd later learned, was a junior member of the Grove. But this couldn't be Jen Davies. Jen, a Jivamukti yoga enthusiast and marathon runner, was a paragon of physical fitness. This woman was at least two inches shorter, stooped, and gray haired.

"Yeah, it's me," the woman said with a self-deprecating

laugh that turned into a cough. "What? You thought I got that ass just by doing yoga?"

"Jen? What happened to you? To all—" My mouth dropped open as I saw the third person in the group. "Phoenix?" I asked incredulously. The last time I'd seen my former roommate, she was being sedated and dragged off to a mental hospital, shortly after Jen Davies had exposed her bestselling memoir as fraudulent.

"I looked for you after you left the hospital," I said, feeling guilty that I hadn't tried harder. "But your mother wouldn't tell me where you were. I was afraid . . ."

"That I'd gone off on a bender?" Phoenix asked, smoothing back her abundant crinkly hair. She'd let it go completely gray—a pale platinum silver that somehow suited her. In fact, she looked remarkably well, especially in comparison with Adelaide and Jen—who, I noticed now, was leaning heavily on Phoenix's arm. "Well, I did," she said, answering her own question. "I was holed up in a hotel room in Hoboken until Jen found me and took me to this marvelous Grove retreat in—" At a glance from Jen, she closed her mouth, but only for half a second. "That's right, I'm not supposed to say. It's kind of a spa for witches who have gone through traumatic events. Jen got me in even though I'm not a witch. Your friends were right about that, by the way. I didn't have an ounce of magic in me—at least not then—but that turned out to be a good thing when those monsters attacked."

"The nephilim attacked a Grove retreat?" I asked. "But why? I thought you were all in cahoots."

Jen laughed at the phrase, but the laugh turned into a hacking cough. "We'll tell you all about it, but your grandmother's right, you know?"

I looked at her blankly.

"You really ought to offer her—and all of us—some tea

and"—she looked past me toward the counter—"some of those scrumptious-looking pumpkin muffins. I'm famished . . . and it's a long story."

Phoenix insisted we all have a hot beverage before she began the story. She asked for a soy chai latte for Jen, and Earl Grey with milk and sugar for Adelaide. She had Frank move Adelaide's chair three times to make sure she wasn't seated in a draft, then settled a fluffy mohair shawl around my grandmother's shoulders. Then Phoenix asked Leon if he could make her a hazelnut half-decaf latte with half skim, half whole milk and just a smidgen of whipped cream on top.

"I know what you're thinking," she said, winking at me. "That sounds like the order of a manic-depressive, doesn't it?"

"Well . . ." I hemmed and hawed. I was still too shocked at watching Phoenix tend to my imperious grandmother as if she were her own beloved granny—and at my grandmother for tolerating the treatment—to be thinking anything at all about Phoenix's coffee order. But now that she mentioned it . . .

She laughed. "I know! But, honestly, it was being bipolar that saved my life."

"And mine," Jen said, laying a gaunt hand on Phoenix's. "If you hadn't been there when the nephilim attacked, I would have been killed."

"What happened?" Moondance asked.

Phoenix opened her mouth to begin, but Adelaide laid a hand over hers and she instantly stopped. I'd never seen Phoenix so easily silenced.

"I think I should tell it," Adelaide said, in a heavy, throaty voice I'd never heard from her before. As she began, I realized that the unfamiliar tone was regret.

"After we left Fairwick this summer, we repaired to the retreat. Closing the door was a monumental effort for us." She glanced at me and blanched. "You underestimate your own strength, Callie. We had to fight your will to work the closing spell."

"I thought it was the nephilim who closed the door," I said, blinking away a tear at the memory of Bill's blood pouring through my fingers, his mortality evidence of my love for him, which had come too late to save him.

"The nephilim have no control over the door," Adelaide replied. "That is their one weakness. When they were banished from Faerie, their fey magic was destroyed—except the Aelvesgold in their wings. The fey took pity on them and left them that, although some say it wasn't pity but cruel irony that they would leave the nephilim with Aelvesgold but without the ability to use it. If they'd known how the nephilim would use their Aelvesgold, the fey would have done it differently. Since the time of the witch hunts, the nephilim have bribed witches to do their bidding with the promise of Aelvesgold. I'm afraid that we were foolish enough to succumb to their bribery."

"And what's different now?" Moondance asked.

"They betrayed us," Adelaide answered. "When we left here, we went to a sanctuary to recoup our powers. The nephilim knew we were at our weakest. They attacked our compound and spread their narcotic incense throughout, rendering all our number unconscious. And then they began to devour us."

"Devour?" I heard Leon and Moondance repeat the word at the same time I did.

"I don't know what else to call it," Adelaide said, her face white. "They spread their wings over their victims first. They have barbs beneath their feathers, thousands of tiny needle-like barbs . . ." Adelaide shuddered, and Phoenix took up the story.

"I saw the whole thing. I was in my six A.M. yoga class when everybody just keeled over in the middle of a sun salutation. For some reason, I was immune."

"We think perhaps because of her particular brain wiring," Jen said.

"Who'd have thunk it? My screwy wiring came in handy for something. Anyway, when I saw everyone hit their sticky mats, I ran out into the courtyard for help and saw those monsters—one had just landed on a sweet little witch from South Carolina. He got his hooks in her and she screamed. I tried to get him off, but when I did she started cracking. It was as if he had drained her of all the vital juices in her body. Then I heard Jen screaming and saw one of the nephilim on top of her, with its wings wrapped around her."

"They start with your memories," Jen said softly. "They dig into your oldest and dearest moments and suck them out of you. It's as if they want to rob you of everything that makes you human before they kill you. I could feel my memories going . . . If Phoenix hadn't gotten that monster off me, I would have lost my mind first and then my life. As it is, I lost whole chunks of my childhood."

She broke off, trembling. Much to my amazement, Adelaide patted her shoulder and made a comforting noise. Phoenix continued Jen's story.

"When I grabbed the nephilim attacking her, I felt Jen's memories being sucked out of her. Then the monster turned on me, but when he sank his claws into me, he recoiled." Phoenix grinned. "Apparently nephilim can't absorb the energy of someone with my unusual brain wiring. As soon as I got rid of Jen's attacker, I went after the one attacking Adelaide."

"The nephilim had its barbs in me for only a few minutes before Phoenix rescued me," Adelaide said, looking at me. "But in that short time I lost your mother's face. It wasn't until I felt it going that I realized how much I had lost by shutting her out—and how little I wanted to lose you, as well."

Her lips were nearly white with the effort it had cost her to make this admission. I knew I should say something but was far too stunned to reply. In all the years I had lived with my grandmother, she was cool and distant, bothering to talk to me only when she had something to criticize. She'd spoken about my mother only to complain that I was like her and that surely I was headed in the same direction—a foolish marriage and an early death caused by recklessness. This summer she'd stood by while Duncan Laird tried to slash my throat. How could I trust her now?

"I don't expect you to believe me, but I've come to make amends."

"If what you say is true, you've come because you have no place else to go," Frank said coldly. "Or you could be here as the nephilim's spies."

"I can't blame you for doubting us," Adelaide answered. "We are willing to bind ourselves to prove our intentions."

"Bind yourselves?" I asked, looking around the group. "What does that mean?"

"A witches' circle can perform a binding spell that holds each member to the good of the group and compels them to truthfulness with one another," Moondance answered. She narrowed her eyes at Adelaide. "Would you be willing for me to say the binding spell?"

"Certainly," she answered without hesitation. "We will submit to whatever binding you deem appropriate. As Mr. Delmarco here so delicately pointed out, we have no place else to go—and we are committed to vanquishing the nephilim."

Moondance looked from Adelaide to me. "What do you think, Callie? She's your grandmother. Do you want to be bound to her after what she did to you—to all of us?"

I looked at my grandmother. I had spent the last ten years trying to free myself of her judgments and criticisms, and yet, in my worst moments, I still heard her censorious voice in my head. Contemplating her now, I saw a tired old woman, and I wondered how I had ever let her have so much power over me. But, I realized, sending her away wouldn't break her hold on me. Maybe having her as bound to me as I was to her would.

"Okay," I said. "Let's do it."

CHAPTER TWELVE

Leon put out a CLOSED sign and reinforced the home-burner spell. He probably didn't need to bother. Main Street, usually bustling on a Saturday late afternoon, was deserted. Fairwick residents were hurrying home as if afraid of being caught out after dark. Glancing at the lengthening shadows as I closed the blinds, I couldn't blame them. When I turned away from the windows and saw the six people arranged in a circle of chairs around a single lit candle, which barely kept at bay the shadows in the corners of the room, I couldn't help wondering if we would be able to stem that outer darkness.

Frank met my worried look and patted the chair next to him. "A bound circle exerts a powerful force, McFay," he said with a level look. "Don't underestimate it."

"Why didn't you bind your circle before?" I asked Moondance as I sat down between Frank and Jen. "Wouldn't that have kept Ann Chase from betraying you?"

"A binding is not to be entered into lightly," Moondance said. "Once we are connected to one another, anything that happens to any one of us will rebound on the others threefold.

Ann always said she was reluctant to bind herself to us because we'd all suffer from her arthritis, but now I wonder if it wasn't an excuse to betray us." I heard the hurt in Moondance's voice and remembered how she had watched out for Ann. The betrayal must have hit her especially hard.

"Do you really want to include me?" Phoenix asked. "When I absorbed Jen's memories I also absorbed her witch's power, but I'm still bipolar—or maybe even tripolar now."

"I think Phoenix will prove to be an asset to us," Adelaide said. "Her brain chemistry allows her to absorb the power of others remarkably well. And as for her mental instability—"

Jen cleared her throat to interrupt. "Who of us doesn't have a little imbalance here or there?" she said, staring down Adelaide. "Anyway, the binding only lasts for one lunar cycle."

"Just long enough to take us through Hallowmas," Adelaide said, returning Jen's stare with a conciliatory smile that surprised me more than anything else so far. "Are we ready?" Adelaide asked, looking around the circle. We each nodded. When her gaze fell on me, her eyes seemed to shine unnaturally bright. It was only when she looked away that I realized her eyes were filled with tears. Was she trying to find my mother's face in mine? Was she sorry she had never performed this rite with her?

Feeling my own eyes fill with tears, I took Frank's hand, which felt warm and strong, and then Jen's. I was instantly struck by the difference in the energy Jen emitted. I'd shaken hands with her before and noticed she had a grip like a mula bandha lock, but now her touch was tentative, her energy wavering. The nephilim attack had depleted her life force dramatically. For a moment I felt my own life force weaken, but when Frank took Phoenix's hand, completing the circle, I felt a satisfying click and a pleasant fizzing sensation, as if I'd just had a glass of champagne.

"That's me," Phoenix said. "I've been riding pretty high since the nephilim attack. To tell you the truth, I've never felt so useful in my entire life. You should also get the benefit of my immunity to nephilim incense. On the negative side, I'm probably due for a mood swing in a couple of days. They're not as bad as they used to be, but I can still get a little cranky around that time of month."

"Good to know," Frank growled.

"I can't say anything positive about my mood," Moondance grumped.

"Someone's been imbibing quite a bit of caffeine," Adelaide remarked.

"Guilty," Leon said cheerfully. "Perks of the job. I pretty much inhale the stuff, morning, noon, and night."

"Great," Frank said. "So we can look forward to sleep deprivation as well as PMS."

I was beginning to see why witches were reluctant to bind themselves to a circle. I already felt as if I had six warring personalities besides my own inside my head. Talk about being bipolar; this felt like being sept-polar. I wondered suddenly what effect *my* energy had on the group.

"Ooh," Jen cooed. "So *that's* what an incubus does for you."

"I don't know what you're talking about," I objected, blood rising to my face. "I haven't seen Bill or Liam in months."

"Yes, but you've been dreaming of him, haven't you?" Phoenix said. "I can feel—"

"Are we going to do this thing or not?" Frank snapped.

"My sentiments exactly," Adelaide said. "Let's get on with it. Moondance, would you do the honors?"

Moondance straightened up in her chair, closed her eyes, and began to chant.

> *"By all the power of goddesses three*
> *this circle as one shall be.*
> *Till Diana turn her face once round*
> *Our wills together shall be bound."*

A pulse of energy surged around the circle. I felt it throbbing through my hands and saw a bright gold filament enclosing the group. All the individual sensations we'd been experiencing—fatigue, anger, lust, sorrow, hope—all merged into one steady *thrum*, containing all the disparate emotions and then overwhelming them into one single connection. We were not alone. The golden thread flared brighter, warring against the darkness rising outside the circle. For a moment, I saw the shadows in the corners of the room writhing away from that light, their shapes distorted into hideous monsters, and then the gold light sank into us and the shadows drained away.

Afterward, we laid our plans. We needed the village to celebrate Halloween. Moondance and Leon would rally the townspeople to resist the anti-Halloween fervor, while Frank, Soheila, and I would covertly urge on the students. Adelaide said that she, Jen, and Phoenix would perform a needfire rite—whatever that was. Everyone else seemed to know, and I was getting tired of being the one to ask all the questions. We would enlist the Stewarts and the vampires to patrol the woods on Halloween night to keep the nephilim from breaching our circle, which would form around the old door. I would be at the center of all those circles.

"The nephilim will exert all their power to stop you from opening the door," Adelaide told me, her eyes fierce now instead of teary. "When you've opened the door and gotten to Ballydoon, you must find the angel stone as quickly as possible and return with it to destroy the nephilim. We'll hold the circle as long as we can, but once it falls, the nephilim will destroy us."

The only problem was that Nan had been unable to tell me where in Ballydoon I would find the angel stone.

It was dark by the time I walked home. Frank insisted on escorting me all the way up to my door.

"Duncan and his cronies will know what we're up to," he said, scanning my front porch. "He'll do everything in his power to stop us. You'll have to be especially careful. Reinforce the wards on your house, never let yourself be alone with him, don't go out alone after dark—"

"Yes, Mom," I replied.

"I'm serious, McFay. I've seen what those monsters can do . . ." His voice cracked.

I looked up, startled, and saw that his face was completely white. The one time I'd seen him like this was three months ago, when he saw the claw marks that Duncan Laird had left on my face. He'd recognized them as the marks of nephilim, but I'd never asked him where he'd seen the marks before.

"You encountered the nephilim before, didn't you?" I asked.

Frank glanced away. In the glare of the porch light, his face suddenly looked old. I knew that, like many witches, Frank could have prolonged his life span with his magic, but I'd never really thought about how old he might be.

"Yes, but I didn't know it at the time. It was during the Second World War. I was assigned by IMP to work with the French underground. We suspected that there was an officer within the SS who wasn't . . . *human*." Frank made a harsh sound that it took me a few moments to identify as a laugh. "As if any of them were really *human*. The sad thing is, most of them were—technically, that is. Some of the worst monsters I've encountered have been. But we suspected that this one SS officer was some kind of demon. To find out, we placed an agent inside the SS, a woman called Nataliya."

I'd never heard Frank's voice so tender—in fact, I realized, I'd never heard Frank talk about any past relationships.

"She was from a small village in Romania, from an old family of gypsy witches, all of whom were sent to the camps by the Nazis. I shouldn't have let her go, but she was determined to avenge them, and she was so powerful that I thought she would be okay. Two months into the assignment, she got word to me that she'd learned her officer's secret. I was to meet her in the woods outside the castle where the officers were quartered. When I got there, I found her nearly dead. She'd been . . . tortured. She had the same claw marks on her face that you had, but that wasn't the worst of it. Her mind had been savaged. I tried to use magic to save her. I connected myself to her to sustain her life, and I felt the agony she had experienced. It was as if her mind had been torn to shreds. The pain was so great, I recoiled . . . I let go of the contact and she died. I *let* her die."

"Oh, Frank," I said, touching his arm. "I'm sure you did everything you could."

"No, you don't understand. I could have kept her alive, but the pain inside her was so great, she didn't want to live, and I . . . I couldn't bear to let her go on with that pain. The last thing she said to me was *angel*. I thought she was saying that I was an angel to let her die, but then when I tracked down the marks on her face I found that they were the marks of a nephilim. We couldn't be sure. The SS officer disappeared. We thought the nephilim were extinct. But I never forgot what those marks looked like"—he turned to me, his eyes dark, bottomless pits—"or what the pain inside her felt like. Those monsters don't just kill you. They make you wish you'd never been born."

Frank's words haunted me in the coming days as I searched through Wheelock's *Spellcraft*, looking for a spell to become the hallow door. There were spells on opening doors and closing them, spells to ward your door, and even one to discourage Jehovah's Witnesses from your door, but nothing on *becoming* a door. But the thing about Wheelock, I was discovering, was that it seemed to grow as you used it. Every time I clicked on a footnote or opened an appendix, the volume grew to accommodate the new material. As I searched, the book grew and grew, until it resembled a summer blockbuster paperback that had gotten waterlogged from being read at the beach.

In the meantime, the folklore club prepared for its first meeting, and my students clamored for a Halloween party. Did I really have the right to encourage my students to celebrate Halloween if it put them in danger? But short of telling them all to drop out and go home, I didn't know how to remove them from harm's way. Besides, along with showing up at my house with supplies of apple cider and cider donuts, they came prepared with a loophole in the administration's no-party rule.

"As long as an event is for instructive purposes, it's allowed," Scott Wilder explained. With the keen mind of a young lawyer, he had combed through the dozens of emails, memos, and minutes issued by the dean's office. "And Halloween teaches us all sorts of crap about folklore, right?"

"Er, I wouldn't put it exactly like that, but, yes, its celebration appears in any number of ballads and folktales."

"Like Tam Lin," Nicky added. "That's when the fairy host rides through the door to Faerie and when the Fairy Queen pays the tithe to hell with a human sacrifice," she continued. "Hey, why don't we do a reenactment of Tam Lin? That would totally make our Halloween celebration school-related. Ruby could play the Fairy Queen, and Scott could be Tam Lin."

"Not if I have to wear a kilt! I went in drag last year and froze my ass off. I don't know how girls wear dresses in the winter."

"Leggings," Nicky and Ruby said simultaneously.

"And Uggs," Flonia added.

"You could wear woolen socks," I suggested to Scott, "but I don't think real Scotsmen wear anything underneath their kilts."

"No way! They went commando? I'm totally up for it!"

The girls dissolved into giggles at that and I went to heat up some more apple cider, leaving them to flirt and plan their costumes. I liked having the house full of laughing young people. Maybe I should rent out rooms to students—or have monthly dinners. Suddenly I saw myself as a female Mr. Chips, growing old in the youthful company of my students. If I never found my demon lover, would I feel, as Mr. Chips had at the end, that I'd led a fulfilling life?

I found myself thinking such melancholic thoughts more as the autumn nights lengthened and filled with the sound of migrating geese and cold winds from the north. I huddled under warm quilts, longing for the warmth of William Duffy's body in my dreams. He was there waiting for me every night now. As soon as I walked through the ruined door into the sun-dappled Greenwood, he would reach for me and pull me down to the mossy bed. His hands and lips moved over me as if memorizing my face, my body.

"Aye, lass," he growled into my neck, "it's you. I'd know you if I were blind and a hundred years went by. Dinna go this time; it's so verra cold when you're gone. Cold as the grave."

It was cold when I woke up alone in bed. I'd try to go back to sleep, clinging to the dream, its warmth fading as fast as heat left a dying body. Even the sprigs of heather that I still found scattered in my sheets were now dried out. It was as if it had turned to winter where William was, and everything was dying there. I began to feel as hollow and dry as the dead cornstalks in the fields. I suppose it was natural to feel this way at this time of year, when the leaves on the trees changed and the grasses in the fields died and the sun itself seemed to be waning. That's why primitive man had built bonfires and made offerings to their dead, to assert that the world wasn't really dying.

But with the nephilim increasing in power around us, I wondered if such tokens meant anything. On campus, fluorescent-green flyers filled the bulletin boards and plastered walls with new regulations and warnings. BAN HALLOWEEN signs were springing up among the jack-o'-lanterns, black cats, and scary witches in town.

By the Friday before Halloween, I had decided that no matter how much I might need the observance of Halloween to open the hallow door, I couldn't endanger my students. I decided to compel all of them to go home for the weekend. Looking through Wheelock the night before, I'd found half a dozen homesickness spells to do the trick. One awakened an unbearable craving for your mother's cooking, and another increased your dirty laundry and made your clean socks disappear. Standing in front of my class, I saw that it would be easy. Although my students affected an attitude of independence and worldly cool, I knew that just below the surface they were still half children. All I'd have to do was remind them of that.

"I thought that today I would read you a story," I said, taking out an illustrated children's book.

There were a few snickers and rolled eyes, but when I perched on the edge of my desk and opened the book, holding it out so they could see the pictures, the students scooted their chairs closer into a circle and leaned forward.

I had stayed up all night, looking for the right narrative strategy to send them home. Finally, toward dawn, I realized it didn't really matter what story I read. As long as I read a story my parents had read to me as a child, they would each hear the story their parents had read to them and they would want to go home. So I read the tattered copy of Tam Lin, with its beautiful watercolors of misty Scottish glens and the deep mysterious Greenwood, of beautiful Jennet Carter in her plaid cloak and the handsome prince she saves from the fox-faced Fairy Queen. At the end, I invested the lines with the compulsion of magic.

"And so Jennet and Tam Lin were married. Together they restored and renamed Carter Hall and they—and their children's children's children—lived there, in the home they made together, happily ever after."

When I closed the book and looked up, I could see in each student's eyes a fire burning—a home fire, a burning desire to be home.

"The last bus leaves at five," I said, casually glancing down at my wristwatch. "Travel safely."

They gathered their books and left in a rush. I saw Ruby talking to Flonia and guessed that Ruby was inviting Flonia to go home with her. Nicky was with them, and I hoped that she would go home with Ruby, too, far away from Fairwick. I doubted that even a homesickness spell would send Nicky running back to the moldering pile her mother and grandmother lived in. She would be safer in New Jersey with Ruby.

I closed my book and rushed upstairs to my office, where I swiveled my desk chair around to face the window that looked over the quad. I raised the sash and leaned my elbows on the sill to watch my students, their brightly hued jackets and sweaters like so many autumn leaves blown by the wind across the darkening campus.

Go home. I willed the spell to spread from student to student. *Go home.*

My words were picked up by a gust across the quad, spinning fallen leaves into red and gold cyclones to carry a few hundred Dorothys back home to Kansas. The wind I summoned smelled like hot cocoa and fresh-baked apple pie, like fires burning in hearths and the sweater your mother wore on cold mornings to fetch the newspaper. It soughed through the trees with the creak of your front door opening and the whisper of slippered feet coming to greet you. It chased the dark clouds out of the west, releasing a crack of sunlight on the horizon that lit up the tops of crimson trees and the brick walls of west-facing buildings with the golden glow of your mother's face when she saw you.

What a surprise! She would say. *I didn't know you were coming home this weekend.*

I was out of socks, you would say.

Or, *The cafeteria food sucks.*

Or, *Everybody else was going home.*

Everybody *was* going home. I could feel the spell spreading across campus, infecting everyone, even the instructors, with the desire to go home. And, like all magic, it rebounded on me thricefold, so that I, too, wanted to go home.

But where was home?

The empty house on Elm Street? My friend Annie's house in Brooklyn, where I knew she and her partner, Maxine, would welcome me to their annual Halloween party? Or Faerie, where my demon lover maybe was or wasn't waiting for me?

I sat at the window until the last light faded from the western sky and the air turned cold.

"Good move," a voice said from behind me.

CHAPTER THIRTEEN

I swiveled my chair around. I hadn't turned on any lights in my office, so the figure in the doorway was silhouetted against the bright hall lights. It was a figure of a man, but the shadow it cast against the wall was of an enormous beast whose wings bristled with a thousand razor-edged barbs. As he stepped though the door, I heard their sharp edges scraping against the wood.

"You can't stop them from going," I said, steeling my voice to hide my fear.

"Why would I want to?" Duncan asked, lifting his shoulders in what would have been a harmless shrug if not for the shadow wings, which flexed out with a series of cracks that sounded like a dozen pistols firing. A nephilim equivalent of cracking his knuckles, I supposed. "Without them, you won't be able to become the hallow door."

"Are you sure?" I asked, with more bravado than I felt. I didn't like that he knew about the hallow door.

His face was suddenly inches from mine, his wings spread out above us, their barbs making a sound on the ceiling like fingernails on a chalkboard.

"You know, now that I think of it, no. I'm not sure. You have grown more powerful than I thought possible. I was hoping that you would eventually see reason and leave your little fairy friends behind to come over to our side. You would make a delightful companion."

He touched my chin with one steel-tipped claw. I'd seen what those claws did to Bill's throat. I searched my mind for a spell that would protect me, but my head was a jumble of confused images. The homesickness spell had weakened me, I thought, but then even that idea twisted in on itself. *Home is what makes you sick.* No, that wasn't right. *Good thing you don't have a home.* The voice seared through my brain with the precision of a scalpel dissecting a frog. I could feel it neatly probing the tender tissue, scraping at all my hopes and fears.

You've sent them all home, Callie, but you don't have a home to go to. Do you think your incubus boyfriend is waiting for you in Faerie? Before killing him, I took a little trip through his soul, and you know what? It was empty. No soul. Nothing but lust. That's what you coupled with. A rutting bull.

Images of a horned creature—half man, half bull—flitted through my head. In each of my memories of making love with Liam and Bill, I now saw the hideous bullheaded monster pumping away at me.

Is that what you're going to Faerie to find, Callie? All your high-minded talk of freeing your friends and finding some mythical trinket to kill me is no better than the fairy tales you tell your students. They're all lies. You want to go to Faerie so you can fuck your incubus boyfriend for all eternity. But you know why no one wants to stay in Faerie? Because after a while there, the glamour falls away and you see how things really are.

An image of Faerie appeared in my mind: the flower-studded meadows sloping down to a crystal-blue lake, a sky of melting purple and rose, my friends—Liz and Diana; Casper and his partner, Oliver; the beautiful Fairy Queen, Fiona, and her king, Fionn. But as I looked at them, they began to change. Sores erupted on their faces, their skin fell from their bones, horns sprang from their foreheads, crooked fangs protruded from their gaping, drooling mouths. They lurched toward me like zombies in a horror movie.

I turned to run from them and ran straight into William Duffy. "Come," he said, holding out his hand to me. I took his hand and we ran down the sloping meadows into the Greenwood, his strong grip giving wings to my feet. If I tripped over a root, he righted me. When I grew tired, he gave me strength. I risked a look over my shoulder and saw that we had left the monsters far behind. We slowed to a walk, William still holding my hand. We had come to the glade and the ruins of the hallow door. William led me into the green circle, to the bed of emerald moss where we had made love. He stopped and turned around . . .

Revealing a monster's face of decayed flesh and bone.

"What did you expect, Cailleach," he said, through rotting lips. "You kept me waiting hundreds of years."

I shrieked . . .

. . . and heard myself screaming in my office. Duncan had pushed me against the window frame, the sill pressing against the small of my back.

That's what awaits you on the other side of the hallow door. Wouldn't it be better to just end it right now, right here? All you have to do is let go.

His claws tapped my hands, which were gripping the window frame. I didn't remember putting them there. Duncan's breath was hot in my face. I could feel the cool air on my back, beckoning me . . . *home.* All I had to do was let go . . .

"Let her go."

I thought the voice was inside my head. It was angrier than the other voices in my head but just as urgent.

"Let—her—go!" it said again, each word sharp as a pistol shot. Frank's voice. It shattered into the mental space Duncan had carved into my brain. I could feel him recoiling, drawing out of my head. His claws, though, were still digging into my hands.

"I said—"

Duncan retracted his claws so quickly, I nearly fell through the open window. He whirled away from me, his wings slapping my face. I leaned away as far as I could, but the barbs still scraped across my face, drawing blood. The pain felt almost good, though, now that he was out of my head. I braced myself against the window and planted my feet against his back—and pushed.

Unprepared for a rear assault, Duncan stumbled. Frank lunged forward and swung something into his face. I heard a dull thud and the crunch of bone. Blue sparks flew into the air. I looked up from the crumpled wings and cringing form of the nephilim to Frank . . . only it couldn't be Frank. This man was a good six inches taller and *glowed.* He held a long, bright object that emitted the blue sparks. Where had Frank gotten a sword? And since when did Frank wear mailed armor? As my eyes adjusted to the glow, I saw that the armor was only an illusion and the object in his hand wasn't a sword at all.

"A baseball bat?" Duncan roared. "You think you can take me down with a baseball bat?"

"Not just any baseball bat," Frank replied smugly. "Bucky Dent's bat. The one he used to hit the three-run home run that beat the Red Sox in '78. Imbued with the faith and devotion of baseball fans everywhere. You touch McFay again and you will feel the wrath of Bucky 'Fucking' Dent!"

Duncan snickered and spread his wings over Frank. I heard a scream—and then smelled something burning. Something that smelled like feathers.

Duncan retracted his wings, their tips singed. Frank was still standing, holding the bat, but his face was pale as death. Duncan drew himself up and folded his wings close to his body, then swept past Frank. In the doorway, he turned to look back at me.

"By the time I'm done, you'll wish you'd gone home with your students," he said. "And, remember, after you're gone, they'll come back. But you won't be here to protect them."

As soon as Duncan left, Frank dropped the bat. Bands of raw red flesh striped his hand.

"Jesus, Frank," I cried, running to him. "What happened to your hand?"

"When I heard you scream, I ensorcelled the bat before I could protect my hand."

Ensorcelled? I wondered, staring at his hand's burned flesh. "Well, that was stupid!"

"You're welcome, McFay. Next time I hear you screaming bloody murder, I'll . . ."

Whatever inane activity he was going to suggest would have to be left to my imagination, as Frank's eyes rolled back in his head and his whole body went limp. I grabbed him in time to break his fall, but I was also weak from the encounter with Duncan. We both ended up on the floor in an ungainly heap, which was how Soheila found us.

"Oh," she said, standing in the doorway, looking embarrassed. "I thought I heard a ruckus."

"You did," I said, untangling my legs from Frank's. "Duncan Laird attacked me, and Frank came to my rescue with an ensorcelled baseball bat. He burned his hand."

I turned over Frank's hand to show her and he instantly came to consciousness, screaming in pain at my touch.

"I've got rose water and aloe in my office. I'll be right back."

Soheila was gone in a gust of clove-scented air. Three minutes later a miniature tornado blew into my office, whirling every paper on my desk into the air and knocking a dozen books off the shelves. The tornado landed by Frank's side and resolved into Soheila, dark hair tossing like a stormy sea, a glass perfume bottle in her hand.

"Hold this," she told me, handing me the bottle. "I'm going to take the heat away first." She gently slid one hand under Frank's injured one, leaned over it, her shapely rose-red lips parted, and blew. Frank stiffened for a moment as the air touched his burned skin, and then he relaxed. His eyes fluttered closed and the lines of pain melted away from his face. He took a deep breath and let it out with a sigh. Soheila held out her free hand for the bottle, and I opened it. The air was suddenly filled with the delicious warmth of a rose garden on a sultry summer afternoon. I handed the bottle to Soheila, and she poured a few drops of the oil onto Frank's hand. Instead of rubbing it in, she gently blew again, spreading the oil across his palm. She repeated the process three times. Each time, Frank sighed and his burns faded from red to pink, then shiny white.

"Is he going to be all right?" I asked.

"The burns will heal, but . . ." She dipped her finger in the oil and touched it to Frank's forehead above and between his eyebrows. A shudder passed through her body. "That monster touched his mind. Healing him will take time." She turned to me, her usually rich olive skin faded to the color of old parchment, her graceful hands trembling. "It's just, I'm afraid . . ."

"Afraid of what?" I asked, thinking of all the terrors we'd faced in the last few months together. Up until now, Soheila had been fearless in the face of it all. What could make her tremble?

"I'm afraid that if I get this close to him, I might not be able to keep from falling in love with him."

I nearly laughed, but I restrained myself and told her in all seriousness, "Soheila, honey, that boat's already sailed. Of course you love Frank—and he loves you. I know you're afraid you'll hurt Frank, but he's a big boy—and a powerful wizard—who can take care of himself. It's time you gave it a chance. Take it from me, you might not *get* a second one."

Luckily, I'd brought my car to campus, so I was able to drive them both to Soheila's house. I'd never been there before and was surprised to find that she lived in a modest 1960s ranch, tastefully but sparely decorated in bleached-wood Scandinavian furniture and muted earth tones. Its only real extravagance was plush wall-to-wall carpeting the color of desert sand. The overall effect was restful—like the Sahara in the moonlight. When I helped Soheila carry Frank to her guest room, I resisted the urge to lie down on the carpet and go to sleep.

"Will he be okay?" I asked.

"I think so," Soheila replied, running her hand over Frank's brow. He murmured under her touch but remained unconscious. "The nephilim barely touched his brain. In time I should be able to heal him."

"I'll leave you to it, then," I said, getting up from the bed.

Soheila looked up. "But what about you, Callie? The nephilim touched you, too. I can help—"

"No, I'm fine," I said. "Frank stopped him before Duncan could do any real damage." The hideously ruined face of William Duffy leered up at me inside my head. I flinched, but Soheila had already looked away, back to Frank.

"What an idiot," Soheila said fondly. "Imagine taking on a nephilim with a baseball bat!"

"Imagine," I said, trying very hard not to think of anything at all.

"But where are you going?" Soheila asked when I was halfway to the door.

"To find another witch for our circle."

I had only forty-eight hours to find a replacement witch. I'd start with the witches I knew. I got in my car and called Moondance on my cellphone. When I told her what had happened, she was silent for so long that I thought I might have lost the connection, but then she said, in a hushed voice that sounded not at all like the robust woman I knew, "He was able to get into Delmarco's mind?"

"Yes," I admitted, "but Frank was distracted. He was trying to save me."

"Still, Delmarco is one of the most powerful wizards I know. If Laird was able to get through his defenses, there's not much hope for any of us."

"Which is why I need to become the hallow door on Sunday night," I reminded her. "So I can find the angel stone and get rid of these creeps. But we'll need another witch. Is there anyone else in town?"

"No," Moondance replied curtly.

"I don't understand. I thought Fairwick was a refuge for witches. Why are there so few?"

"There was an incident back in the fifties that cleared out a lot of witches. That was before my time, so I'm not sure what happened. Ann would know . . ." Her voice trailed off wistfully.

"Do you think there's any chance Ann could be persuaded to rejoin the circle?"

"I don't know. I've tried calling her. The last time, she answered the phone but didn't say anything. She might listen to you, though."

"Why me?"

"I think she feels bad about what happened to Bill . . . Anyway, it's worth a shot."

Moondance gave me Ann's number. Then I recalled seeing Ann and her daughter coming out of their house on Mulberry Street, just a couple of blocks away from my house. I decided to drive there instead of calling. I drove slowly down the street, hoping I'd recognize Ann's house, but at night all the houses on Mulberry looked rather alike—quaint 1930s bungalows with low overhanging porches that seemed to close the houses off from the lane. I recalled that the path to Ann's house had been lined with flowers, but then it had been summer . . . I stopped in front of a house whose path was lined with jack-o'-lanterns. A dozen cardboard gravestones sprang up from the lawn, along with a gruesome rubber hand. An entire family of imaginatively carved pumpkins squatted on the porch steps. This couldn't be it, I thought. Not only was the taste far too garish for Ann, it wasn't likely she would decorate for Halloween while in league with the nephilim.

Still . . . the house looked just like the one I remembered from this summer. I parked the car and walked up the path.

About halfway up, one of the jack-o'-lantern tops opened and a screeching black cat popped out. I jumped and let out a high-pitched squeak. From inside the house came the faint titter of giggles.

Regaining my composure when I ascertained that the cat was an animatronic creation of wire and fake fur, I continued up the path. On the porch steps, a goblin erupted from a pumpkin and a diaphanous ghost flew out of the shadows. I yelped obligingly and brushed past spider-laden cobwebs and dripping green ectoplasm to ring the doorbell. Deep moans and chain rattling ensued. The door was swung open by a witch in green face paint.

"You're early!" she screamed gleefully. "Halloween's not for two more nights."

I easily recognized Ann's daughter, Jessica, from her eager smile and the epicanthic fold in her almond-shaped eyes.

"Early? Clearly I'm too late! I was looking for Jessica Chase and her mother, but I suppose you've already turned them into frogs and eaten them!"

Jessica collapsed into giggles. "Silly, *I'm* Jessica!"

"No! Are you sure? The Jessica I know works at the newspaper and saves lost cats. She's not a witch." *But her mother is,* I thought. I wondered how much Jessica knew about her mother's vocation.

"You can be both!" Jessica crowed. "And I can be anything I want to be," she added a bit more defensively.

"Yes, you can," Ann said, coming up behind Jessica. Although not in costume, Ann was wearing an orange turtleneck and a necklace made up of plastic pumpkins. "Can I help you, Dr. McFay? Jessica's right that it's a little early for trick-or-treating."

"I was hoping we could talk," I said.

"If your dean knew you were here, we could both be in trouble," Ann said, darting her eyes toward Jessica.

"I think my dean would be surprised to see your house all decked out for Halloween," I replied.

I didn't mean it as a threat *exactly*. I'd never tell Duncan Laird on her, but Ann didn't know that, and I was desperate.

"Okay," she said, her face grim. "Come on in." And then, turning to Jessica and giving her a smile that completely transformed her face, she added, "Jessica will make some of her hot mulled spider for you."

While Jessica went to prepare the hot mulled spider—"Don't worry," Ann told me, "it's just hot apple cider with cinnamon and cloves"—Ann took me into the living room and closed the pocket doors. The room, decorated in Stickley Mission furniture, had even more Halloween decorations in it.

"It's Jessica's favorite holiday," Ann said, moving an orange-and-black pumpkin pillow over on the couch and sitting down next to me. "I couldn't bear to tell her she wasn't supposed to celebrate it this year. But if the nephilim find out . . ."

"They might cut off your supply of Aelvesgold for Jessica?"

Ann nodded grimly. "Do you know what the life expectancy is for a child with Down syndrome?"

I shook my head.

"Mid-forties. And that's an improvement over the mid-twenties prognosis I was given when Jessica was born. She's forty-four. I suppose some would say I'm lucky to have had her this long and that a life with Down syndrome isn't worth prolonging further—"

"I would never say that," I broke in. "Jessica's . . ."

"Special?" Ann suggested with a wry smile. It had, in fact,

been the word that had come to mind. "That's the euphemism, of course, but with Jessica it's . . ."

"True?" I finished for her. "Jessica's a witch, isn't she?"

Ann looked around, as if suddenly wary that the ceramic black cats and grinning ghouls on the coffee table might be listening. She spoke in a low whisper. "You must promise not to let the nephilim know. I've kept it a secret, afraid others would take advantage of her power. At first I refused to even admit it to her, but then I saw that it was just confusing her to have so much power and not train it. So I began working with her." A tentative smile appeared on her face. "She's the most powerful witch I've ever encountered. But if the nephilim found out . . ."

"They would use her power for their own ends. I understand," I said, getting to my feet. "And you're right. I'm putting Jessica in danger even being here."

"But why did you come, then? You came here to ask for my help, didn't you?" Ann asked, grabbing my hand.

"Yes." I explained why I needed a witches' circle for Halloween night. "But I see now why it would be too dangerous for you. I'll figure out some other way—"

"No!"

I looked up. The voice came from the now-open pocket door. Jessica stood there, holding a tray of steaming apple-shaped mugs. "No. You need a witch. I'm a witch. I want to help."

"Jessica—" Ann began.

"No, Mommy!" Jessica stamped her foot, rattling the mugs. Other things in the room rattled. Ann got up to take the tray from Jessica's hands.

"You're always saying I can be whatever I want. You're always telling me to act like a grown-up. Well, I'm a witch, and I'm grown up enough to make my own decisions. I want to help Callie and her friends get rid of the neff-ums."

"Your mother's right," I said. "It's too dangerous."

"Isn't it too dangerous to let these bad men bully everybody in town?" Jessica asked, looking from me to her mother. "Besides, Mommy only told them *she* wouldn't be part of your circle. She never said *I* wouldn't," Jessica concluded with a sly, proud smile.

"Ann," I said, "I didn't come here to involve Jessica."

"I know," Ann said with a sigh. "But, as usual, Jessica's right. It's always more dangerous to give in to bullies. Jessica and I will both join your circle on Halloween night."

CHAPTER FOURTEEN

I didn't sleep that night. Every time I drifted off, I was back in the Greenwood. I knew William Duffy was there with me, but which William Duffy? The tender lover of my dreams, or the one Duncan Laird had shown me? I was afraid that if I saw the monstrously hideous version, I wouldn't be able to go through with the ceremony and open the door, so I stayed up with my Wheelock's *Spellcraft,* LaFleur's *History of Magic,* and half a dozen other magic books. Ralph pored over the pages of the books with me as I studied all the spells I could possibly need to become the hallow door. I was running out of time. It was time to cram, as I had for my PhD orals. I'd stayed up three days straight then, and my life hadn't literally depended on a thorough knowledge of English literature.

It turned out, though, that my body had different needs than it had three years earlier. I made it halfway through Saturday night before I started to crash. I brewed more coffee and combed Wheelock for stay-awake spells. There was one for keeping sleep at bay for forty-eight hours, but it came with a host of dire warnings that ranged from mood disorders to a weakened immune system to hyperanimation (whatever the hell that was!). But what choice did I have? I needed to stay up until I found the door spell. I mixed the ingredients for the stay-awake spell in the kitchen while Ralph ransacked the cabinets for a snack.

"Sorry, guy," I told him. "I promise that once this is over I'll go shopping."

My bare cupboards reminded me that I needed to buy candy for Halloween night. And decorate. Everything I read insisted that the observance of Halloween was crucial to the success of opening the hallow door. Besides, maybe doing something other than reading Wheelock would unlock my brain enough to figure out a strategy, so I spent the early hours of Sunday morning up to my elbows in raw pumpkin gunk.

I carved three jack-o'-lanterns. Having read in Wheelock that properly made jack-o'-lanterns were threshold guardians for your house, I uttered the words of a warding spell while I carved. First was a traditional jack-o'-lantern with triangle eyes and a snaggletooth smile. *Protect my home,* I asked him. Getting into the mood, I made the second pumpkin into a warty-faced witch. *Watch over all who are in it,* I asked her. I was amazed at how well it came out. On the third I carved a scary cat so realistic that, when I showed it to Ralph, his fur stood on end and he ran away.

"Scaredy-cat," I yelled after him. But when I turned the pumpkin back around, even I was surprised at how lifelike the cat appeared. I took the three jack-o'-lanterns out onto the front porch. As I arranged them on the steps, I spotted Evangeline Sprague, my nonagenarian neighbor, retrieving the Sunday paper from her front lawn.

"Happy Halloween!" she shouted, waving to me.

She had tied white cloth ghosts to the branches of an old apple tree by her front porch and had her own little family of jack-o'-lanterns on her stoop. Inspired by her example, I went back in to get more decorating supplies. I found an old pair of jeans and a flannel shirt, which I stuffed with the straw I'd picked up last week to use as mulch. I arranged the makeshift limbs of my scarecrow in a rocking chair and placed the snaggletooth jack-o'-lantern on top. Then I found a black dress and leggings, stuffed them with straw, and propped them under the witch-head pumpkin. I just needed a witch's hat . . .

I ended up going downtown to McGuckin's Variety Store and buying a slew of decorations and candy. I spent most of the day decorating my yard and front porch, hoping some inspiration for the door spell would come to me while I warded my home. As I draped spiderwebs over my front porch, I wove in another protection spell. And as I attached plastic ghosts to pulleys, I called on the spirits of my ancestors to watch over me. My efforts inspired my neighbors. Cheryl Lindisfarne from two doors down dropped by to say she was glad to see I was getting in the spirit.

"With all the fuss, I felt a little funny putting out decorations this year, but now that I see you doing it, I'm going to tell Harald to pull out all the stops. He's got a coffin with a zombie in it whose eyes bug out when it opens."

"Ooh," I said, jealous. "I'll come by later to see it."

By five o'clock, my house looked like it belonged to the Addams Family. Standing back to admire it, I noticed that all my neighbors had followed my lead and decorated their homes with the trappings of Halloween. Down the street, a troop of diminutive fairies, ghosts, and goblins was shrieking with delight at Harald Lindisfarne, who was dressed as Herman Munster.

Yikes! There were already trick-or-treaters. I'd forgotten that parents took their little kids out before dark—and dark was not so far off now.

In fact, it was just that moment when day slid into evening. The sun setting behind the mountains in the west lit up the east side of the street but cast the west side, where Alpha House stood, into shadow. It looked as if the street were divided down the middle. Where the two sides met, the air shimmered and crackled with energy. I could feel it from my toes to my fingertips—the *turning*. This was the moment when the year turned from light toward dark, the *hinge* of the year, as Moondance had called it, a liminal time when boundaries—between light and dark, seen and unseen, death and life—could be crossed. I felt the weight of a world teetering on the edge. Would I be able to become the hallow door and cross over to Faerie and into seventeenth-century Ballydoon?

My mind, like the planet, seemed to be turning toward the dark, but then I noticed an odd assortment of trick-or-treaters heading my way. Three women dressed in long black robes, the middle one carrying a lantern, were walking down the middle of the street, along the dividing line. The lantern carried by the middle figure swayed back and forth, casting an orange glow that pushed away the edges of the dark just a little and lit up their faces. I recognized Adelaide, Phoenix, and Jen.

They stopped opposite the Lindisfarnes' house. Jen took a long taper from beneath her robe and lit it from the lantern. She walked slowly, cupping the flame with her hand, into the Lindisfarnes' yard and spoke to Cheryl, who was dressed as Lily Munster. Cheryl nodded yes to whatever she had been asked. Jen walked up to the front-porch steps, knelt beside the jack-o'-lanterns, and lit each of them with the taper. As each flame was kindled, a warm glow spread outward from the pumpkin. It lit up the faces of my ordinary, down-to-earth neighbors with something decidedly *extra*ordinary. I felt the warmth of that glow two doors down.

Jen rose to her feet, rejoining Phoenix and Adelaide, and they proceeded to Evangeline Sprague's house, repeating the same ritual. I saw Evangeline's old face suffused with that otherworldly glow.

As the three women approached my house, I noticed that the brothers of Alpha Delta Chi had come out to their porch to watch the procession. They stood with arms crossed over their broad chests, expressions inscrutable in the shadows. For the first time, I thought about who these boys really *were*. Their fathers were nephilim, but presumably they had human mothers. Were they all completely unreachable?

I walked to the middle of the street to meet the women and inspect the lantern more closely. It looked like an ordinary hurricane lantern, the kind they sold at McGuckin's Variety, but the flame inside glowed fiercely.

"We kindled it from a needfire," Jen told me.

"That's a fire you make by rubbing two sticks together," Phoenix added. "We did it at a crossroads at dawn while saying a spell to protect the town, and now we're carrying it through the whole village, lighting everyone's pumpkins."

Phoenix herself was lit up like a jack-o'-lantern. I wondered what the crash from this high would be, but I reminded myself that the former addict wouldn't have to worry about that if we didn't succeed against the nephilim.

"The needfire protects the house where it's lit," Jen said more soberly, as she withdrew a long thin piece of wood from her cloak. "We'll light yours now."

I walked with Jen to my front porch and watched her light the three warded jack-o'-lanterns, each seeming to leap to life. As we returned to the other two women, I saw that the Alphas were still watching us. "I have an idea," I told Jen. "Can you give me one of those tapers?"

Jen handed me a long piece of wood, watching me curiously as I lit it from the lantern and then crossed over to the dark side of the street. The flame sputtered and I felt a corresponding shudder inside, as if I'd become a hollow pumpkin and the needfire had been kindled inside me. I cupped my hand around the taper, sheltering the struggling flame, and kept going, feeling the light inside myself growing with each step. The boys on the porch shifted uneasily as I approached. At the foot of the porch steps, I paused, the flame cupped in my palm, and looked up into the face of Adam Sinclair.

"It occurs to me that you probably haven't had much choice about what side you're on," I said.

Adam's upper lip twisted into a sneer, but his eyes, I noticed, were focused on the flame in my hand, which was burning steadily now.

"We're on the winning side," he said.

"Maybe," I replied. "Or maybe not. But it's going to be a long night. Who knows what will wander out of the woods? Why not take what protection you can?"

"We don't need . . ." Adam began, but then his eyes widened. I turned to see what he was looking at. The last light had faded from the street. The woods loomed dark behind my house, but not entirely dark. There were small flickering lights in the shadows and, when the wind stirred, the sound of creatures moving through the shadows—a *scritch* of nails and a heavy leathery thudding of wings. Turning back to Adam, I saw that his face had turned white. Suddenly he looked very young. "Sure, why not?" he said, shrugging. He picked up one of the tiki candles left over from their luau party and carried it down the steps to me. He tilted the glass sideways and water ran out of it, nearly extinguishing the taper. I heard a gasp from one of the boys on the porch. I steadied the taper, which was barely long enough to reach the wick inside the glass. The flame hissed and sputtered when it touched the damp wax. I held it against the wick, waiting for it to light, my fingertips beginning to burn.

"I'm sorry I've been such an ass in class," Adam said, so softly I wondered if I'd heard right. But then the wick caught, and in the glow of the flame I saw a look of contrition on his young face. At the same instant, I felt something click inside myself. What had Nicky said? *A good teacher is a door to other worlds.* I'd opened up a new world for Adam—a possibility of becoming something other than what the nephilim wanted for him—and in doing so I'd become a doorway. This was how I'd be the hallow door.

"That's okay, Adam," I said, feeling grateful to the boy for what he'd unwittingly done for me. "You've got plenty of time to make it up to me. Just keep your brothers safe tonight and we'll get a fresh start tomorrow, okay?"

He nodded and turned away, carrying the lit candle up the stairs. I turned and walked across the street, where the three women waited for me on my front porch. Adelaide was shaking her head at me. "Why did you do that?"

I shrugged. "I don't know. It felt . . ." I looked back at Alpha House. Glass tiki candles lined the railing of the front porch, their glow a barrier against the dark. ". . . right," I finished. "Now, if you'll excuse me, I've got to go check something in Wheelock. I'll see you in the circle at midnight."

In Wheelock's section on teaching magic, I found what I was looking for. When I opened the footnote, I located the spell to become a doorway. It turned out I had already completed the first two steps: make a blood bond to the door you want to open, and empty yourself of all prejudgments. The third step was simply a spell I had to recite at the moment I wanted to open myself. I committed the spell to memory and changed into a long green skirt, body-hugging bodice, and white lace blouse, with a tartan shawl I'd had since childhood wrapped around my shoulders and pinned with the Luckenbooth brooch. A sprig of heather in my hair from the heap of them I found strewn over my bed and, voilà, I was Jennet Carter, off to the Greenwood to rescue Tam Lin. When my doorbell rang, I was ready with a bowl of miniature Kit Kats and Hershey bars.

I swung open the door, ready to greet my first tiny ghouls and goblins, and found a crew of slightly older trick-or-treaters—a rather large Scot in a kilt, with an assortment of fairies.

"Scott!" I said, hardly recognizing my student, with his hair neatly combed back in a ponytail and with a clean white shirt tucked into a plaid kilt. "What are you doing here?"

"Man, Prof, did you forget our folklore party?"

"No, it's just that I thought . . ." I turned from Scott to the woman dressed as the Fairy Queen at his side. "Ruby? I thought you were going home?"

Nicky, wearing a Tinker Bell outfit and carrying two large reusable grocery bags, laughed and pushed past Ruby. "You know, we almost *did* go to New Jersey with Ruby, but then when we all met up at the bus station we realized we didn't really want to go."

"Yeah," Flonia said, carrying more bags over the threshold. "We wanted to be here—you know, with friends."

At the word *friends,* a crowd of my students came up the front path. "Is this where the party is?" asked a girl dressed as Alice in Wonderland.

"Yeah," Scott called back, "this is it. We hope you don't mind, Prof; we invited a bunch of your students we ran into at the bus station. When they heard there was a party at Professor McFay's, they all said that sounded better than going home. Hey, cool jack-o'-lanterns, Prof, especially the way you've got them wired for sound."

Scott edged past me to answer Ruby, who was calling him to come in and help, so I didn't get to tell him I'd done nothing of the kind. Then I was too busy welcoming students to my house to figure out his meaning. I was touched to see how many of my students had come dressed as their favorite fairy tale characters.

"You inspired us," Tania Lieberman, dressed as Snow White, told me. "We were all planning it, and then we almost forgot and went home. Can you believe that? But then I remembered how much I was looking forward to my first Halloween at college, and ... wow, your house is, like, totally cool! It looks like something out of *Paranormal Investigations*."

Stephanie Moss, a girl who never spoke in class, thanked me for the comments I'd written on her Beauty and the Beast paper. "I was feeling kind of homesick earlier today, but then I remembered what you said about how the heroines of fairy tales find their real homes in these stories, and that made me think . . . well, that Fairwick's my new home. Anyway, I baked you some chocolate chip cookies from my mom's favorite recipe."

About twenty of my students had resisted my homesickness spell and stayed—or, rather, they hadn't had to resist the spell, because they had found a new home with their friends here at college. As they filled my house with laughter and loud voices, the smells of apple cider and fresh-baked goodies, I realized they'd turned my house into a home, too. I didn't want to leave it, but as it drew closer to midnight I knew I had to. I waited until they were all in the living room playing a game of fishbowl (a version of charades that allowed talking—or at

the moment some kind of wolfish howling), and I slipped out
the front door.

A chill wind bit into my skin as I left the warmth of the
house. I wrapped my wool tartan shawl tighter around my
shoulders and hurried down the steps before I could change
my mind and turn back. The howling and laughter from inside already sounded far away and from a different world. I
was alone in the cold and dark . . .

Or not quite alone.

Something squeaked at my feet. I knelt and picked up
Ralph. Someone had tied an orange ribbon around his neck.
"Thanks, little guy. But are you sure you don't want to stay
here and cadge some caramel apples?"

But as I looked up at the house, I saw that neither of us was
going back. Three sentries stood on the front porch—an ancient stooped woman in a black dress, a tall redheaded man in
patched jeans and a flannel shirt, and a black cat grown to the
size of a panther—my jack-o'-lanterns kindled into life.

"You'll watch over them?" I asked, worried about my un-
suspecting students.

The witch, scarecrow, and cat inclined their heads in assent.

"All right, then," I said, slipping Ralph into my skirt
pocket.

I started to go, but the scarecrow stepped forward and
handed me a lit lantern like the one Adelaide had held.

"Thank you," I said, taking the light from his hand. Then
I turned and headed into the woods.

CHAPTER FIFTEEN

The needfire lit my way through the woods, its glow carrying a little bit of the warmth I'd left behind in my home. And not just the warmth of my home but the combined goodwill of the community. Its glow split the darkness and sent the shadows skittering off the path into the woods. I knew that some of the creatures were the ones who had been trapped here when the door closed. They were most likely watching me to see if I'd be successful in opening the hallow door, waiting for a chance to slither through the door before they perished without Aelvesgold. I thought of the creatures Volkov said were lurking in the tunnels and in the woods. Mostly I hoped there weren't nephilim—although the rustle of wings in the branches above me suggested otherwise.

The deeper I went into the woods, the lower the branches were. I was in the honeysuckle thicket, where the bare branches intertwined above my head like bony hands clasped together. The creaking they made as they rubbed against one another sounded like knuckles cracking—or like nephilim flexing their razor-barbed wings.

At each crack, I ducked my head, and I nearly dropped my

lantern more than once. I didn't like to think what would happen if my lantern went out . . . but of course I *did* think about it, imagining how quickly the nephilim would be on me, how their barbs would sink into my flesh and mind, how they would suck the marrow out of my bones and my hopes and memories out of my soul. *Those monsters don't just kill you,* Frank had said. *They make you wish you'd never been born.*

I'd miss Frank in the circle, I thought. Moondance had said that Frank was one of the most powerful wizards she'd ever encountered. Would we be strong enough without him? Had Duncan attacked him to take out our most powerful member, so we'd be too weak to succeed without him?

A fluttering above my head made me flinch. I had the sensation that I was being herded down this path to my death—like cattle driven through a chute to slaughter. Once all the remaining witches of Fairwick were gathered in one place, the nephilim would be able to destroy us all . . .

What if this is a trap?

The question so startled me that I stopped abruptly, caught my foot on a root, and tripped. I slammed hard onto the ground, the lantern rolling away from my hands, glass shattering, its light sputtering . . .

Darkness rushed in around me with the sound of wings. The nephilim crashed onto my back and dug his claws into the nape of my neck. He took my breath away, and then he started to take my *self* away. The pointy barbs were in my brain, scraping away its tender parts: memories of my mother and father, Annie, my college boyfriend Paul, Liam, Bill . . . I could feel them all begin to slip away . . .

Then I heard a strange yelp. The nephilim's hold loosened enough for me to twist around to see what was happening. The creature was still straddling my back, but he was sitting up, his hands flailing at something behind him, his wings beating—something was crawling on the wings. Ralph! I saw the flash of tiny sharp teeth. Ralph was biting the nephilim to distract him, but how long would he be able to?

I had to help. I unpinned the Luckenbooth brooch from my shawl and jabbed it into the nephilim's thigh. He let out a bloodcurdling scream and reared back. I was surprised that it hurt so much—maybe these nephilim weren't so tough after all. But then the nephilim bared his fangs and I revised my opinion. Those fangs were heading straight for my jugular—and then he was flying backward through the air. The nephilim landed on his back, wings pinned beneath him, Anton Volkov crouched on his chest. The vampire's fangs were bared, his eyes flashing red in the fire's glow . . .

Fire?

I looked behind me and saw the honeysuckle thicket in flames, kindled by my broken lantern. The fire was quickly spreading from the ground up to the arching canopy. Soon we'd be encased in a fiery tunnel.

"Go!" Anton hissed. "I can't hold him forever. Go to the circle."

It startled me to realize that Anton couldn't kill the nephilim. We needed the angel stone to do that—which meant I needed to get to the circle and open the hallow door.

"Will you be all right?" I asked.

Anton's amber eyes flicked to mine. Reflecting the fire, they seemed huge and inhuman—a tiger's eyes. "Your concern is touching," he said hoarsely. "I will . . . manage. Now . . . *go!*" He roared the last word, putting some compulsion into it, which got me to my feet and had me running down the path before I remembered that Ralph was no longer with me. But it was too late to go back, even if I had been able to resist Anton's compulsion. Ralph was forged in fire; he'd find a way out—but I might not. The fire raced with me, devouring dry wood like a hungry animal. At least I no longer needed a lantern to light my way. The woods were bright with the clear orange glow of the needfire. Above the crackle of the fire, I heard retreating wings. The nephilim couldn't reach me in my tunnel of fire, but they wouldn't need to if I burned to death.

When I reached the entrance to the glade, though, I saw a welcome sight. Mac Stewart and his clan stood in a circle around the glade. Every man, each in a flannel shirt bearing the Stewart tartan, stood with his arms stretched out to his sides. Filaments of red, blue, green, and yellow ran from fingertips to fingertips, forming a shimmering plaid hanging in the air. Sparks from the fire sizzled and died when they reached the plaid. The Stewarts were protecting the glade from the fire—and no doubt from half a dozen other threats.

Mac smiled at me when I reached him. "Callie, we were worried you wouldn't make it! It's almost midnight."

"A nephilim tried to attack me, but Anton Volkov stopped him."

"Oh," Mac said, his smile fading. "I would have whomped that winged bastard if I'd've been there, but I had to keep the circle safe."

"And a brilliant job you're doing of it. Can your family hold the plaid against the fire?"

Mac puffed up his chest. "The plaid can withstand anything," he bragged.

"Not forever, you dunderhead," Mac's father, Angus, interrupted. "Best let the lass go, son; she's got a job to do."

"That's right," I said.

Angus and Mac did something with their hands to make an opening in the tartan field, and I stepped through it. As I did, I stood on my tiptoes and kissed Mac on the cheek. "Thank you, Mac. Try to find Ralph and take care of him—and of

Fairwick—if I don't . . . well, if things don't go according to plan in there."

Mac's eyes widened and he began to object, but I pinned him with a look I used in class when a student gave me a lame excuse for not turning in a paper.

"I will," he promised.

"Good. I feel better knowing Fairwick's in your hands." I started to go in but thought of something else. "And Mac, the Alphas—some of them may not be as bad as their fathers. Keep that in mind."

Before Mac could ask me any questions, I stepped through the plaid and into the circle. I could tell when the plaid closed behind me, because I could no longer hear the fire or smell the smoke. Looking back, I saw that the predominantly red tartan was glowing with the reflection of fire, but inside the circle it was cool and still. For a moment I thought I was alone, but then seven figures in black cloaks stepped out of the shadows of the thicket. The one nearest to me pushed back her cloak, and I recognized Moondance.

"We haven't much time," she said brusquely. "It's almost midnight. Are you ready?"

I'd been repeating Wheelock's spell for the last few hours, but at Moondance's question I suddenly felt, as I had when I sat down for my orals, that my mind had been rinsed clean of every scrap of knowledge I'd ever imbibed. This time it might actually be true. What if the nephilim attack had erased the spell from my brain? Around me were the hopeful faces of the seven people who had come to help me. They were all looking to me with complete trust. Moondance had let go of her wariness, Leon had dropped his habitual hipster attitude, Phoenix appeared calm and composed for a change, Jen seemed as if she didn't even have a probing question, the look of worry in

Ann's eyes had been replaced with pride as she stood by her daughter, and Jessica . . . Jessica's faith glowed with a purity of trust that took my breath away. Even my grandmother, who had rarely regarded me with anything but a mixture of annoyance and disappointment, was looking at me with complete faith. Each face, glowing in the reflection of the fire that ringed us, was like a smooth white stone dropped into a deep well. A feeling of quiet and calm came over me, and with it, like a stone dropping into the well, fell the words of the spell to become the hallow door.

I nodded to Moondance, then to each of the others, and stepped into the center of the circle, to the empty place where once stood the door and where Bill's blood had been shed. I took off the brooch, pricked my finger, and let a drop of blood fall on the ground. I recited the first part of the spell.

"My blood binds me to the door." A red mist rose from the ground and arched over me. I felt Bill's love for me, so strong that he had sacrificed himself. That love bound me to the door.

"I empty myself so that I contain all things." I closed my eyes and became hollow inside. I'd felt like this before: when my parents died, when Liam left, when Bill perished. But each time I had been emptied, there were people who stepped into my life to fill that void. Annie, after my parents died. My friends and students, after Liam and then Bill had gone. I thought of all the *good neighbors* in Fairwick who had filled my life and who were depending on me to save them. They were inside me now. I had only to make myself a bridge from Fairwick to another world. And to do that I had to open myself up to the possibility that somewhere there was still love for me. That was the hardest part of the spell. Since Bill died, I had not allowed myself to think that there could ever be anyone else. It was too painful to hope. I had closed off a part of myself so that I'd never be hurt again. That was the part I had to open now.

"I open myself to love," I said.

The red mist began to swirl around me. I felt a wrenching pain and then a dizzying lightness. I was inside a maelstrom. Around me, my friends stood in a circle of protection, and outside that circle stood the Stewarts, but none of them could protect me from the hurricane. I was alone here, open, un-guarded, at the mercy of every fear and emotion, so torn by the currents of time that for a moment I didn't seem to exist. In that moment, I became the door. I stepped through my own self, through my own pain and fears, and found myself stand-ing on the threshold of Faerie, its iridescent dusk stretching out below me. I stepped forward . . .

. . . right into the path of a galloping horse.

I barely had time to throw myself to the side to escape being trampled. I fell to the ground beside a curved stone wall as the horse thundered past me, its silver hooves flashing mere inches from my nose. I looked up to see its rider glancing dis-dainfully over her shoulder at me, then tossing her silver-white hair and green cloak as she rode on. Another mount followed close behind, this one gold with jet hooves, its rider cloaked in gold. I recognized them both—Fiona, the Fairy Queen, and her king, Fionn. More horses followed in their wake, all decked in gold and silver and glittering jewels. It was the fairy host riding out on All Hallows' Eve, just as they did in the ballads of Tam Lin and William Duffy.

William. Was he here with them? I struggled to my feet, pulling myself up on the damp stone wall to scan the faces of the riders as they rushed past me, but they were all cloaked and hooded. How would I recognize him? But then I remembered the ballad and the sign William Duffy had promised his beloved—that he would leave one hand ungloved.

I watched for a rider with a missing glove . . . and saw him at the end, on a white horse the color of moonlight, cloaked in black, one hand gloved, one bare.

I stepped into the path of the horse, which reared, diamond hooves flashing in the air inches above my head. The rider's cloak fell back, and I saw his face in the moonlight against the shadow of the cloak. That is how he came to me first, as moonlight and shadow. I reached up, grabbed a handful of cloak, and pulled.

He slid off his horse and landed right on top of me. We both tumbled to the ground, tangling in our cloaks. As we rolled, I felt him changing in my arms, his long, lean muscles lengthening and wrapping around me. When we came to a halt, I saw that I no longer held a man but was held instead by a huge serpent. Its eyes were still William's, though, so I held on, remembering the story and bracing myself for the next transformation, which, if I remembered correctly . . .

Dagger-length teeth snapped at me as slippery scales turned to deep fur in my hands. The lion's great jaws opened wide and roared in my face, but the eyes were still William's, so I held on . . .

And was engulfed in flames. I had no eyes to look at this time, and I recalled from the story that this was where the heroine tossed her lover into a holy well.

Which, if I wasn't mistaken, lay just behind that damp stone wall I'd fallen against. I blindly groped my way to the wall, pulled myself up by my burning fingertips, and dove over, headfirst. As soon as I hit the water, I felt another body in the well with me, arms and legs flailing and dragging me down. There was nothing in the story about the hero drowning the heroine. But then he was pulling me out of the water, pushing me up on his shoulders so I could fling myself back over the top of the well. I turned and reached for him and pulled him, sputtering, sopping, and stark naked, out of the well. His long, lean torso and limbs gleamed like marble in the moonlight. For a moment I was dazzled at the sight of him—I knew that smooth chest, those strong legs—and then I thought to toss my sodden tartan over his shoulders, just in time to cover him before the Fairy Queen rode back to stare down at William from her silver horse.

"If I had known you would leave me for a human girl, William Duffy, I would have plucked out your eyes and heart and replaced them with eyes and heart of wood. If you ever step foot in Faerie again, I'll do just that. And you." She turned her eyes on me. "I condemn you with the same curse. You may never step foot in Faerie again."

Then she turned and rode off, leaving me with a shivering half-naked man atop a bare and windswept hill.

CHAPTER SIXTEEN

"Are you all right?" I asked the shivering half-naked man beside me.

In answer, he sank to his knees. "I am now, my lady. You have saved me. I have been a prisoner of the Fairy Queen for seven long years, and tonight she was supposed to sacrifice me to the devil. At the last minute, she decided to keep me as her slave, but then I would have become a demon myself. You have saved me from that fate." He took my hand. "And for that, you have my undying gratitude and love, dear lady."

His hair, still wet from his dunk in the well, hung in dark waves around his face. Drops of water clung to his pale flesh, glistening in the moonlight. The hand that grasped mine was cold and trembling, just as Liam's flesh had been before I'd breathed life into him. His expression, though, was like Bill's when he returned to make up for how he had hurt me as Liam—a look of pure gratitude. But this man's face was younger—and his skin was goose-fleshed with cold.

"You're human, aren't you?"

He laughed. "What else would I be, lass? Did ye think you'd snared a kelpie or a phouka?"

"You haven't . . . been changed yet. You're William before he became the incubus."

The amusement in his eyes faded, and his face became still as marble. "An incubus? A creature that ravishes young maidens? Aye, the Fairy Queen told me that's what I'd become if I remained with her in Faerie. Once she sucked all that was human out of me, I would have to feed off human girls to survive." He took his hand from mine and turned it back and forth in the moonlight. I recognized the hand, remembered the feel of it caressing me. I reached out my hand and took his. His skin was still cold. For a moment I thought I was too late, but then, beneath the chill flesh, I felt the warm pulse of human blood. I squeezed.

"See," he said, "I *am* human. You saved me before I could become a monster. Just as you said you would."

"Just as I said . . ." Of course. He thought I was my ancestor, the first Cailleach, the fairy girl he laid with in the Greenwood, who promised to come back for him in seven years. I looked around us, at the wild heath covered with long grasses and flowers. I sniffed and smelled—yes, the same scent that had been haunting my dreams, the flowers I'd been finding in my bed—*heather*. The humpbacked mountains that surrounded us were taller than the Catskills that surrounded Fairwick, and perched atop one were the ruins of a castle. I had done it! I'd gone back in time to Scotland in the time of William Duffy. But where was the angel stone?

I looked down at William and noticed something glimmering on the ground. We both reached for it at the same time, our fingers touching. I withdrew my hand, and he held up a silver heart identical to the one still pinned to the tartan wrapped around him. He held the two halves of the heart together.

"Aye," he said, "you told me that someday these hearts would be rebound."

"I'm not that girl . . ." I began to explain to him, but then I noticed how badly he was shaking. It was colder here than in Fairwick, and we were on a bare hillside with no visible shelter—and no angel stone. I'd hoped somehow that the stone would be waiting for me when I walked through the door, but clearly I would have to go looking for it. "I'll explain all that later," I told William, "but for now I suppose we'd better find someplace warm, before we both freeze to death."

We walked down the hill, into a narrow valley where a stream flowed through a copse of beech trees. We followed the stream for more than a mile in silence, until we came to an unpaved road marked by a massive stone cross carved with intricate Celtic designs. Normally I'd be fascinated by an ancient monument such as this one, but I was cold, wet, and confused.

"Do you recognize where we are?" I asked William, whose teeth were chattering even more than mine were. Despite his cold, he'd offered twice to give me my plaid shawl back, which he'd craftily wrapped like a kilt around his waist with one end draped over his chest. I'd refused on the grounds that being seen walking with a naked man wouldn't help my reputation any in the seventeenth century.

"Aye," he said, "that stream is Boglie Burn. It runs into the Tweed, just beyond Ballydoon. And the forest we came out of is the Greenwood, an ancient enchanted wood. That castle on yonder hill is Castle Coldclough, but nobody lives there and it's haunted. But that wee croft up there belongs to a cousin of my auntie's, Mordag MacCready."

He pointed up a hill that rose to our right. All I could see was a stone outcropping, but when the clouds cleared from the moon, I made out the shape of a stone cottage built up against the hillside. Its windows were dark, but that could be because its inhabitants were asleep.

"Do you think she'd put us up for the night?" I asked.

"No Christian soul would turn us away," he said, already climbing the hill. There was a narrow dirt path between the bushes, clear enough to indicate that it had been in use recently. I caught up to him, wondering what Mordag Mac-Cready would make of a naked man knocking on her door in the middle of the night, cousin or no. Would she think he was one of the boggles or haunts that everything around here seemed to be named for? As we approached the house, though, I began to doubt there was anyone home. The place had a forlorn, derelict look to it. A gate had been left open, swinging on its hinges, an empty bucket lay in the yard, and there was no smoke coming from the chimney.

"It looks deserted," I commented to William.

"Aye, maybe Mordag is pasturing her sheep in the hills overnight, although it's getting late in the year for that."

Now that he mentioned sheep, I could detect the not-unpleasant aroma of manure mingled with hay and wet wool coming from an empty stone-walled enclosure beside the house.

"How do you know so much about sheep?"

William snorted. "As a wee lad, I watched the flocks—before I ran away to the city."

"If you were living in the city, how did you get kidnapped by the Fairy Queen?" I asked.

"Och, I'd come back," William answered. "Do ye want to know my whole life's story standing here freezing on the doorstep, or would ye mind if I continued the tale inside by the fire?"

"Do you think we should break in? Won't Mordag think we're burglars?"

But William had already opened the door. I stood nervously on the threshold until William found a lantern and lit it by striking something that looked like a primitive lighter. With the lamp lit, I saw that the cottage was plainly and sparely furnished but clean. And cold. It was hardly warmer than it was outside.

"Are ye going to stand there all night letting in the cold air?" he asked, holding the lantern up. "Or are ye afraid of me? I'll no' turn into a lion again."

With the coarse wool shawl draped over one shoulder and his long hair bushing out around his face, he resembled one of the wild men that peasants believed roamed the woods of medieval Europe. As I looked at him, it came home to me that I really didn't *know* him. I knew the man—or creature—that he would become: the incubus Liam, who came to me as moonlight and shadow and became flesh through my breath; then Bill, who came back to me to make amends and died when my love made him human. But this man—William Duffy—I had dreamed of him, but I didn't *know* him. Could he be trusted?

A cold breeze brushed against my back, insinuating itself down the neck of my damp blouse. I shivered at its touch . . . but then felt it warm as it crept down my back. It felt like a hand, as if the breeze had turned to flesh as it met my flesh—as Liam had gained flesh with my breath. And as the warm breeze coiled around my waist, I smelled heather.

William lifted his head and sniffed the air. His eyes met mine and I felt a spark of recognition. Pulled by that spark—and the invisible hand at my back—I stepped over the threshold.

While William went to work lighting a fire, I looked around the cottage. The central room contained the fireplace, with a settle and two chairs set before it. A spinning wheel had been knocked over, the wool from its bobbin strewn all over the floor. There was also a rudimentary kitchen consisting of a cupboard, an iron basin, and a cast-iron stove. There were two small rooms in the loft upstairs, one with an antique brass bed covered with wool blankets and a sheepskin, the other with a loom, more trunks, and piles of blankets and sheepskins. Mordag was a weaver as well as a shepherd, which made sense.

I grabbed an armful of blankets and sheepskins, then came upon a trunk full of clothes. I put the blankets down and stripped out of my wet clothes, carefully spreading them out over the loom to dry. I put on a long white cotton shift and picked out a nightshirt for William—there were no pants— then carried the blankets down the stairs. I found William crouched on the stone hearth in front of a roaring fire.

Here," I said, tossing him the nightshirt. "Put this on while I see if there's any food."

"There isna but a stale bannock or two, but I did find this."

He held up an earthenware jug. I took it and smelled the peaty aroma of malt whiskey. Good scotch had been Liam's weakness. Some things never changed, I supposed. Certainly the golden skin of the man before me . . .

I took a swig of the scotch to keep from looking at those long golden limbs. Turning away, I felt unaccountably shy. I'd been making love to this man in my dreams for weeks now— I'd made love to his incarnations for longer than that—but I didn't know him. He looked at me as if he knew me, but that was because he thought I was the first Cailleach. He'd never met me—and he wouldn't, I suddenly realized. I'd saved him before he became the incubus, so he would never come to me as Liam or Bill. I felt a sort of hollow feeling in the pit of my stomach, but perhaps that was an aftereffect from emptying myself out to become the door. Certainly I should feel glad that I'd rescued William Duffy before he could become the incubus, but I didn't. The man I'd fallen in love with—whatever combination of Bill and Liam that had been—had never existed. I'd rescued a total stranger.

A hungry and cold stranger.

I searched the cupboards for food. I found a number of glass jars full of dried herbs and a covered earthenware canister half full of oatmeal and another with hard biscuits—the bannocks William had spoken of, no doubt, although they didn't resemble the warm, flaky biscuits my father used to make. Either seventeenth-century fare was spare or Mordag had planned to be away for a while and hadn't stocked her kitchen before leaving—although I noticed that there was a bowl on the table half full of dried oatmeal, a wooden spoon congealing beside it. It looked as if Mordag had been having her morning porridge when she'd been interrupted and left suddenly.

I hadn't come across any indoor plumbing on my exploration, so I went out back to relieve myself, squatting behind a lilac bush. In the moonlight I could see a pump, a neat garden sheltered in the lee of a stone wall, and an apple tree, all well tended and trimmed back for winter. Mordag hadn't been gone for long.

I washed my hands at the pump and filled a tin bucket that hung beside it with water. The water was ice cold and tasted like snow, which I noticed was covering the tops of the moonlit mountains surrounding the cottage. There hadn't been any snow in the Catskills when I left Fairwick. It gave me a hollow feeling that time was moving on, even though I knew that was absurd. The gulf of time separating me from my friends in Fairwick was far wider than a few weeks.

Shivering, as if I'd felt that wide gulf of time opening up

under my feet, I hurried back into the cottage, which felt toasty warm now. William had arranged the sheepskins and blankets into a sort of couch in front of the fire and was re-clining lazily, his bare legs ruddy in the firelight. I brought the water and bannocks over and busied myself filling a cast-iron kettle.

"I thought ye might've run away, lass," he said when I fi-nally sat down beside him. "Ye seem more scairt of me now than when I turned into a lion."

"You remember that?" I asked, avoiding the question of me being afraid of him. He was right—I was. But why?

"Aye," he said, his eyes glowing with mirth and reflected firelight. "I didn't have any choice about it, mind, no more than I had these last seven years, but I knew how brave ye were—and how kind. To risk your own neck for a man ye'd only met that once, although . . ." He drew his legs under him and knelt in front of me, studying my face. "It was a *once* that I would never forget." He leaned forward. His loose hair, fall-ing in soft waves around his shadowed face, was lit red by the firelight behind him, making him look for a moment like the lion he'd turned into back at the well. When he touched my face, his hand felt as soft and warm as the lion's fur.

I swallowed, feeling the pressure of his strong fingers on my skin. My voice sounded hoarse when I spoke. "There's some-thing I have to explain to you . . ." I began, before his lips touched mine. He leaned back on his heels and looked at me, a line creasing his brow. I resisted the urge to smooth it away.

"I'm not that girl," I said, "the one you met in the Greenwood—Cailleach. I have the same name—although I go by Callie more often—but I'm not her. I'm . . . her descendant. I've come back through time."

"What happened to her, then? The other Cailleach?"

"I don't know," I said. "I think she had to leave Ballydoon

because the witch hunters came and she tried to get back to Faerie, but it wasn't the right time. I've dreamed about her. I think she saw you and tried to come through the door, but then she faded . . ."

A pained look crossed his face. "Aye, I half-remember that, but I thought it was a dream—I've had some awful dreams in the time I've spent in Faerie. If she didn't come for me, then what happened to me?"

"You became an incubus," I said. "You came to me twice as that creature, each time in a different guise."

"Did I hurt ye, lass, when I came to ye as a demon?"

"No—or at least not physically. You rather broke my heart as Liam, but then when you came back as Bill you tried to make it up to me."

"As if there were any way to make up for treating a lady badly!" He jerked away and flung himself back against the piled blankets and stared into the fire. "There were things I did when I was in Faerie . . . things I remember . . . I don't know if they were real or no'. There were great feasts at which we ate and drank like kings for days and nights on end, only there wasn't any difference betwixt night and day, so no telling how long our debaucheries went on—or where they might lead. I remember riding through the woods, horns calling the hounds to the hunt, chasing a white deer, only the deer became a girl . . . a frightened human girl."

He turned to me, his eyes glowing blood red in the firelight, his face pale as ash. "I don't like to think of what became of that girl, or the others. The queen brought them to me. She said I must learn to feed on their life or I'd no' be any good to her." He looked back at the fire, his profile white against the shadows. He was no longer cold, but he was trembling. I wanted to reach out and touch him, but I was afraid that when he looked at me he would see one of those girls he'd

hurt. I remembered that after I'd banished Liam to the Borderlands, he spent his time there trying to help creatures
across safely, to make amends for the souls he'd drained of
life. And when Bill showed up at my door to fix my roof, he
constantly told me that he was sorry. I saw now that it wasn't
just for the hurt he'd caused me. He'd been trying to atone for
the things he was forced to do to survive in Faerie.

"I didn't know what she meant," William went on. "I . . . I
lay with those girls, but I never meant them any harm. Still,
they would grow paler and weaker and thinner . . . and then
they would be gone. I told myself they had been released back
into the world, but when I asked, the queen would only laugh
and take me into her bed again—" He broke off and lowered
his head. "Ye must think me a monster," he said in a low,
desperate voice.

I started to speak, but my throat was so dry I gagged. I
reached for the water and took a long drink, wishing the clean
cold of it would wash away the images of William in the Fairy
Queen's bed. I remembered that before I knew that Liam was
the incubus, he told me a story about a lover who had led him
into debauchery, with whom he had done things he didn't like
to remember. That, I saw now, had been his way of telling me
what had happened with the Fairy Queen. But that story
hadn't come close to the raw details of this tale. Soheila had
first told me the story of how a mortal became an incubus
because he lived so long in Faerie that he had lost his human-
ity and then had to feed off the life force of human women,
but I had not imagined exactly what that process entailed. I
had not pictured the Fairy Queen feeding live girls to him, as
one might feed a pet snake live mice. Nor had I pictured her
taking that pet—replete with the strength he'd sucked out of
those girls—back into her bed. I knew I should say something
reassuring to him, but I couldn't think what.

William looked up again and helped me hold the pail to my lips, but he wouldn't meet my eyes. He took a sip of the water himself, put the pail aside, and looked back at the fire. "Aye, I don't blame ye. I became a monster in my own eyes. The worst of it was, I began to hunger for those girls. I looked forward to the hunt. When I saw ye standing on the road tonight, I thought you were tonight's prey, and . . ." He turned to me, his eyes wide and staring. "I cannot lie to ye—I wanted you. I want ye now, but I'm afraid of what I might do to ye." His hands twisted around my arms as the serpent had coiled around me. His hair, dry now, waved around his face like a lion's mane; his eyes burned like a fiery brand.

I shook one arm from his grip. I saw the pain in his eyes as I broke away, but he didn't try to restrain me. He let my other arm go and sat back on his heels. My arms free, I stroked his hair and wrapped my arm around his trembling shoulders. I coaxed his head down to my shoulder, stroking his hair and kneading the knotted muscles along his back. His whole body began to shake, but I held on to him fast as I had at the well, only this time I wasn't so sure what I'd be holding in the end.

CHAPTER SEVENTEEN

We fell asleep in front of the cottage's fire. At some point, when I felt William's body relax, I stretched out beside him and brushed the damp hair from his brow. Fresh washed with tears, gilded by the light of the smoldering embers, he looked like a boy, not a monster. I felt like Psyche gazing at her lover by lamplight, astonished to find a beautiful youth instead of the beast she had feared. But as beautiful as he was and as much as this man looked like Bill, he wasn't Bill. And now that I'd saved him from a cursed existence as an incubus, he would never become Liam or Bill. I should have been glad that I'd spared him years more of servitude to the Fairy Queen, but all I felt was a pang for the man William would never become. I let slumber overtake me, my own tears falling on his breast like the oil from Psyche's lamp, all the while feeling the beat of his heart under my cheek.

From the warmth of the fire, I drifted into the dream-heat of the sun filtering through the trees of the Greenwood, the crackle of the dying fire becoming the snap of branches as I frantically ran through the dense underbrush, the beat of William's heart becoming the pounding of horses' hooves in pursuit.

The hunt was on my heels. I heard the baying of the hounds, their jaws snapping, hungry for my blood. If they got to me, first they would rip me limb from limb. But they weren't the only creatures hungry for me. The horses' riders wanted to devour me, too. I fled in terror. Heedless of branches slapping my face and thorns tearing at my flesh, I left a trail of blood behind me. I could smell it—and smell the excitement of the hounds as they picked up the scent. Any second they would be upon me, their sharp teeth sinking into my flesh . . .

A white horse crashed through the brush in front of me, splitting the dark-green leaves like a beam of moonlight slicing through the night. The rider, cloaked in black, leaned down and scooped me up in his arms. He swung me onto the back of the horse with a supernatural ease that should have alarmed me but only made me glad to be above the snapping dogs, sheltered behind the rider's broad back. As we rode through the woods, I held on to him without knowing what I held on to. Only when we came to the glade with the stone ruins of a door did I begin to remember. He helped me down from the horse, murmuring reassuring words. We were safe, he told me; the hunt couldn't find us. His lips were warm on my skin, his hands gentle as he laid me down on the soft green moss. The sun was behind him, his hair falling in loose waves that hid his face. I reached up and pushed his hair away . . . and found myself looking into the hungry eyes of a savage beast.

I startled awake in the cottage, in William's arms. I felt the jerk of him waking, too, saw his eyes widen in the dim glow of the coals from the dying fire.

"You!" he gasped. "You were with me in the Greenwood. I became a monster!"

I lifted a shaking hand to his lips to quiet him. "It was just a dream. You're not a monster."

I felt his breath on my hand as his lips parted and he kissed my fingertips. "Only because you saved me." He lowered his lips to mine. They were soft, not the hard, snapping jaws of a monster. I opened my lips and tasted him. He tasted like honeysuckle and heather. When I closed my eyes, I saw the Greenwood ringed around us, keeping us safe from the hunt. His arms gathered me up, strong as the serpent's hold, not crushing me but encircling me with his warmth. I wrapped my arms around him, pressing myself against his smooth, hard chest. No lion's fur, but a lion's heart beating hard and steady as I wrapped my legs around his waist. I wanted to be the serpent encircling him, the lion ravishing him, the fire branding him. I wanted to burn away everything that had happened to him in Faerie these last seven years. I heard him gasp as my legs locked around his back. He dragged my shift over my head and his nightshirt over his so we could press bare skin against bare skin, our hearts pounding as fast as hoofbeats. I felt him hard against me. He slid his hands under my hips and gathered me up as he'd scooped me up onto the horse in my— *our*—dream. Were we dreaming now? I wondered as he hovered above me. The moment seemed to stretch as I opened up for him—as if we both had left time and gravity behind, outside the circle of the Greenwood, where the dogs bayed for our blood and winged monsters beat at the trees above our heads and we were always together on the brink of him entering me . . .

And then we came together, meeting in midair like dragonflies mating, and I felt the strong hot length of him entering me, and I knew it wasn't a dream. *This* was real—us rocking together on the hard stone floor beside a dying fire, kindling our own heat from flesh and blood. Even if the cry he made as he came inside me didn't sound quite human, that was okay. Neither did mine.

When I awoke in the morning, I was alone. I sat up, pushing aside a wool blanket. A fresh log burned on the fire. Something bubbled in a cast-iron pot hanging from a hook in the fireplace. I sniffed and recognized the comforting aroma of oatmeal.

The back door opened and William entered, wearing the long nightshirt I'd found for him last night and a blanket tied around his waist like a kilt. I was suddenly aware that I was naked beneath the blankets—and remembered *why*. Memories of last night came rushing back—the soreness between my legs told me that part hadn't been a dream. Probably the second time we'd done it hadn't been a dream, either.

I pulled the blanket up over my breasts, feeling completely abashed. In some ways I'd known this man forever, but in other, more *practical* ways, I'd met him for the first time only last night. Worst of all, I felt disloyal to Bill.

"Ah, you're awake!" William said, coming to sit on the stone ledge in front of the hearth. He kept his back to me as he stirred the oatmeal in the pot. Maybe he was also feeling a little shy after our impromptu lovemaking in the middle of the night. Or maybe he'd forgotten . . .

He turned to me and smiled. "I thought ye might be hungry after . . . weel, the exertions of last night." He blushed—or perhaps it was the glow of the fire on his face. He rubbed his chin. "And I found I needed a shave. I'm afraid I'm a wee bit out of practice. My hair never grew in Faerie. What do ye think?" He slid down beside me, taking my hand and holding it up to his smooth shaven cheek. "Do I feel like a beast to you this morning?"

"You're not a beast," I told him.

He brought my hand to his lips and kissed it. "I was afraid ye would think I was after how I behaved last night. I promised myself I wouldn't take advantage of you, and then I ravished you like a wild animal."

I started to laugh, but, realizing that he was serious, I cleared my throat and pretended it was a cough instead. "As I recall, I did some of the ravishing."

He grinned. "Aye, I thought so! But then I told myself this morning I must have conjured up that part. I didn't wish to presume . . . weel, I feel as if I have known you a long time, but perhaps you do not feel the same for me."

"I feel as if I've known you for a long time, too," I said. "But . . . well, I suppose it will take some time before we figure out what we know and what we don't know about each other, and I'm not sure how long we'll have."

His face darkened. "And where will you be off to then?"

"Back home," I said. "My friends are in danger. I have to find the angel stone and return to save them."

"Back through Faerie?"

"Yes . . ." I began.

"But did ye not hear the Fairy Queen's curse?" he demanded. "She cursed us both. She said if ye ever set foot in Faerie again, she'd pluck out your eyes and heart and replace them with eyes and heart of wood."

I smiled at the arcane language of the curse, but I felt a chill remembering the Fairy Queen's blazing green eyes. "When it comes time, I'll deal with Fiona," I said with more conviction than I felt. "But first I must find the angel stone."

"And do you know where to find this stone?"

I admitted I didn't.

"Weel, then," he said, his mood restored. "You'd best eat your parritch to keep your strength up. Who knows how long it will take to find one wee stone amongst all the stones in Scotland? But I know where we'll start. We'll go and ask my auntie."

Besides a prodigious collection of vintage underwear and nighties, Mordag possessed no other clothes, so I had to put on my costume from last night. William found an old, much patched and baggy pair of trousers—that he referred to as *breeks*—which he wore with his nightshirt tucked in and a pair of misshapen clogs he'd found by the back door. No doubt we looked a strange sight as we headed down the road, but there wasn't anyone to see us.

"Are there always so few people around here?" I asked.

"Well, it's no' the Royal Mile of Edinburgh, but there's usually a farmer taking his wares into town." He pointed down the road in the opposite direction from where we'd come last night. "This is the way to Ballydoon."

We headed in that direction, William whistling along the way. Gone was the young man who'd been woken by nightmares.

"You seem happy," I said, slightly envious that even in borrowed shoes he strode along with less effort than I did.

"Aye, and why not? I'm strolling along a country lane with a beautiful lass on a fine day."

The sun had burned off the morning mist and was warming the air. A gentle breeze rustled the yellow birch leaves on the side of the road and the purple heather on the hillsides. Magpies chattered in the heather, sunlight glinting off the blue iridescent stripes on their wings. The road climbed at a slow and steady incline. At the top of a rise, we looked down at a small village nestled in the next valley. It was really only a few dozen stone houses around a town square with a market cross and an old church. The ruins of a castle perched on the opposite hill, casting its shadow over the stone houses—the ruin that William had identified last night as Castle Coldclough. It looked like the idyllic Scottish village one might see on the label of a single malt or a tin of shortbread. Or, I thought uneasily, like the bewitched village in that old Gene Kelly movie, which appeared only once every hundred years.

"Brigadoon," I said aloud.

"Nay, this is Ballydoon," William said. "At least, it *was* Ballydoon. There's something queer about it."

I gazed back down at the village. It seemed picture perfect to me, like a model under glass or a movie set—and then I saw what he meant.

"Where is everybody?" I asked.

"Aye," he said. "That's what I'm wondering. The sun's been up more than an hour. The market should be full. The farmers should be bringing their wares into town, the goodwives should be washing down their front steps, having a gossip . . ."

"Do you think they've all left?" I asked, staring hard at the stone houses, as if I could pierce their thick walls with the intensity of my gaze.

"Nay," he said. "There's smoke coming from the houses. The folks are still there, they're just staying close to home."

I noticed now the trails of smoke rising from a few houses.

"What would keep everybody at home?"

"The pest," he answered in a hushed whisper, as if the word could conjure such a thing. I shivered as though a shadow had passed over us, blocking the warm sunshine and blotting out the beauty of the day.

"William, do you know what year it is?" I asked.

He scratched his head. "Weel, it was 1652 when I left, so if it's been seven years . . ."

I ran through my patchy knowledge of British history, trying to remember if there was still plague in 1659. Had there been an outbreak in Scotland at this time? But all I could recall was the date of Defoe's *A Journal of the Plague Year*, which took place in 1665. It was certainly possible.

"What should we do?" I asked. "Should we go back to Mordag's?"

He turned to me for the first time since we'd seen the village. The fear I saw in his eyes was not reassuring, but there was something else—a flash of steel that I recognized from when Bill had gotten angry after Duncan Laird hurt me.

"Perhaps you should go back to the cottage and wait. My auntie who raised me is down there, and I need to know if she's all right."

"We'll go together," I said quickly. After all, we'd already braved the Fairy Queen and William changing into a monster. "You said she might know something about the angel stone."

William nodded. "Aye, she's a wisewoman."

"Let's go, then," I said, putting on a bright smile that felt false on my face. Only as I followed William down the hill toward the village did it occur to me that *wisewoman* might not refer to his aunt's sagacity. In these times, it was what witches were called.

As the dirt road turned to cobblestone, it remained deserted, but I sensed movement behind the closed shutters of the houses we passed, a stirring that might have been townspeople pressing their eyes to the cracks and peepholes—or rats scurrying in the walls, carrying plague.

"There are no quarantine signs to mark a house condemned," William whispered. "And no reek of dying. There's something else amiss."

"Fear," I said, sniffing the air. The clean scent of heather and running water was gone now, replaced by a metallic tang that I could taste at the back of my throat. "The people here are afraid of something, but what?"

As we continued, I saw up ahead a town square with several open-air stalls—perhaps a farmers' market. But the stalls were deserted, save for a half-empty basket of rotting potatoes and a bit of undyed wool snagged on a wooden contraption set up in front of the market cross. As I looked around the abandoned square, William read a sign affixed to the front of the church. A bright scrap of cloth drew my attention to the far side of the square. Coming closer, I saw it was a crudely made rag doll. Black stitches marked its eyes; undyed wool made up its hair. I picked it up and winced as something stung my hand.

"Leave that!" William cried, grabbing my arm. "Let's get out of here—"

"William? William Duffy? Is it really you?"

William's grip on my arm tightened, and I felt his body tense. I could sense him on the verge of bolting, but then he steeled himself and turned around to face the speaker. She was a young woman, perhaps in her early to mid twenties; her long blond hair was pulled back on top but then worn loose in long ringlets flowing over a royal-blue cloak, which was clasped at the throat with a silver pin. Her eyes were Wedgwood blue and grew even larger as they fastened on William.

"It *is* you. We thought ye were dead. Instead you're with"— her eyes swiveled to me—"another . . . *woman*." She managed to inject a note of disdain into the word *woman*. She might as well have said *slut*.

"So there is someone alive in this godforsaken place," I said. "Maybe she can tell us what's going on. Do you know her?"

The girl's eyes grew even wider. "Know me?" she asked, affronted. "I'm Jeannie MacDougal. William Duffy and I were—*are*—engaged to be married."

"Engaged? But he's only just arrived."

"Aye, he vanished seven years ago. He left me standing on the kirk steps, feeling like a fool." Her glance shifted from William to me, her china-blue eyes traveling from my unkempt hair to my stained and wrinkled green skirt, then to my muddy boots and back up again to meet my gaze.

"I recognize you! You're the demented girl who wandered out of the Greenwood just after William vanished and whom Malcolm Brodie took pity on and married. But then you up and deserted him and your own bairn when the witch hunters came to town. You ran back to Faerie, didn't you, where you'd left poor William? Weel, never you fear, William, the witch hunters are here in Ballydoon, and they'll know what to do with this witch."

CHAPTER EIGHTEEN

I looked around the square again—at the sign on the church door and the contraption in front of the market cross. It was a wooden T, the top bar made from two long pieces of wood with a large hole in the center and two smaller holes on either side. I recognized it from history books as a pillory for holding prisoners and humiliating them in public. The sign on the church door announced a kirk session to investigate charges of witchcraft. We hadn't wandered into a plague-ridden village: we'd wandered into one in the throes of a seventeenth-century witch hunt. No wonder everyone was hiding behind locked doors. However, Jeannie's tirade drew a few cautious souls out of their homes to see what was going on. Meanwhile, William was stumbling for an explanation for why he'd skipped out on his fiancée (whose existence he'd conveniently forgotten to mention last night) and disappeared for seven years.

"Jeannie, I was kidnapped the night before our wedding by . . ." I saw a frantic look in his eyes. Did he dare tell his fiancée and the assembled townspeople that he'd been taken by fairies? Did the citizens of old Scotland still believe in fairies?

" . . . by pirates," William concluded.

"Pirates?" Jeannie echoed. "Do ye think I'm daft, William Duffy, that I'd believe sech a story?"

William looked unsure of how to answer that question, so I stepped in for him.

"Actually, pirates were quite active in the . . . er . . . right about now. The Barbary corsairs were—*are*—still raiding European coastal settlements, more commonly in Spain, France, and Italy but also in England, Ireland, and Scotland, well into the late seventeenth century. In fact, in 1631, a Dutch corsair captured nearly an entire village in Ireland and sent them to North Africa, where most lived out the rest of their lives as galley slaves or in harems—"

"Aye," William interrupted, "that's where I found this poor lass, enslaved in a sultan's harem. So, you see, she can't be the girl you spoke of who married Malcolm Brodie. I was about to be slain when she came to my rescue and pleaded for my life. Only because she was the sultan's favorite was she successful. Together we escaped and came back here!"

I wasn't sure that I relished being made a harem slave, even in a fictional account. Fortunately, I had recently reread a Dahlia LaMotte book called *The Barbary Beast,* in which an Irish girl was abducted by an English corsair who sold her into a sultan's harem. I recalled the details of the plot now to give me a more active—and virtuous—role.

"Yes, I *was* sold into a sultan's harem, *but* I was able to fend off the sultan's advances by telling him part of a story each night, which again and again I left unfinished, with the promise that I would tell him the end of the tale the next night if he, er, left me alone. I did this for one hundred nights, until

I was able to escape with"—I almost said *Jack Wilde,* the Barbary pirate of LaMotte's book, who had secretly listened to the Irish girl's tales and fallen in love with her wit and eloquence, but I caught myself—"William."

"I thought ye said she saved you," Jeannie said coldly.

"We saved each other," William replied, with a look that made me blush—and that enraged Jeannie.

"And in all this did ye forget that ye were betrothed to me, William Duffy?"

William tore his eyes from me. "Nay, Jeannie, I didn't forget, but I dared not hope that ye'd remember me in all the long time I'd been away. And I knew that surely a lass as beautiful and well favored as yourself would have married another in these seven years." William ended with a hopeful look that he quickly masked as a sorrowful one, but Jeannie had turned bright red at what I imagined was an unwelcome reminder of her spinsterhood. If she'd been ready to wed seven years ago, she must be in her mid-twenties by now—in this period, an old maid.

"Weel," she said, tossing a lock of her gold hair over her shoulder. "It's not that I didn't have my share of suitors, but I held out hope that you would come back. And now . . ." Her red lips parted to reveal a dazzling smile. "Ye have. My father— and brothers—will be glad to see ye, William. You'll come with me now. I'm sure your"—she gave me an icy stare—"*lady friend* can be accommodated at the tavern."

William glanced at me imploringly, willing me to come up with some story that would save him from his fiancée, but I was too angry at him for not telling me about her last night to feel inclined to help. Fortunately for him, someone else came to his rescue: a middle-aged (although I realized that middle-aged here might mean thirty) woman who looked strangely familiar.

"I'll no' have ye takin' my nephew away before I have a chance to box his ears for making us all worry these long years."

"Aunt Nan!" William exclaimed. The woman's hair was longer and not yet gray, her blue eyes unclouded by cataracts, but she was identical to Mac Stewart's nan, whom I'd met at Shady Pines Assisted Living a few weeks ago—or, rather, three hundred plus years from now.

"Nan Stewart?" I asked.

She narrowed her keen blue eyes at me. "Aye, do I know ye? You look a bit like Katy Brodie."

I realized my mistake. This woman must be an ancestor of Mac's grandmother. I didn't want the village thinking I was Katy, which I assumed must have been the name the fairy girl had gone by. "No, it's just that William's spoken of you."

William gave me a quizzical look. The number of falsehoods being bandied about was making me dizzy. Nan Stewart may not be Mac's nan, but she was the closest thing to a sympathetic face in the crowd. I nudged William. "And I'm sure he wants to explain to you where he's been. Don't you think we should go with your aunt *now*?"

"Aye, a good idea—"

"You're not going anywhere, William Duffy," Jeannie announced, with a stamp of a pretty, slippered foot, "before ye tell me whether or no' you have come back to fulfill your promise and marry me."

"Aye, I'd like the answer to that question, as well." A broad, grizzled gentleman dressed in finer clothes than the rest of the townspeople had appeared at Jeannie's side. Her father, no doubt. "Or should I be summoning my lawyer to draw up charges of breach of promise?"

I looked at William and noticed that he had turned a slightly greenish hue. I felt sorry for him until he opened his mouth and said, "I cannot marry ye, Jeannie, as I'm already wed to this lady here." He took my hand and held it up so that the sun struck the emerald and diamond ring I wore on my right hand—the ring Liam had given to me. *The emerald is the color of your eyes when we make love,* he had told me when he put the ring on my finger. I felt a strange stab of disloyalty as William claimed it as proof of our engagement, a feeling that mingled with the rather petty enjoyment of watching Jeannie's face turn livid with jealousy, and that finally resolved into pique that William had claimed me as his own in the marketplace without consulting me.

"If that be the case, then you will be hearing from my lawyers. And," Jeannie's father added over his shoulder as he steered his outraged daughter away from the square, "the kirk session will be interested to hear this story of pirates. To me, it sounds suspiciously of witchcraft."

William opened his mouth to reply, but his aunt put a warning hand on his arm and answered instead. "I'm sure the lad only did what was right, Hamish MacDougal. As for the kirk, I haven't heard yet that being kidnapped by pirates is proof of witchcraft." She steered William, who still gripped my hand, in the opposite direction from where Jeannie and her father had gone, leading the way down a narrow alley. When we'd gotten away from the square, I turned on William.

"How could you claim me as your bride in front of all those people without asking me first?" I demanded.

William's mouth dropped at my question. "It was all I could think of to keep from having to marry Jeannie Mac-Dougal. After last night I didn't think you'd mind."

"Last night I didn't know you were engaged to another woman!"

"I didn't know it myself! I had no idea that Jeannie Mac-

Dougal would be waiting for me all these years. Her father is the richest man in town and an elder of the kirk. When I was courting her, she was the most sought-after girl in all of Bally-doon. I'd have thought she'd wed a month after I vanished."

"Clearly she isn't as fickle as you are."

"Fickle? Me? I didn't notice you worrying overmuch last night about your Bill or Liam."

"What are you talking about? Bill and Liam were *you!*"

"I don't see how they can be me if I don't remember them and I have been in Faerie all these years—"

"Fucking everything that moves!"

William's eyes flew open wide at the expletive. "Only be-cause the Fairy Queen made me!"

Nan, who'd reached her front door, wheeled on us. "Do the two of ye dunderheads want to be taken as witches right this minute with all your talk of fairies?" she cried. "Do you not know that traffic with the fairies is considered an admis-sion of witchcraft?"

I did, in fact, remember something of the kind from a class I'd taken on the European witch hunts. From 1597, when James VI proclaimed in his work *Daemonologie* that any occurrence of the supernatural came from the devil, witch hunters throughout the first half of the seventeenth century prosecuted anyone who admitted—often under torture—that they'd had contact with the *gude neighbors*. The furor culmi-nated in a massive witch hunt that claimed more than three hundred lives . . .

"In 1659!" I said aloud. "Nan's right. The country's on the verge of one of the worst witch hunts in Scottish history."

Nan stared at me for a moment, then wordlessly turned, opened her door, and pulled me through it into a small, neat, homey parlor with cushioned chairs by a fireplace, a spinning wheel, and bunches of fragrant herbs hanging from the low

roof beams. She locked the door behind us, drew the lace curtains at the windows, and poked her head into an adjoining
room—presumably to check if we were alone. Then she took
me by both hands, drew me down onto a bench in front of the
hearth, and stared hard into my eyes.

"Who are ye?" she asked. "You do look a mite like that
demented girl who wandered out of the Greenwood, but I can
see you're not her. How do you know what will happen in the
future, and how did you know me? Are ye one of . . ." She
licked her lips and looked nervously around the room. "One
of the fair folk?"

I looked up at William, who was hovering nervously above
us. "Nay, Auntie, she's the one who saved me from them."

"So that *is* where ye've been. I thought it might be the case
when ye went missing and that girl showed up in the village
the next day."

"Was her name Cailleach?"

"Aye," Nan said, eyeing me suspiciously. "That's what she
said her name was, but it's not a Christian name, so we called
her Katy. She was not right, puir thing. She was ravin' about
having lost her way to a door and that all her folk would die.
I asked her about William, and she just wept the harder and
told me he'd been taken by the Queen of Elphame and it was
all her fault. I didn't know, though, if she were raving or telling the truth—and I knew that, if it were the truth, if she kept
on like that she'd be taken as a witch. I looked after her until
Malcolm Brodie, whose own wife had died the year before
leaving him with two motherless bairns, fell in love with her
and married her. We thought she'd settled down when she had
her own bairn, but then the witch hunters came and she ran
away. We never did see her again." She looked at me. "If
you're not her, what are you? Witch or fey?"

I considered lying, but I felt an instinctive trust of Nan, perhaps because I knew her descendants in the twenty-first century and there were no people more trustworthy than the Stewarts. "A bit of both," I replied, and then proceeded to tell her my story as honestly as I could, translating the details of the twenty-first century into terms a seventeenth-century woman would understand. She listened patiently, stopping me only when I got to the part about the nephilim. She made me go back and describe them.

"Aye, I know their ilk. I believe that some of the witch hunters may be those devils. Their kind have been abroad in the country for many years now. They are the ones behind the war on the auld folk and all who hold the old ways. They have outlawed the minstrels and tale-tellers—all those who tell the old stories—because it's in those old stories that lie the secrets to destroy them. They're the inquisitors who trick hapless old women into telling tales of the little folk and then accuse them of consortin' with the devil, because they are afraid that any who know the old ways will know how to destroy them."

"That's what Nan Stewart—your descendant—told me. She said that I had to find the angel stone that would destroy them, but I don't know where to look. The girl you call Katy must have had it. Did you ever see her with a milky-white tear-shaped stone?"

"Aye, she wore it in a brooch just like the one you're wearing." She pointed at the pin on my shawl and then flicked her eyes toward William and saw the one that he was wearing. "When the witch hunters came and Katy ran away, she left the brooch for her daughter, little Mairi, but it no longer had the stone in it. Malcolm thought she must have taken it to sell. The witch hunters stayed six months, turning neighbor against neighbor, sister against sister. By the time they were done, twenty-four men and women were hanged for witchcraft. And now they're back again. They've taken my cousin Mordag—"

"Mordag?" William asked. "Why, she's a harmless old woman. We stayed in her cottage last night."

I thought of the unfinished bowl of oatmeal and the spinning wheel knocked over on the floor and the beautiful woven blankets I'd slept under. Although I'd never met Mordag, I felt a pang for the woman being yanked out of her quiet life by those monsters. "Where have they taken her?" I asked.

"To the dungeons of Castle Coldclough," Nan replied with a shiver.

I felt a chill, remembering how the dark ruin seemed to loom over the village, casting a malignant shadow.

"We'll rescue her," I said. "Once I have the angel stone, we can use it with your magic plaid."

Nan snorted and plucked at my ordinary and decidedly *un-magical* plaid shawl. "A magic plaid, what nonsense! I've never heard tell of one of those."

It was hard to disguise my disappointment. "But your descendant told me that her family used the plaid against the nephilim. She said a fairy woman taught them. Are you sure Caill—I mean Katy—didn't teach you?"

"Nay, she couldn't even spin or knit or weave. Whenever she tried, the wool tied itself into knots. As for the stone . . . well, you'll just have to stay here until you find it, I suppose. In the meantime, I suggest the two of you stay out of sight. That pirate story you spun in the town square fooled no one, and this lass looks enough like Katy Brodie that folks will say she's a changeling. If the witch hunters get ahold of you, it won't take them long to discover you're not who you say you are."

The idea of being interrogated by a seventeenth-century

counterpart of Duncan Laird made my knees go weak. I was remembering the details of that class I'd taken on European witch hunts and the horrific torture devices they used to extract confessions. I suddenly had had enough of the seventeenth century. It had been foolish to think I'd be able to find the angel stone with no clue to its whereabouts. And as for William . . . I looked at him regretfully. He might look like the incubus, but he wasn't the man I'd fallen in love with in the twenty-first century.

"I'm sorry," I said. "There's no guarantee that I'll ever find the stone here. After all, it's just a fairy tale . . ." My voice cracked on the last words. What was any of this but a fairy tale? My life, my love for Bill—it was all a fairy tale that had evaporated into the mists. "I have to get back and help my friends." I turned away from the look of hurt in William's eyes and, like my ancestor before me, fled Ballydoon.

CHAPTER NINETEEN

I ran through the narrow alley, my bootheels echoing on the cobblestones. When I reached the square I turned to look back, but William hadn't followed. I squelched the pang of disappointment, raised my shawl over my head, and hurried through the square, ignoring the curious looks of the few remaining stragglers. Most townspeople had scurried back behind their shutters, but a few old women lingered by the market cross in the center of the square, gossiping—probably about the scene I'd played a part in earlier. They'd go back to Jeannie MacDougal, no doubt, and tell her they'd seen William Duffy's *queer wife* fleeing the town alone. Jeannie would decide I'd fled in shame at finding myself married to a man who'd been betrothed to another—or that William had repudiated me in favor of his beautiful first love. It irked me that she would interpret my leaving as proof of my shame and her own superiority, but I couldn't worry about that—or whether or not William and she would end up married. I could look it up in the history books when I got home.

I hurried fast out of the town, fueled at first by my urgency to get home and then by the need to keep warm. The sunny day that William had extolled on our way into town—it already felt centuries ago—had become gray and overcast. When I got to the top of the hill, it was raining. By the time I reached the stone cross, I was soaked. I glanced up toward Mordag's cottage, where William and I had spent the night. The memory of the warmth of the fire—and the heat of his hands on my body and his mouth on mine—flashed through me. He wasn't Bill. He wasn't the man I had fallen in love with, but leaving him behind seemed a final admission that I would never see Bill again. Even as I'd seen Bill's throat cut, watched his blood seep into the ground, I'd clung to a remnant of hope that something of him remained in Faerie that I could reclaim.

But now I knew in my heart that Bill was really gone. Since I'd saved William from becoming an incubus, Bill would never exist. When I got back to my own time, I might not even remember him.

Perhaps that was for the best. I pulled my shawl more tightly around my shoulders, bowed my head against the now driving rain, and turned away—into the path of a heavily laden cart. The rain had covered the sound of its approach and it was nearly on top of me, so close I could feel the hot breath of the horses steaming the air. I veered sideways, my ankle twisting in the mud, and stumbled into the ditch on the side of the road.

The wagon wheels narrowly missed my foot but ran over a corner of my shawl and splashed muddy water over my face. I squawked in protest, my cry taking in all the agonies of the day, a sound so pitiful that I was sure the cart driver would stop immediately and get down to help me, but he only cast a baleful glance in my direction and snapped the reins over the horses' backs to drive them harder. Anger quickly replaced self-pity. I struggled to my feet, prepared to give this road hog a piece of my mind, but my gaze met not the driver's eyes but the dazed and hopeless eyes of three women standing in the back of the cart. They were bareheaded in the pouring rain, hands chained, feet hobbled, unable to even huddle close together for warmth. Wet hair plastered their heads and turned their faces skeletal and their staring eyes into empty sockets—as if they had already been tried, convicted, garroted, and burned. Clearly these were more women accused of witchcraft, being transported to the dungeons of Castle Coldclough.

Their jailer told me that. I knew immediately that he was a nephilim. He loomed over the prisoners, ramrod straight and stock-still despite the rocking of the cart, in a long black cloak and a ghastly mask. It had a long black beak and red glass eyes that stayed on me as the cart continued on its way down the road. But it wasn't the horrible mask, which I recognized as the kind plague doctors wore, that held me riveted; it was the brooch pinned to the nephilim's cloak. It held a cloudy white stone big as a goose egg and shaped like a tear. As I stared at it, it began to glow, piercing the gray steaming air like the moon appearing from behind clouds. *The angel stone.* Every atom in my body called out to it. The light from it seemed to be filling my body, cold water pouring into my bones as if the rain were coming in through my pores. With it came an overwhelming sorrow—the grief of the creatures who had fathered these monsters and the shame of the children whose fathers had turned from them. This sorrow made the grief I'd been feeling for Bill a moment ago seem like a drop in the ocean, but it also made that grief swell into a flood that threatened to drown me. Every sorrow I'd ever felt—the death of my parents, the shame of my grandmother's coldness and disapproval, the moment I believed Liam had betrayed me, Bill's death—rose up inside me. It was unbearable. I wanted to throw myself under the wheels of the cart or lie facedown in the ditch until I drowned. I wanted to . . .

"Callie?"

The voice behind me barely pierced the fog of grief. I still couldn't take my eyes off the stone as it receded down the road. I saw the cloaked man touch a gloved hand to it, and beneath the beaked mask he smiled wolfishly. My grief acquired barbs.

"Callie!" A hand shook me roughly, the voice louder now in my ears. He was trying to turn me around, but tearing my eyes off the stone felt like ripping something inside me. William's face loomed out of the rain, as hollow-eyed as the skeletal masks of the condemned prisoners.

We'll all be dead if I can't get that stone away from those monsters, I thought, and then William's face bobbed like a balloon over me, getting farther and farther away, as if he was floating over me—or I was sinking down beneath him.

I sank deep into the darkness, into a waking dream, as if falling into a pit. Far above the pit hung a gibbous moon that looked down on me with a cold and pitiless eye. I could feel the angel stone pinning me down—its gravity pushing me ever deeper into the dark.

But then I was being lifted and carried out of the pit. I struggled to open my eyes and saw William's face instead of the cold, heartless moon. I couldn't keep my eyes open for long, though: the force of the angel stone was dragging me down into a nightmare world where, instead of being carried by William, I was taken to a dungeon. I wasn't alone there. The skeletal faces of the condemned women in the cart were with me, as were my friends from Fairwick—Frank and Soheila, Nicky and Ruby Day. All of us had been condemned by the nephilim to this cold dungeon, where our hands and feet were bound by cold iron and the beaked-faced creatures came and took us one by one to another room, where someone screamed and screamed and screamed . . .

When I was able to open my eyes, I caught glimpses of William and Nan. I saw that they had carried me to Mordag's cottage and put me in the upstairs bedroom under layers of wool blankets and sheepskins, but when I closed my eyes I was back in the dungeons and nothing could keep me safe or warm—not the hot tea that William held to my lips or the broths that Nan brought. Just by looking at the angel stone, my soul had been pierced. How could I ever have thought I could wield it as a weapon against the nephilim? How could I ever have thought I could save my friends back in Fairwick when I couldn't even save myself?

"Foolish girl," my nightmare inquisitor said when at last they came to take me to the torture room. "You didn't come here for this." He touched the stone and I felt a cold weight against my breast, as if a heavy stone had been laid there. "You came for your demon lover, to consort with him. Look, here is his devil's mark on you."

I looked down and saw the dark circles on my wrist where Liam's hand had encircled mine when I banished him to the Borderlands. As he dissolved, the shadows had bitten into my wrist.

"You see what trafficking with the devil has gotten you," he sneered.

The weight on my chest grew heavier, crushing my lungs. My hands clawed at the stone, trying to push it away, but it was too heavy. It held the weight of every regret—banishing Liam, loving Bill too late to save him, failing to save my friends and students from the nephilim back in Fairwick.

Somewhere I heard a woman's voice say, "She can't breathe,"

and I knew that in a sheepherder's cottage on a Scottish hill-side I was strangling to death.

"I'm sorry," I gasped with my last breath. "I couldn't save you."

"But you did." I heard a man's voice. "You saved *me*."

I felt something press into my hand. In the cottage room, warm fingers gripped my hand. In my nightmare dungeon, I looked down and saw the heart-shaped brooch, then looked up and saw the red glass eyes of my inquisitor fastened on it. The mask couldn't hide his surprise. I wasn't supposed to have the brooch.

I curled my fingers around it. In the cottage room, a hand closed over mine. In my nightmare, the inquisitor opened his mouth and let out a raucous caw. Black glossy wings filled the room with wind and noise. I could barely lift my hand in the tumult, but then I felt another hand on mine, guiding it to my chest. As soon as the cold silver heart touched my chest, the weight burst. I opened my eyes, gasping for breath, in the cottage. William was by my side, holding my hand.

"She's back," I heard Nan say.

When I saw the look of relief on William's face, I didn't have the heart to correct Nan. I wasn't back. I was trapped in the seventeenth century. But I did manage to squeeze William's hand and whisper before I fell into a deep and dreamless sleep, "I think I know how to get those bastards."

Once the immediate danger to me was past, Nan came less often, leaving William to care for me. I felt bad that William was stuck watching over an invalid—and worse that, while I lay in a warm bed, Mordag and eleven others were in the dungeons of Castle Coldclough. Nan had told me that the number of the accused was up to twelve, but she was right that I was too weak to face the nephilim now. I had to gather my strength. I sat up when William brought me oatmeal—my *parritch,* as he called it—in the morning and broth in the evening. During the day I watched out the window at the foot of the bed. In the morning, I followed his progress through the heather as he led Mordag's sheep, which a neighbor had been tending since she'd been taken, into their pastureland; in the evening, I waited for the moment when I'd spy him silhouetted against the lilac sky, a lithe shape like some pastoral figure on an antique vase. In between, I thought about the vision I'd had of the inquisitor. The angel stone he wore had exerted great power over me. I didn't even like to think of how it had made me feel, but I forced myself, remembering the cold weight of despair that had nearly crushed me. Despair, guilt, regret—the stone had evoked every mistake I'd ever made. It seemed to pull them out of me like a magnet. Only the Luckenbooth brooch had broken the spell and released me. I lay in bed each day trying to figure it out, my thoughts spinning in fruitless circles.

Then one day after a week or so, I got up to meet William downstairs as he came in the door. His eyes lit up at the sight of me; his cheeks glowed red as apples from the cold air. I felt a corresponding flare in my own heart but then a pang, because I was planning to leave as soon as I was able to get the stone away from the nephilim.

"I've been thinking about what happened when I saw the witch hunter," I said, as I spooned out the stew that William had made for us.

"Are you sure you want to be thinking about that?" he asked. "You were raving as if you were being tortured . . ."

He paused and looked up at me, his eyes shining in the firelight, and I suddenly wondered if he spent his days thinking about his captivity with the Fairy Queen. "I mean," he continued, "I know you are worried about your friends and that you must get this stone to save them; but perhaps it's better if you use this time to get your strength back for when it is time to go."

"Is that what you did when you were in Faerie?"

He looked surprised but then nodded. "Aye. I thought of what I should do if I had a chance to escape. I even dreamed sometimes of the lass who would save me . . ." He looked away, embarrassed. Since we'd returned to the cottage, he'd studiously avoided touching me more than he had to in the course of nursing me back to health. Sometimes I wondered if that first night we'd spent here, when we'd come together so urgently in front of the fire, had been as much a dream as the dreams of the Greenwood. "But those dreams of mine were a great deal more pleasant than the ones you were having," he said. "I don't like to think of you dwelling on them."

"I have to," I told him. "I have to understand how I broke the angel stone's spell, so that I can get it away from the nephilim. Not just for my friends back in Fairwick but for everyone here—for Mordag and the rest."

He nodded. "Aye, I don't like to think of what those bastards are doing to them. But I don't see how we can help. They're deep in the dungeons of Castle Coldclough and guarded by a squadron of those cloaked bastards. The whole town is terrified of them, everyone afraid to speak up in the kirk session lest they're accused next. And when someone does speak, they're struck dumb. I went to the kirk session on Sunday and watched Donald McCreavey try to speak up for his sister, but he fell on the floor in a fit. The minister said he'd been possessed by a demon and had him taken to the dungeons to join his sister. He was babbling all the while about all the sins he'd committed, how he'd stolen from the collection plate and watched the girls swimming in the burn naked.

Harmless things, but he took on like he was the devil himself."

"It's the stone," I said, guiltily thinking how much worse than Donald McCreavey's were the stains I had on my own conscience. "It makes you remember all the things you've done wrong—and makes them worse—until you feel like your own guilt is crushing you."

"That's why you were gasping for air?" he asked. "But what could you have done . . ." He stopped as the blood rushed to my face. "Oh," he said, "did it have to do with me—or who I became?"

"Yes," I admitted. "I'm afraid I caused you a lot of pain."

William smiled crookedly. "I imagine I deserved it—and I can't imagine whatever you did to me wasn't worth the time I got to spend with ye." He reached across the table and took my hand. "Dinna fash yourself, lass." As he squeezed my hand, I remembered how I'd felt his hand in mine during my vision.

"That's how I was able to break the angel stone's hold," I said, looking down at his hand. "You put the brooch in my hand . . ."

"Aye." He reached under the collar of his shirt and pulled out a leather thong. Hanging from it were both brooches. "I was unpinning your shawl when you started thrashing about, so it was in my hand when I grabbed yours."

"I saw it in my hand in my vision, and the witch hunter saw it, too. I could tell he was surprised—and frightened. When I laid it on my heart, I was able to break the angel stone's hold."

"Then you ought to be wearing it now for protection," he said, pulling the thong over his head. As he leaned closer to put the thong over my head, I smelled heather. A sprig was in his hair. I pulled it loose . . . and was flooded with the memory of the dreams I'd had of making love in fields of heather and the sprigs I'd find in my bed afterward. Perhaps he was remembering those dreams, too, because he blushed as he saw the flower in my hand.

"Och, aye," he mumbled awkwardly, "that's a queer thing. I fell asleep on the hillside today and awoke to find myself surrounded by heather, though it's too late in the year for the stuff to be flowering."

I thought about the beds full of flowers I'd awoken to back in Fairwick and wondered what William had been dreaming about. I looked down so he wouldn't see me blush and fingered the brooch he'd put around my neck. I fitted the two hearts together. I remembered the part from the ballad of William Duffy when the fairy girl breaks her brooch in half and gives one half to William.

"Tell me what Cailleach—the first Cailleach—said to you when she split the brooch in half," I said.

"*Keep this as a token of my love,*" he said, so quickly that I guessed he had repeated the lines many times. "*My heart will be halved until we are together again.* And . . ."

"There's something else?" There wasn't anything else in the ballad.

"Aye, she said that when the two halves were joined again, nothing could hurt us. What? What does it mean?"

"It means," I said, holding the two halves of the brooch up together, "that I have an idea how to get the stone and destroy those bastards. But I'll have to speak to your auntie first."

CHAPTER TWENTY

The next morning, after William had left with the flocks, Nan appeared on my doorstep. I wondered how William had gotten word to her so soon that I wanted to see her, then, looking past her up the hill, I saw the smoke of a bonfire rising in the still, cold air and realized they must have arranged a signal for her to come. The signal wouldn't have told her of my purpose, though. She was carrying a basket with food for us and another large basket full of unspun wool, which she said she'd brought for us to spin.

"We haven't time for that," I said, trying not to sound as irritable as I felt. I hadn't slept well the night before, agitated by thoughts of how to steal the angel stone—and by thoughts of William asleep in the next room.

"'Twill calm you," she said, giving me a keen look that took in my agitation. "You're as skittered as a cat that's misplaced its kits."

That was true enough. I'd asked William to send for Nan so I could tell her what I'd figured out about the power of the angel stone, but now that she was here I wasn't sure how much I should tell her. Her friends and neighbors were being rounded up as witches. Would she trust me—a stranger—to know how to help Ballydoon? Or might she turn me in to the witch hunters to save her relatives and friends? I supposed it wouldn't be a bad place to start by going along with her request.

I helped her pull the large spinning wheel from the corner and set it up near the fireplace—the only place in the house that stayed warm now that the days were getting colder. Nan placed the basket of wool under the wheel and explained that Mordag had already combed and carded it. The stuff resembled a cloud of dirty white cotton candy and felt, when I stuck my hand in it, faintly sticky. Nan took a handful of it and, with a series of quick and mysterious finger movements, drew out a thread, which she fixed to the bobbin of the spinning wheel. As Nan pumped a pedal with one foot, the wheel began to spin, drawing more of the creamy thread onto the bobbin. I watched, mesmerized, as the amorphous blob yielded a solid thread of yarn.

"Here," Nan said after a few minutes. "You try."

She showed me how to pull the wool back in one hand while pinching the thread between the fingers of the other with just enough slack to let the spinning wheel twist the yarn, but when I tried, it was like sticking my hand in a cloud and trying to wrest something solid out of it. Like trying to pull a rabbit out of a hat. No wonder the old wives who wove were sometimes taken for witches.

After I'd failed at several attempts, Nan made a sound low in the back of her throat—a sort of *mmppff*—and wrapped her own worn and capable hands around my weak and clumsy ones, guiding my fingers in the pulling and pinching motions. When she took her hands away, I could still feel their touch guiding my fingers in the same motions, coaxing a thread out of the clumps of wool and onto the spinning wheel's bobbin.

"Hey!" I said, delighted at the sensation of making something solid out of so much fluff. "This is fun!"

"*Mmpppff.*" Nan made the noise again and sat back with a hand spindle to work on another clump of wool. "Glad ye like it. There's a barn full of the stuff Mordag left unspun when they took her."

"Oh," I said, my fingers fumbling at the thought of Mordag and the others trapped in the dungeons of Castle Coldclough. "Have you had any news of her?"

"They say she confessed."

My fingers snared in the wool and the thread broke. Nan clucked her tongue, whether over my clumsiness or Mordag's confession I wasn't sure, and showed me how to twist a new thread onto the old. When the wheel was spinning again, I asked Nan how Mordag came to be accused.

"Are you asking me if she is a witch?" Nan asked.

"It doesn't matter to me. Even if she is a witch, she doesn't deserve to be locked away in a dungeon and tortured."

"Nay," Nan said, dropping her spindle from her hand to pull out a long thread of yarn. "That's true enough. But Mordag's no witch. She's only a wisewoman who uses her plants to heal folks and animals alike. She has a deft hand with the wee beasties. Three years ago, when the blight wiped out most of the local flocks, Mordag kept her own flock alive. She offered to tend the MacDougal flocks, as weel, but Hamish MacDougal was too proud to consult a wisewoman. All the MacDougal sheep perished, which drove up the price of wool next season. It made Mordag a rich woman—but a hated one. I told her she ought to leave off healing, but she wouldna say no to anyone in need." Nan shook her head and wrapped a skein of yarn around her arm, twisting it into a knot and dropping it into a basket. She'd woven twice as much with her hand spindle as I had with the wheel. "She brewed a special dip for Fergus MacIntire's sheep last spring, and a few of them died. Fergus accused her of hexing them. *Mmppff*. Like as not the creatures died from Fergus skimping on their feed."

"But why has she confessed?"

"Why do ye think? That man ye saw on the cart? The one who wears the moonstone pinned to his cloak? That's Endymion Endicott. He's a famous witch finder. Any man or woman he interrogates ends by confessing. By the time he's done with them, they confess to crimes committed in their dreams. They confess to all the petty acts we each think of doing but don't. Mordag admitted that she had seen the auld folk riding in the moonlight on All Hallows' Eve. Same as we all have in these parts. Mordag didna know that the judges didn't see any difference between the devil and the fey, but the real devil was that monster Endicott, who tortured her into confessing. By the end, he had her sayin' that she'd kissed the devil's arse. But she wouldna name any members of her circle, so she will not be given the mercy of a quick death. She's to be burned alive three days before Christmas Eve."

I shuddered but somehow kept the thread moving through my fingers—as though I had to do something to keep the horror of Mordag's fate at bay. Nor did I want to look at Nan when I asked her my next question.

"Not that it really matters," I said, trying to keep my voice casual, "because where I come from it's not a crime . . . even if anyone believed in it . . . so I just wondered . . ."

"If I'm a witch?" Nan asked, looking up from her spindle.

The thread broke in my hand and I met Nan's gaze. "Well, you see, I *am*, so if you are . . ."

"Aye, I suppose you could call me a witch. My gram said

we were wisewomen and *buidseach*. I wouldna ever do harm to anyone. That is one of the verra first rules I learned at my gram's knee."

"An' it harm none, do what ye will," I quoted the Wiccan credo from one of Moondance's bumper stickers. "Although I'm not sure all the witches I know abide by that rule." I thought of my grandmother and the curse her grandfather had put on Nicky Ballard's family.

"Nay, not all do, but the harm they do always comes back on them."

"Thricefold," I said. "Yes, I've heard that, too. I wonder how many of those convicted and killed by Endicott are actual witches."

"I do not know for sure. Some of the accused belonged to our circle and some did not."

"Your circle?"

"Aye, our *spinning* circle, ye ken. Perhaps you'll join us when ye've gotten your strength back."

"And this witch finder—Endicott—do you think he's a nephilim?"

"I dinna ken what he is, except he must be some kind of monster to do what he does to the poor souls he questions. It's like he breaks something inside them."

"It's the angel stone," I said, stealing a look at Nan. She was watching me, but her eyes were on my hands, not my face. I had somehow gotten the hang of the spinning now, and the repetitive motion of feeding the wool into the wheel made it easier to go on. "The stone makes every transgression seem far worse. The story I heard from my colleagues was that the nephilim were elves that were thrown out of Faerie because of how they abused human women—although, now that I think of it, I don't see how what they did was any worse than what the Fairy Queen did to William." The spinning wheel whirred faster as I thought about the abuse William had suffered. "Anyway, when they came here to our world, they bred with humans, and their offspring were born . . . *deformed* somehow—*monsters*. They were so horrified that they disowned their children, and the children in turn were so ashamed of their fathers' horror that they killed them. The last of their fathers shed a tear that became a stone—the angel stone. It's supposed to be the one thing that can destroy a nephilim. It's what I came here to Ballydoon to find."

"And that's the stone Endicott was wearing?"

"Yes, and he's using it to force witches to confess. But if we can get the stone, I think we can use it against the witch hunters."

"That's a mighty big *if*. How do you figure you can get the stone from Endicott? He always wears it, and he's not likely to hand it over to you."

"No, but there is one thing that can break the stone's power. Look there on the settle . . ." I pointed with my chin to the china saucer I'd put out on the bench in front of the fireplace. I didn't want to break the rhythm I'd fallen into. Nan was right: the spinning was not only relaxing me, it helped me think. Nan gave me a curious look, then put down her spindle and picked up the two halves of the Luckenbooth brooch I'd left in the saucer.

"While I was in my trance, William put my half of the brooch in my hand and it appeared in my hand in the vision. The inquisitor—Endymion Endicott—was scared when he saw it. I was able to break the stone's spell with it and escape from him."

"Aye, but only in a dream . . ."

"If it was that powerful in a dream, it will be more powerful in reality—and twice as powerful when the two halves of the brooch are fit together. There's a space between the halves that's just the right shape and size for the angel stone. If we can fit the angel stone into the brooch, it will become a weapon to use against them. And if we can figure out how to use the plaid, too, we can destroy the bastards."

Nan looked up from the brooches to me and grinned. "Aye," she said, "I think ye may be right. And I've got an idea about that magic plaid you've been nattering on about." She lowered her eyes to the bobbin on my wheel. I followed her gaze . . . and gasped, breaking off the thread. The undyed wool I'd been spinning had turned fiery red on the wheel and was glowing.

That evening, when William came home, I had the table set for his supper. I'd made bannocks and a stew from some mutton and carrots Nan had brought. I'd swept the hearth and scrubbed the wide-planked floor and arranged some dried heather in an earthenware jug—although I supposed since William spent his days in the heather he might be tired of looking at it. But I wanted the house to look and smell nice.

"What's all this?" he asked, his cheeks ruddy from the cold, his dark hair dusted with a sprinkling of snow. He reminded me of Liam when he would come in from his walks in the woods, and I found myself leaning toward him to catch the scent of pine and wood smoke that had clung to Liam's clothes. But William smelled of heather and peat and sheep.

"I know you've been working so hard," I said. "I wanted to do something for you."

"That's very kind of ye, lass, but you shouldn't trouble yourself. I see you've been spinning with Nan . . ." He cast his eye toward the spinning wheel. The yarn had stopped glowing after a little while. I wasn't sure yet how to make it glow again, or how we would make a magic tartan, but Nan had promised to come back tomorrow for us to spin some more.

"Yes, she taught me to spin," I said, spooning out a bowl-ful of stew. "And I told her about the angel stone. We think we might have a way of getting it." I told him about the magic tartan that the Stewarts had used in my time.

"You mean it's like a pen you'd make for your sheep—only made out of glowing thread?" he asked skeptically.

"Yes, and in my time the Stewarts were able to use it to keep the nephilim out of the circle long enough for me to open the door . . ." I paused, wondering what had happened after I'd disappeared from the circle. Had the tartan held—or had my friends been overwhelmed?

"You're back with them, aren't you?" William said softly.

"What?"

"Worrying about your people."

"Yes," I admitted. "I'm sorry."

"You don't have to be sorry, lass. I understand. I've been thinking how ye being here must be a wee bit like me being trapped in Faerie. It isn't the place you're meant to be, is it?"

"No," I admitted, taking a quick swallow of the ale Nan had brought.

"Aye, I suspected as much. I know verra weel what that's like. In fact, I have a wee confession to make."

"Oh?"

"Aye. When I was taken by the fairies seven years ago, I wasn't in the Greenwood just to see what would happen there on All Hallows' Eve. I was on my way out of town, heading for Edinburgh."

"You mean you were planning to leave Jeannie at the altar?"

William blushed. "I know it's no' honorable, but, aye, I

saw what my life would be like tied to her and the Mac-Dougals, and I knew that I wanted something different. I wanted . . ." He leaned forward, his eyes shining in the candlelight. "My plan was to go to Edinburgh and ship out aboard a merchant vessel, although I would not have been averse to joining up with a band of pirates if I happened upon them. I suppose that sounds foolish."

"How old were—are—you?"

"I was nineteen when I was taken, so I suppose I'm twenty-six now, although sometimes I feel I lived a hundred years, not seven, in Faerie."

He was a year younger than me. At nineteen, the age when he'd run away from Jeannie, I was in college at NYU. My biggest decision was what class to take and what major to declare.

"I guess you got an adventure after all," I said.

"Aye, but not the kind I wanted. Being slave to the Fairy Queen wasn't so different from marrying Jeannie MacDougal after all. So I understand what it's like to feel trapped. I want you to know that what happened between us that first night . . ." He blushed and looked away. "Well, I understand you were most likely thinking of your fellow from your own time—Bill, ye called him?"

"Yes, Bill," I said through a tightness in my throat.

"And I know I look like him, even that someday I'm supposed to be him, and that's why you . . . er . . . might have confused the two of us. But I know I'm *not* him and this is not your time and place . . . so you needn't fash yourself about me. I won't stand in your way. I'll help you get the stone you need from those bastards, and after we've run them out of Ballydoon I'll help you get back to your own time, to your friends."

I stared at William. I'd spent the whole day working up

speeches to explain how I couldn't get attached to him because I had an important mission and would have to leave when it was accomplished. And he—for all intents and purposes a nineteen-year-old boy who'd run away to join the pirates—had beat me to it. Clearly if he could be practical enough to see we shouldn't fall into each other's arms, I should be.

"Thank you, William," I said, the words feeling as cold in my mouth as the cooling stew. "I appreciate your understanding and your offer of help. We'll need it. Nan and I are going to learn how to weave the tartan to protect us, then we'll need as many men and women as we can find to carry the tartan to the castle. I'll use the brooch to get the stone away from Endicott, then I'll destroy the nephilim and free their prisoners. It will be dangerous."

"A raiding party against a castle guarded by a host of winged monsters?" William grinned. "It sounds better than being a pirate any day."

CHAPTER TWENTY-ONE

The days seemed to move faster once William and I had made our pact to work together to defeat the nephilim. We may not have been a romantic couple, but we were united in a shared mission. He proved to be a far better roommate than most of the ones I'd had in college, one of whom had borrowed my clothes and left them in stained clumps on our suite floor, and another who hacked into my Facebook account and posted spurious nude photos on it. William was courteous and neat, sleeping each night on a sheepskin pallet by the fire, which he rolled up when he left in the morning. Most mornings he rose before I did and headed out to milk the cow. When I heard him go out, I got dressed and made our breakfast. He'd have built the fire up and drawn a pail of water from the well, so all I had to do was set the oatmeal to cooking over the fire and make the bannocks, which I'd discovered were the mainstay of the local diet.

Soon after William left with the flocks, Nan would appear on the doorstep with her basket of wool and sundry gifts of food. I had the feeling that she waited until William was gone to give us some privacy, although I'd tried a number of times to make clear to her that our relationship was platonic, lest she get the idea that I was planning to stay in Ballydoon or that I was taking advantage of her nephew.

"I'm not blind or daft," she complained one day when I'd pointed out for the eleventh time the pallet where William slept. "I can weel enough see that a city-bred lass such as yourself would have no truck with a simple country boy such as young William—although he's a good lad now that he's gotten his silly notions of being a pirate out of his head."

I laughed and broke the thread I was spinning, which I was trying to get to glow again. We'd spun baskets full of wool, attempting to replicate the glowing multicolored thread I'd spun the first day, without success. Nan had me trying a hand spindle now. "You knew about that?"

"Och, aye, when he was a wee boy he used to make ships out of bits of wood and scraps of my best linen and launch them on the Boglie Burn while singing shameless sea chanteys he'd picked up hanging around the tavern."

I laughed at this image of a young William, which brought to mind how Liam would collect twigs and stones on his walks in the woods and bring them back to Honeysuckle House. The story also reminded me of a song I'd heard Bill singing once.

"Did any of those chanteys sound like this . . ." I hummed the tune. The words had been in another language I couldn't reproduce.

The thread broke in Nan's fingers and her face softened. "Och, that's no sea chantey but only a lullaby my sister used to sing to him when he was a bairn." Picking up her thread, Nan began to sing, keeping time to the rhythm of the song with the foot pedal of her spinning wheel. She sang it first in Scots and then in English.

"Hush, hush, my bonnie sweet lamb.
Tho' my ship must sail in the morning,
I will be with you
When the salt spray fans the shore,
I will be with you
When the wind blows the heather,
I will be with you when the dove sings her song,
Sing ba la loo laddie, sing ba la loo dear
Hush, hush, my bonnie sweet lamb."

Nan's eyes were shining when she came to the end of the song. For a few moments, the only sound in the room was the pedal knocking against the floor and the whir of the spinning wheel.

"What happened to her?" I asked. "William's mother . . . your sister."

"Ah, Jenny. The pest carried her away, along with William's father. William was only a wee lad. I took him to live with me and did my best, but it's never the same, is it?"

Having lost my own parents when I was twelve, I knew that well. "At least he had you. I went to live with my grandmother after my parents died, and she was not half so kind. I can see you really care for William."

"How could I not, him looking so much like my poor little sister." Nan's voice grew hoarse, but instead of lapsing into silence, she sang the lullaby again, this time in a stronger voice, as if she were singing it for her lost sister. I thought of Bill singing that song more than three hundred years later—remembering it across time and all the shapes he had assumed—and felt an electric charge that ran from the back of my neck to the tips of my fingers and down the thread I was spinning . . . which began to glow a brilliant crimson. I looked over at Nan to see if she'd noticed. She had stopped spinning and was staring not at my thread but at hers. It was glowing a deep emerald green.

"The color of Jenny's eyes," she whispered. "That's what I was thinking on."

I plucked a length of the scarlet thread from my bobbin, and Nan, understanding, unspooled an equal length of hers. We held them alongside each other—the red and the green thread, my love for Bill and hers for her sister—and they clung like socks just out of the dryer and then coiled around each other, forming a multicolored thread. Nan gave it a tug.

"It's strong," I said. "Stronger than one by itself."

"Aye," Nan said. "But to make that tartan, we'll need more than the two of us."

Nan left early that day, telling me she had an idea or two of who she might ask to spin with us. We had to be careful with our choice. Any one of the women might turn us in to the witch hunters for doing magic. "Folks are scared," she said, "but some are also weary of being scared. And there are those whose mothers or daughters are amongst the accused, who will take the risk to save them."

After Nan left, I decided to walk out to meet William as he came down with the sheep. I'd watched him often enough to know where to find him, and I needed the air and exercise. I was excited about the progress Nan and I had made but a little tired of being indoors, doing "women's work."

I wrapped my shawl around my shoulders against the cold and tucked its ends into my skirt, as I'd seen Nan do. I walked briskly across the meadow and up the path William took into the hills, my bootheels crunching the dried stalks of heather. The air had a bite to it, with a tang of peat smoke and snow coming. There was already snow on the mountaintops rising

206 · JULIET DARK

above us in every direction. Ballydoon was in a valley—or a glen, as it was called here—protected by those steep mountains. One road connected it to the outside world. Behind me, to the north, the road curved between two hills and led to Edinburgh. In front of me, the road twisted through the village of Ballydoon and then headed toward England. Looming over it, above a dark ravine that looked like a gash in the hillside, was Castle Coldclough. Its stones, turned black with time, seemed to have grown out of the native rock, but it didn't look as if it belonged in the peaceful valley—it looked like a malignancy that had grown on the hills. Even the ravine below it, cut so deep in the rock that it served as an impassable moat between the village and the castle, looked as though nothing had ever grown in it—as if the earth had shriveled under the cold hard stare of the nephilim's castle.

"Do ye know what *Coldclough* means?"

I turned to find William standing behind me.

"The word makes me imagine a beast with icy claws," I said, "but I don't suppose that's what it really means."

"A clough is a narrow ravine," he said, pointing to the deep rift below the castle. "That bit o' land afore the castle has always been a queer place, colder than everything else surrounding it, even the higher mountaintops. The sun never reaches the bottom, and nothing ever grows in it. Some say it's where Lucifer landed when he fell to earth."

I shivered looking at it, and William unwound his scarf from his neck and draped it around my shoulders. It held the warmth from his body and the smell of dried heather. "No wonder the nephilim chose it for their stronghold," I said. "We'll have to go through it to reach them."

William shook his head. "You'll no' find anyone from these parts willing to step foot in it, even with your magic plaid.

How is that progressing, by the by? Have ye worked out how to make it?"

"We managed two different color threads today," I said, turning away from the view, grateful for a change of subject. I told him about our progress as we walked back to the cottage. "Nan's going to find some more spinners, and then she'll teach me how to weave and knit."

"Och, are ye saying you don't know how to knit!" William exclaimed, looking scandalized. "I can teach you that."

"You know how to knit?" I asked.

"And spin and sew," he replied. "What do ye think a shepherd does with himself in the evenings? Are ye telling me Liam and Bill sat on their hands all night and did not make themselves useful?"

"Well, Liam was always restless," I admitted, recalling the way he'd pace around Honeysuckle House, "but Bill was quite good with his hands." I blushed, remembering the feel of those hands on me. "We didn't have much time together, but in that little time he was always fixing things." I remembered Bill removing a splinter from my finger and telling me he was sorry he had hurt me. "I think he came back that way to make amends for what had happened before . . . for hurting me."

"And well he should have," William proclaimed heartily. "To tell ye the truth, the two of them sound like a pair of dunderheads. If they could not keep ye, they did not deserve ye." William huffed and turned to walk back to the cottage.

When we reached the house, he produced a handful of dried heather and put it in the jug on the table. After dinner, while we sat by the fire, William taught me how to knit. I was so clumsy at it that he had to hold both my hands in his to guide me. I thought about whether these hands on mine were the same that had once touched me—or would someday touch me—until my head felt dizzy with trying to figure out what I wanted from those hands. He may have felt the same. After a few minutes, he let go.

"It's the fault of these big clumsy needles," he grumped. "Delicate hands like yours need finer needles. I'll make you a pair."

He spent the rest of the evening carving a pair of fine wooden knitting needles out of a branch of hawthorn wood, while I practiced knitting. It kept my eyes off his agile hands turning the wood and my mind from imagining the touch of those hands on me.

The next day I opened my door to find Nan and three other women—at least, I assumed they were women. They were all swathed so heavily in shawls and scarves that they looked like woolly mummies. When everyone was unwrapped, Nan introduced me to Beitris, a plump middle-aged woman and Nan's cousin on her mother's side from o'er Erceldowne way; Una, an ancient-looking crone; and Aileen, Una's daughter-in-law, who disclosed a baby beneath her copious wrappings. If Nan had told them that they'd come to weave a magic tartan, they didn't let on. Beitris remarked it was good to be out of the village and the prying eyes of the witch hunters.

"They've taken Bess MacIntire, have ye heard?" Beitris said. "Dorcas MacGreevey accused her of bewitching her husband. If you ask me, it wouldna take a witch to make a man stray from a dried-up stick like Dorcas."

Aileen looked scandalized. "But it's a mortal sin to commit adultery! Surely Dorcas's husband wouldn't do it unless he'd been bewitched."

Una snorted. "Poor lass, ye think that because you're new married and my Ian's fair besotted with ye."

Aileen blushed prettily at mention of her husband's affection for her and jostled the baby, whom she managed to nurse while spinning, a feat I couldn't help but admire. I leaned forward to peer at the baby's plump face, his pink mouth pursing like a sea anemone.

"What a pretty baby," I said. "What's his name?"

"Ian, like his da," Aileen replied, her cheeks turning as pink as her baby's mouth. She leaned forward so I could see him better, and a fold of his swaddling cloth fell over his face. Instinctively, I pushed it away, stroking the velvet softness of little Ian's cheek.

"What a handsome young man," I cooed.

Pleased, Aileen jostled him again and began to sing—the same song that Bill had once sung, the one William's mother sang to him as a baby. Little Ian laughed and crowed at the song and at being bounced up and down. We all laughed, and the atmosphere in the room lightened. When we'd all gone back to our spinning, I noticed a faint shine to our threads— Aileen's was the pink of her baby's cheeks, Beitris's was a vivid yellow, Una's a dark navy, Nan's a forest green. And mine was heather purple—the color of the flowers William brought home for me. I looked around to see if the women noticed, and Beitris winked at me. Una and Nan nodded, but Aileen seemed oblivious, humming her lullaby to baby Ian.

Throughout the rest of November and the beginning of December, the spinners came to the cottage. Beitris always had news of who'd lately been accused of witchcraft and who was rumored to be next. Nan would shake her head and suggest we dwell on cheerier topics. Baby Ian always provided a few items of good news in the form of a new tooth, sitting up for the first time, and, on an overcast day in mid-December, his first step. All our threads turned bright gold when that happened.

Nan observed that the thread glowed after I touched the

spinner. "It's your magic combined with our feelings," she said. But the results were erratic and unstable. The thread would glow for a bit and then grow dull. If the spinner became angry—as Aileen did once when Una chided her not to let baby Ian suck his thumb—the thread might suddenly break. Once, when I was thinking about how William had brushed against me the night before, my thread went up in flames. Even Aileen seemed to notice that, and Nan gave me a guarded look and stayed after the others had left.

I was afraid she'd guessed what I'd been thinking about, but when we were alone she said instead, "It's almost the time of the trial, and we don't know how to make this tartan of yours. We don't have enough thread."

"I'm not even sure we're going about it the right way," I said, discouraged. "The Stewarts in my time were able to weave the tartan out of thin air. They didn't need wool and spinning wheels and looms."

"It's queer you don't know how to do it, seeing as you're the one who taught them."

"The whole thing is queer," I said, exasperated. "How could I have been the one who taught the Stewarts how to make the tartan when they already knew how to make it when I met them?" When I thought about the tangle of time, my thoughts became as snarled as knotted yarn.

"Aye, 'tis a puzzle. But that's not all I wanted to talk to you about. I've noticed the way William looks at you when he comes home, and I saw how you were looking when your thread caught fire. Were you thinking of William—or were you thinking of the creature he became?"

"I don't see how that's your business," I snapped.

Nan gave me a level look. "It's my business because I care about the lad and I would not see him trifled with after all he's gone through. He's been the plaything of one woman already."

I bristled at being compared to the Fairy Queen, but then I met Nan's steady gaze and saw the genuine concern there. In her eyes, I might be just as much a threat to William's happiness as was the Fairy Queen.

"I *was* thinking of him," I admitted. "I've come to care for him. How could I not? He's a sweet boy and he will become the man I fell in love with—and lost."

"But you still intend to go back to your time when you've gotten what you came for, aye?"

"What choice do I have?" I cried more shrilly than I'd meant to. "My friends are waiting for me back in Fairwick."

"Do ye know for sure they are, lass?" Nan asked. "From the stories I've heard about travelers in Faerie, there's no telling when you might come back. Perhaps it will be a moment after you left or a month or a year or two hundred years, like Oisin when he returned to his country to find his castle in ruins and all the folk he knew long dead and gone. And then, when he stepped foot on the ground, he turned into an old man and died."

"I know the story," I said. "Do you think I haven't wondered about that? No, I have no idea what will be waiting for me when I get back to Fairwick—or even if I'll be able to get past the Fairy Queen's curse to get there—but I can't just abandon my friends no matter how I feel about William."

Nan's face softened. "Aye, I thought as much. Then I beg you to be careful not to break the poor lad's heart."

When William came home that night, I did not walk out to meet him. After dinner, I picked up my knitting to keep my hands busy and kept my eyes on my stitches to keep from meeting his gaze. When he asked about the spinning, I told him, "Well, we're going to start weaving tomorrow. We'll have the tartan soon, and then we'll use it to get the angel stone from the witch hunters."

William got up to poke the fire, hard enough to make it nearly go out, then with his back to me said, "Good. I'll start collecting a few lads brave enough to carry your tartan to the castle."

"Are there men willing to risk it?" I asked, knitting faster to resist the urge to knead the tightened muscles in his back.

"There are sons and husbands of the accused," he answered. "What kind of man would not be willing to risk his neck for the woman he loved?"

Without waiting for an answer, William walked out the back door, muttering something about needing to check on the sheep, leaving me to wonder why William was willing to risk his own neck carrying the tartan to Castle Coldclough.

CHAPTER TWENTY-TWO

The next day we set up the loom in the central room, and Nan and Beitris took turns teaching me how to weave while Aileen and Una took turns knitting a blanket for baby Ian and rocking him by the fire.

"He's fretful today," Aileen complained as she handed him over to Una and stood to stretch her back. "He might be cutting a new tooth."

"I could brew him a tonic," Una said, crooning to her grandson.

Aileen sniffed. "Reverend Fordick says if ye say your prayers and attend kirk regular, ye have no need of herb craft and sech witchery. Put yer faith in the Lord, he says."

"That's all very well," Una replied, "but if the Reverend Fordick didna spurn my dandelion tonic, he wouldna look like a man who's not moved his bowels since Whitsunday."

Beitris and Nan laughed, but Aileen looked scandalized to hear the reverend's bowels discussed.

"And I wouldna have ye hanging scissors over his cradle anymore," Aileen added.

"Why, the scissors are meant as a charm to keep the baby being taken by the auld folk—"

"Hish!" Aileen hissed, and took baby Ian from Una. "Reverend Fordick says it's a sin to believe in the fairies. And look what ye've gone and done. You had Ian so close to the fire you've fair smothered him. He's hot as a roasted hickory nut!"

I got up from the loom to peer at baby Ian, moving the blanket aside to look at him. Aileen flinched and jerked him away from me. I was startled. I'd never been sure that Aileen was comfortable with me, but she acted as though I was going to hurt her baby.

"I only wanted to see if he was warm . . ."

"He's weel enough, he's just teething." Aileen gathered Ian to her bosom and he wailed piteously.

Nan got up from the loom and bent over the baby, her face creased with concern. Una's face was also lined with worry, making her look as if she'd aged ten years in the last ten minutes. "I'm afraid it isna just the fever," Nan said. "I'm afraid it's the pest." She tilted Ian's fat baby neck, and I saw that his throat was dark and swollen.

"Don't you be saying such a thing!" Aileen cried, horrified at the thought of plague. "And layin' a curse on him. All he needs is to be home." She was gathering her basket and strapping Ian to her chest under a layer of shawls.

Nan nodded, but she and Una were murmuring to each other in hushed voices, consulting over the best treatment. I wished that I'd paid more attention in science classes. I knew the plague came from fleas, which were carried by rats, but William had gone on a rampage against rats in our first week in the cottage and we were relatively free of them; Nan had also shown me what herbs to use to keep away fleas.

As Aileen opened the door, a gust of cold air entered the

house and swirled around the room. I shivered—it felt like the cold fingers of death searching for their next victim. A brief, uncharitable thought flashed through my head—*better she take the sickness away from here*—but I instantly banished it. "You don't have to go," I said, laying my hand on Aileen's arm. "It would be better to keep him warm here. We could tend to him together."

She flinched away from my touch. "They all say in the village you're a fairy enchantress. Jeannie MacDougal says you've put a spell on William. Just like the spell you've put on my Ian now." She spat in the doorway. "I'll no more cross your threshold, witch, and if Ian comes to harm, the witch hunters will hear of it."

With that, she was gone. I stood, stunned by her speech, watching her swaddled form disappearing in the gray twilight. Although not much past three o'clock, the day was already turning dark, and the heavy gray clouds over the mountains looked swollen with snow.

"I'd best go after her," Una said, joining me at the door. "She'll need help tending to the puir bairn."

"You'll let me know if there's anything I can do," I said.

Una squeezed my hand in thanks but answered, "Nay, lass, you'd best stay out of the village. This sickness will only feed the frenzy of the witch hunt. And it's true what she said about Jeannie MacDougal. She has been spreading stories about you." She shook her head and hurried away, much faster than I would have thought a woman of her age could go, spurred on by her need to aid her grandson. Beitris left, as well, but Nan stayed on.

"I'll bide till William's come home," she told me. "So you'll not have to be alone."

"You can help me, then," I told her, going to the sheep shed for the large iron cauldron that Mordag had used for washing fleece. "We should boil all our clothes and bedding and bathe ourselves."

"In this weather?" Nan complained. "We'll catch our deaths!"

"We'll catch our deaths from fleas and germs," I told her. While we boiled water over the fire and I stripped my bed and tossed William's pallet out into the yard, I proceeded to give Nan a lecture on germs and infectious diseases. She looked skeptical—she who believed in fairies and witches and who had accepted the idea that I came from the future found it hard to believe that invisible "wee beasties" carried sickness from house to house—but she helped me scour the cottage and hang all our clothes and bedding on a clothesline. When I'd pinned the last sheet to the line, I looked up as though someone had called my name. A last bit of sun had sneaked out from beneath the clouds and lit up the western ridge of mountains, turning the sky a fiery red and each line of mountains a different shade of lavender, lilac, and purple. The closest fields were the deep purple of dying heather. Just as the sun sank beneath the farthest ridge, I saw William appear along the closest ridge, his outline recognizable to me even at this distance. *I'd know him anywhere,* I thought, my heart feeling heavy in my chest. Even across the distance of time. Even if he took another shape, as he had when I pulled him from his fairy steed. Or if he became another man, as Liam and Bill had. Would I really be able to leave him when the time came? But I couldn't think of that now. When William reached the house, Nan and I told him about baby Ian.

"Aye," he said grimly, "I heard the plague bells tolling from the village. Things will get even worse now."

"We can help," I said. "If people knew to boil their clothes and burn the ones they can't wash, it might keep the sickness from spreading."

"I could go from house to house to tell them that," Nan said.

"I'll go with you," I said.

Nan and William exchanged a look. "Best you stay here, lass," Nan said. "You're a stranger in these parts, and Aileen and Jeannie are not the only ones who think you're a fairy enchantress."

"Aye," William agreed, "folks will say you're spreading the pest with your strange ways. I'll take Nan and see what we can do to help."

"But what about you?" I cried. "Won't they suspect you of witchcraft if you visit the houses of the sick? And you could get sick!"

"I'm no' so frail, lass," he said, smiling at my concern.

Nan went inside to look through Mordag's pantry for herbs that might relieve illness. William put a reassuring hand on each shoulder and chafed my cold skin. Without thinking whether I should or not, I leaned into him and pressed myself against his broad chest. He was warm and solid, not the insubstantial creature that had come to me in moonlight and dreams, but a flesh-and-blood man. A mortal man who could die of plague just as easily as anyone. "Be careful," I told him, ruing how inadequate the words were. Wasn't there a spell I could cast to protect him? I searched my memory for something out of Wheelock but instead recalled one of that sorcerer's admonitions.

The strongest protection a witch can give anyone is the mantle of her love.

And I did love William. As much as I'd tried not to fall in love with him, I knew now, with the possibility that I would lose him, that I had. I wrapped my arms around him and pictured my love draped over him like a cloak. I closed my eyes and envisioned the threads I'd spun these last two months, each one a different color, each thread a moment we had shared—a meal eaten together, a walk over the hills, his hands over mine when he taught me how to knit.

"Dinna fash yerself," William whispered into my ear. "I'll be safe."

When I lifted my head, I saw that the threads I'd spun were woven together into a luminous multicolored tartan that lay across his chest and over his shoulders like a Highlander's plaid.

I heard a gasp from behind me. Nan had come out of the cottage. She was staring at William. "You've done it!" she cried. "You've woven the tartan!"

When William came home late that night, he told me baby Ian had died and there were three more cases of the pest in the village. Even though I'd seen how sick Ian was, I was shocked. "Poor Aileen," I said.

"She was wailing like a *ban-sidhe*," said a saddened William.

"How about Una?" I asked. "Has she gotten sick?"

"Nay, but she's so stricken with grief I would not be surprised if she fell sick next. Aileen has thrown her out of their house because she said she would not have a witch under her roof."

"She called Una a witch? But Una loved that baby every bit as much as Aileen did."

"Aye, she called Nan a witch, too. I fear it's only a matter of time before others join her. The miller's family has fallen ill, and the miller's wife was heard calling Nan and Una out as witches in the marketplace. Last fall Una accused the miller's wife of giving her short shrift on her grain, and Nan tended their youngest wean when she fell and broke her leg."

"I guess I can understand why the miller's wife might suspect Una if she thought Una had a grudge against her—although I've heard Beitris and Nan complain of the same—but why would she accuse a woman who had helped them?"

"I don't know why, lass, but I know that's the way of folk." William shrugged and sat down at the table, sighing deeply. His shoulders slumped in a way that made him look older. A day in the fields with the flocks had never made him as tired as a few hours in the village had. The glowing tartan was still around his shoulders, but it had grown fainter. When I laid my hands on his shoulders and massaged his knotted neck muscles, the tartan glowed brighter and his sigh turned into a moan of pleasure. "Och, it feels good to be touched. When I left Nan's house, I felt the eyes of all I passed upon me, giving me a wide berth. I could tell they were thinking I carried the pest on me . . ."

The muscles tightened beneath my hands and he flinched away from me. "Ye shouldn't be touching me! I would not carry the pest to you."

I sat and took both his hands in mine. "First of all, Ian was here when he came down with it. If I was going to catch it, I would have caught it from him. But I don't think I will," I added quickly when I saw the look of worry in his eyes. "I traveled a lot with my parents when I was little, and I was vaccinated against a whole host of diseases."

"Vaccinated?" he asked. "Is that some kind of magic?"

"No, it's science, but it *is* sort of magical when you think about it. It's a type of medicine that prevents you from getting certain diseases. I can't be sure that I was vaccinated against whatever this is, but my mother was a witch, so I think she might have strengthened those vaccines with magic. I just don't think I'm going to get this—and neither are you. Before you left today I wove a kind of protective spell around you. I think it will keep you from getting sick. It's the tartan that Nan and I have been trying to weave." I touched the glowing plaid that still mantled William's shoulders. "You can't see it?"

William glanced over both shoulders, looking comically like a dog trying to chase his tail. "Nay, I canna see anything but the dust I picked up on the road . . . only . . ." He held up both arms and looked from one to the other. His right arm, which hadn't been covered by the tartan, was coated with a fine brown dust, but his left arm, which had been covered, was clean.

"It kept the dust off you," I said. "And I think it will keep the pest off you, as well. If only I had been able to make it before. Perhaps I could have saved baby Ian—"

"Do ye think ye could make this sort of cloak for other folks?" he asked, cutting short my litany of regret.

"I don't know," I admitted. I'd been asking myself the same question the whole time he was gone. "The Stewarts in my time are able to protect Fairwick with their tartans. I think that's because they consider the whole village their responsibility. I suppose if I felt that way about Ballydoon . . ."

William snorted. "I wouldna blame ye if ye didna love the place. It's no' been verra friendly."

I shrugged. "Nan and Una have been kind. And Beitris. That's a start. And Nan cares about the village. If she can weave the tartan, then together we may be able to protect more people—and if we can save the village from the pest . . ."

"Then we can take the tartan to Castle Coldclough and destroy the witch hunters," William finished for me.

CHAPTER TWENTY-THREE

We waited until midnight to return to the village. The fewer people who saw us going near the houses of the sick, William explained, the better. Even if we managed to help them, suspicion of witchcraft might fall on us, and if we failed and people died, we'd be blamed for that.

We went first to Nan's house. When we knocked on the door, the curtain over the window twitched, then we heard something heavy being moved away from the door and a bolt being drawn. Finally the door opened and Nan motioned for us to come in quickly. The room was so dark that at first I thought she was alone, and then I made out a crooked old woman huddled by the hearth, bent over her knitting in the faint light of the dying embers. When I got closer, I saw that it was Una. She appeared to have aged ten years since I'd seen her. She was still knitting the blanket she'd been making for baby Ian.

"I'm so sorry about wee Ian," I said. "He was a sweet little boy."

"Aye, he was a braw lad," she said, wiping an eye with the

back of her hand, "but Aileen willna let me sit vigil o'er my own grandson."

"I'm sorry," I said again, feeling foolishly unable to think of any better words.

Una clucked her tongue. "Dinna fash yourself, lass, there wasna anything you could have done."

Una's words, excusing me as if I had only been unable to prevent a jug from breaking, brought tears to my eyes. I looked up at Nan and she saw the look of panic in my face.

"Come down to the root cellar with me and help me mix a draft to ward off the pest," Nan said.

William moved to the seat I had vacated and offered to help wind the yarn that lay in loose skeins at Una's feet. I followed Nan to the root-cellar door, where I looked back to see William holding a skein of yarn like some henpecked husband from a sixties sitcom and Una placidly wrapping the yarn into a ball. I could hear the soft murmur of Una's voice and make out the name Ian repeated like a refrain. While engaging in a mutual chore, Una could more easily share her memories of her dead grandson. I noticed that a bit of the glow from the tartan I'd woven for William was carried along the thread and into Una's hands. The glow seemed to bring some vestige of life and warmth back to Una's face—at least she no longer looked like a corpse.

"The tartan you cast over William is moving to Una," Nan said softly from behind me. "Can ye show me how to cast it?"

"I can try," I said, following Nan down into the cellar. "It starts with the desire to protect someone . . ." I looked at Nan and thought about how all these weeks she'd come to my house to teach me how to spin and weave, even though associating with me—a stranger who'd appeared out of nowhere—would open her to the charge of witchcraft. She had risked her safety for me and to save her village. She cared about

Ballydoon the way I cared about Fairwick. I held out my hands and she held up hers, our fingertips touching. I thought about my friends back in Fairwick and my students and what would happen to them if they were left at the mercy of the nephilim. My hands grew warm and sparks leapt from my fingertips, but they fizzled in the damp cellar air, unable to cross the divide between us.

"Think about those you wish to help," I told Nan.

"Aye, what else do ye think is on my mind—a recipe for sheep dip?"

I laughed in spite of the gravity of the situation, and multi-colored motes danced in the air. I could hear William humming upstairs as he helped Una wind the yarn. It was the lullaby I'd first heard Bill sing, the one William's mother lulled him to sleep with when he was a baby. Now he was singing it to poor bereaved Una. Would Una want to hear a lullaby, I wondered, after losing her grandson? But after a few minutes I heard Una's voice join in, weak and quavering at first but growing stronger. Nan, too, began to hum the tune and then sing, her eyes shining in the dim cellar. I knew she was thinking of her sister but also of William and baby Ian and all the others whom she had loved and lost. I began to sing it, too. I thought of Bill crooning this song more than three hundred years in the future. I thought of the words of a simple child's lullaby connecting the two men—the one I had loved and the one Nan loved—across time. As I sang, the colored threads leapt from my fingers to Nan's—a luminescent skein binding us together.

The glow lit up Nan's face, washing away her fatigue and grief. "It feels . . . *alive!*" she said with wonder, a small, tentative smile beginning. "Sometimes when I am spinning a thread from wool, I can feel the life of the sheep it came from and the sun that beat down on it and the grass and heather it chewed and even the bees that buzzed about the flowers. *This* thread . . ." She spread her hands wide apart, and the threads separated from mine and formed a skein, much like the one that William held upstairs for Una. As Nan pulled her hands in and out, the skein thickened. "*This* feels as if it contains *all* of life in it—the sun and the moon, the barley growing in the fields, the creatures in the wood, each beating heart in the village . . ." As she named each type of life, I saw a new-color thread spring to life. I reached out and pulled a thread of each color from her skein.

"I was able to use my love for William to protect him, but you can use your love for the whole village to protect everyone in it," I said.

"Mmppff." Nan made a soft sound in the back of her throat. "I'm no' so sure I love every soul in Ballydoon, but, aye, I love the place, and I know that if this madness has its way, it willna be the same for many a year. If I could weave a mantle of this stuff to protect all of Ballydoon, I would. But we canna do it just the two of us. Together we make the warp. We need someone to be the weft."

"Who do you think we can trust that would be able to do it?"

Nan tilted her chin up to the floor above us. "Una could, only . . ."

"Do you think she's too grief-stricken over baby Ian?"

"I dinna ken. It isna just the grief. When she knows there would have been a way to save Ian if we had known it afore . . ."

"Do ye think I'm that puir an auld woman as I would begrudge the life of my neighbors because I couldna save one of my own?"

Una's voice came from the top step of the cellar. Nan and I

looked up at her guiltily. Her shape in the doorway was back-lit by a golden glow that I thought was the lamplight behind her, but when she came down the steps she brought the glow with her. The mantle I'd spun for William had spread over her. She walked toward us, her eyes on the threads spread out between us. When she reached us, she held out her hand and cast a thread that intertwined with ours. Another motion pulled it taut. I felt the threads between Nan and me grow heavier and brighter, strengthened by the power of Una's love for baby Ian. Some might let their grief turn them away from the needs of others; some would use their grief to save others. I saw in the fierce determination of Una's face that she would honor Ian by saving who she could. Her grief—and the memory of baby Ian—was our weft.

We worked until dawn, weaving four cloaks made of light. When we were done, we each draped one over our shoulders. William went to rally the men of the village. Nan said we ought to start with the miller's house.

"There are others who are sicker," Una protested, "who live closer and are more worthy."

"We can't go judging who we'll save by how they've treated us," Nan snapped.

"Verra well," Una said, bristling, and quickened her step. When Una was a few paces ahead of us, Nan spoke in a low voice to me.

"There's another reason we must start with the miller's family. Perhaps you do not know that the miller's surname is Brodie."

"No, I didn't, but why—" Then I remembered. "The same Malcolm Brodie who married the first Cailleach?" I asked.

"Aye," Nan replied. "He's no' been a happy man since Katy left him, but he's raised her bairn along with his two other children."

"Mairi?" I asked. "Cailleach's daughter?"

"Aye. I canna say I understand these matters, but if I understand what you told me, then I know that if Mairi dies . . ."

"I'll never be born," I finished for her, my mouth going dry. *Nor my father or his father* . . . "That's why you want to start with the miller's house."

"Aye. You willna be of much help to us if ye vanish into thin air. I only hope we're not too late." She pointed to the small stone cottage that sat beside the river Tweed. The mill wheel that would ordinarily be spinning was still, and there was no smoke coming from the chimney.

Nan knocked on the door, but no one answered. Giving me a worried glance, she turned the knob, and the door yawned open with an ominous creak. Nan and I looked at each other again, but Una squared her shoulders and marched past us, the mantle around her shoulders blazing like a battle flag.

Hers was the only light inside the dim, fetid cottage. The hearth was cold, and heavy homespun cloth hung over the windows. On the floor by the fireplace, the same cloth was draped over a mound that looked like a sack of potatoes. But it wasn't a sack of potatoes. I knew that even before Una knelt and pulled aside the cloth, revealing the blackened face of the miller, Malcolm Brodie.

"Puir lad," Nan said, kneeling beside him. "He never had much luck. He lost two wives and now this had come on him." I heard a low moan. I thought it came from Nan, but she looked up at the sound, as startled by it as I was. It seemed to be coming from directly above our heads.

"The loft," Una said.

The ladder that ordinarily would have led up to the loft

had fallen over. We righted it and Nan started up first. I followed her into the unlit upper story as if climbing into a dark cloud. A *stinking* cloud. The reek was so strong it seemed to have weight—a rank combination of excrement, vomit, and blood. When the odor entered my nose and mouth, it felt as if someone were stuffing fouled gauze down my throat. Taking one hand off the ladder, I drew the glowing tartan over my mouth and nose. The smell receded just enough to make it . . . well, I wouldn't call it *bearable,* but somehow I did bear it. The glow from my tartan illuminated the scene in the loft. Three bodies lay on a straw pallet—the miller's three children, one of whom was my multi-great-grandmother. I stooped—the slanted ceiling was too low for me to stand—over the first one and looked into the blackened face and staring eyes of a teenage girl. Too old to be Cailleach's child, who would be only six now—the age of the girl who lay by her side. They had pushed their pallets close enough so that they could hold hands. Their fingers were still intertwined. The younger girl, Mairi, grasped in her other hand a cloth doll. Her eyes were closed, but when I knelt by her side, they flew open.

I sat back on my heels, startled by those light-blue eyes staring out of the darkened swollen face. Sightless eyes. She had been blinded by the disease.

"Mairi is alive," I called to Nan and Una.

"Aye, and so is Tom, but barely." Nan and Una were crouching over the miller's son. In the glow of Nan and Una's cloaks, his face was soaked with sweat. Nan took a fold of her tartan and used it to brush his tangled hair away from his face. He let out a low moan, his cracked lips working to speak, but all that came out was the sound *Mmmmaaa,* like the bleat of a sheep.

The girl stirred and strained toward the young man, her limbs trembling convulsively.

Mmmmaare . . . Tom moaned again. He was calling Mairi.

"He wants her," Nan said, struggling to keep Tom from getting up, "but he's too weak to move."

"I'll bring her to him." I bent down to gather Mairi in my arms. A fold of the luminous tartan fell as I did. I wrapped it around Mairi, and her trembling stopped. The glowing threads pulsed and molded to her frail body like a cocoon. I felt her relax in the warm folds. *What a strange thing!* I thought. I was holding my own ancestor. As I started to lift her up, though, something tugged her back. The girls' hands were still intertwined. Gently, I disentangled their fingers, but Mairi's hand thrashed in the air like a fish flapping against dry land. It thudded against me with surprising force. Only when I intertwined my own fingers with hers did she stop flailing.

I carried her over and laid her by Tom's side. As I put her down, a length of the tartan separated from the cloak around my shoulders and coiled around Mairi. It seemed to pulse in the same rhythm as Mairi's shallow fluttery breath.

"Mairi," Tom said, turning his head toward the little girl.

"She's here," I told him. "And I think she's getting better."

I wasn't just saying it to comfort him. Mairi *did* look better. The swelling around her throat was going down, the bluish tinge in her skin was replaced by a flush of pink, her breathing had deepened, and the pulse in her wrist had strengthened. The tartan was healing her.

"Wrap your cloak around Tom," I instructed Nan. "There will be enough to surround him and still cover you."

She did as I said, with Una's help, and encircled Tom's body with the glowing cloth. Just as it had with Mairi, the piece of tartan detached itself from Nan's cloak and then fitted itself to Tom's body. Within minutes, color returned to Tom's face and the black swelling at his throat receded.

"Thanks be to the Lord," Una murmured, crossing herself.

I was momentarily surprised by the gesture, as I'd come to think of Una as a witch who followed "the auld ways" instead of Christianity, but then I realized that there was no separation between the two for Una. She could follow the auld gods and the new, recite a psalm in Latin or a spell in Gaelic. It was all the same to her, but I didn't think Reverend Fordick would see it that way.

I called her name, and when she turned to me I saw that, while the lines her grandson's death had carved into her face were still there, now her skin was pink and her eyes had life in them. I took Mairi's small soft hand, still intertwined with mine, and laid it in Una's worn one. Like a bud opening, Mairi's fingers released mine and opened up in Una's hand. A tremor passed over Una's face—a little struggle that I thought I understood. After losing all she had, caring about someone else opened her up to loss—the loss she'd already suffered and the possibility of more loss. I knew because that was what it felt like caring about William after losing Bill. I could feel her resistance in her old crabbed fingers. But then those fingers grasped Mairi's hand with the fierceness of a much younger woman.

"Puir bairn," Una cooed. "Una's here to watch ye now. Close yer een and go to sleep."

Obediently, Mairi closed her sightless eyes. So did Tom. I looked at Nan and she nodded. "It's best ye bide here with the two of them to make sure they're safe," Nan said. "Callie and I will go visiting and see who else is sick."

Una nodded but didn't look up. She was gazing at Mairi's face, stroking her tangled red hair back from her brow. As Nan and I went down the ladder, I heard Una singing softly. "Hush, hush, my bonnie sweet lamb," she sang.

At the bottom of the ladder we were greeted with the body of Malcolm Brodie, my own great-something-grandfather.

"If I'd figured out how the tartan worked before—"

Nan tsked. "Aye, 'tis no use cryin' o'er spilt milk, lass. Not when there are others who need saving. Half the village will have passed by here in the last fortnight to have their grain ground. There'll be others fallin' sick with the pest as we stand here ditherin'."

The thought of more households besieged like this one turned me cold. How would we know where to go first? Would people die while we took care of others? We had no phones or Internet to track the contagion. And what if the pest was carried out of the town while we went from house to house? It could spread over all of Scotland . . .

"There's too much to do for the two of us," I said, turning to Nan. "We need help."

"We can help."

The voice came from the doorway. I turned and saw William, resplendent in his glowing tartan, like an electric Highlander. The plaid wasn't the only thing that was glowing. His skin, hair, but most of all his eyes, burned with a fierceness I'd never before seen. What I saw in his eyes wasn't magic or fairy dust—it was purpose and determination. This was the man he'd been meant to become before the Fairy Queen stole him.

"We?" Nan asked.

"Aye," William replied, giving her a brilliant smile. "I've rounded up a few of the lads." He stood back and Nan and I moved to the door. Outside was a small troop of Ballydoon men.

"What did you tell them?" I whispered to William.

"I told them we were going to save the town," he replied. "They didn't care how we do it."

I turned to Nan, wondering if she was thinking the same thing I was—that if we told these men we were outfitting them with a magical tartan that could heal the sick and protect the well, we opened ourselves up to charges of witchcraft. Nan's forehead was creased, her solemn blue eyes raking the faces of each man. She looked less like the kindly middle-aged woman I'd come to know than a general surveying her troops. Under her stern regard, the men straightened their shoulders and stood up straighter.

"James Russell Gordon McPhee," she called, as if the men did indeed stand across a battlefield from her. A pimply, gawky lad stepped forward, surreptitiously wiping his nose. "Can ye be trusted with the Order of the Plaid?"

"Aye, ma'am."

"And do ye solemnly swear to uphold the honor of the plaid and to never divulge the secrets of the plaid to any save your brothers in the plaid?"

"Nay . . . I mean aye, I swear it."

"Mmppff," Nan huffed, looking at Jamie McPhee dubiously. But then she cleared her throat. "I do hereby endow you with the Order the Plaid." She plucked the edge of her own tartan and measured out an arm's length of it into the air. It separated from her cloak without leaving hers any smaller. Then she swirled the glowing plaid over Jamie McPhee's shoulders. At first he only looked confused, but then a change came over him. He held his head up higher and squared his shoulders. A glow came into his sallow cheeks and dark-brown eyes.

"God bless ye, lad," Nan said softly. Then she moved on to the next recruit. She repeated the procedure with each man. When Nan was done, the shambling motley crew had been transformed into a glowing honor guard. Nan regarded them with a look of fierce pride. "I declare ye all to be brothers in the Order of the Plaid, Stewards of Ballydoon."

I'd thought that the Stewarts I'd met in Fairwick had inherited their ability through family, but now I saw that the origin of their clan came from this small group of ordinary men who were willing to risk their lives to save their neighbors. Somehow it made them seem even nobler.

"There's one more thing I must tell ye," Nan said, the pride in her eyes wavering. "If we do this, the witch hunters will come for us."

A tremor moved through the group, like wind passing over a field of grass, riffling their glowing tartans. It was only right for Nan to warn them of the danger, but I was afraid now that they would back down and disband. But then young Jamie McPhee stepped forward, his tartan glowing like a beacon.

"Then we'll have to go for them first," he said.

CHAPTER TWENTY-FOUR

We split up into two groups—William and me with three of the men, and Nan with four of them—and went from house to house. When we found ailing folk—and we found plenty—we wrapped them in the tartan. When we were done, a man of the newly formed order stood at each corner of the house and stretched his arms out to his comrades on either side, making a protective shield to surround the house.

A few didn't let us in. The MacDougals would not permit us into their fine castle—but we spread the tartan over it anyway. Nor would the Reverend Fordick let us into his manse. When we tried to surround it with the tartan, he came out brandishing a crucifix in one hand and the King James Bible in the other, and he ordered us "sinners, witches, and demons to be gane."

Only those initiated into the Order of the Plaid could see the tartan. The people we helped didn't know how we helped them. We brought salves and herbs and broths. We told them that the men who stood outside their houses were there to make sure no one entered with infection. When we'd gone to every house, we joined back with Nan's group. To cast the plaid over the whole village, she directed us to a spot along the town walls.

When we were done with the protective plaid, William and I walked back to our croft. We were both so tired we didn't talk much at first. William put his arm around my shoulders and I leaned against him, grateful for his strength and warmth. I looked up at his face, which still glowed with the light of the tartan—and with something else. Today I'd watched him tending to the sick, carrying the bodies of the dead to burial, rallying the young men to seek out every household in the town and every ailing citizen. He was no longer the young boy I'd saved from the Fairy Queen. He'd changed shapes then—to a snake, a lion, and a firebrand— but now he'd changed into a man.

"Do you think the town will be safe?" I asked when we got to the top of the hill. For answer, he turned me around to face Ballydoon. For a moment it seemed the sun was rising, even though it was cold winter dusk. Nestled in the folds of the surrounding snow-rimmed hills, the village glowed like a handful of jewels cupped in a velvet cloth. All the colors of the tartan I'd woven with Nan and Una had spread throughout the town, burning like rubies, sapphires, emeralds, and yellow citrines. Rays of the jeweled light soared up into the sky and swirled together like the aurora borealis—beacons in the dark, shielding the town from harm and proclaiming its survival.

But above the town still loomed the ominous shape of Castle Coldclough, like a black crow perched over its prey.

"What do you think they'll do when they see the tartan?" I asked.

"I think they'll come for us—but not until tomorrow, the darkest day of the year. But we'll be ready, because of you."

I felt something cool kiss my cheek and then William's hand brushing a snowflake away from my face. I turned and looked at him, his face glowing in the swirling snow like a lamp lit in a window. Snowflakes clung to his hair and eyelashes. "Not because of me," I said. "You rallied the men."

"Aye, but only because I had your magic tartan."

I shook my head and stepped forward to brush the snow from his hair. "I wove the tartan by thinking of you."

As our eyes met, I felt something click inside me, like a key turning over the tumblers of a lock. Unlocking something. I heard the words of the spell I'd said to become the hallow door. *I open myself to love.* For a second, I wanted to turn the key back. If I loved William, I would open myself to pain. I stepped into William's arms and lifted my face to his. He pulled me to him, crushing me against his chest. His mouth latched on to mine so hungrily that for a moment I thought he *was* the incubus, come to suck the very life out of my flesh. But then I was returning his kiss with equal force. His hands slid down my back and pressed me so hard against him that my feet came off the ground and I thought we would fall, but we didn't. We were surrounded by a cocoon of warmth and light. The tartan I'd woven out of my love— and that he wore, I saw now, out of his love for me—wound around us like a fiery cloud, buoying us above the ground and sheltering us from the now-driving snow. I felt as if we had been lifted above the hills—above Ballydoon and the horrible sickness we'd seen today, far away from the monsters we'd have to face tomorrow, and outside time itself, so that the man I kissed contained the man he would become, the man I'd someday love. But when I looked at him, I saw and loved only William.

· · ·

There was a moment after we came back to the cottage when William paused uncertainly by the hearth, where he usually unrolled his sheepskin pallet, but I held out my hand to him and drew him upstairs to the bedroom. Outside, the blizzard raged, but in our bedroom William and I made our own heat, burrowed beneath soft layers of sheepskin and wool, like two animals gone to ground beneath the snowdrifts. We had been given this brief time together before we would have to deal with the nephilim. In the pale white light of our snow cave, he touched me and looked at me as though he was trying to memorize my body. I traced his long lean back, his hips, his thighs, as if I could read his future in the lines of his body. When he hovered over me, his face blurry in the dim snow-lit room, I felt for a moment that if I took my eyes off him he might vanish. He must have seen the fear in my eyes, because suddenly we were surrounded by the tartan glow. It illuminated his face, and as he came inside me he said, "I'm here with you, lass. I'm not going anywhere else."

We made love surrounded by the tartan glow, the multi-hued threads binding us. By dawn we had woven something new between us, a tapestry of our history together—our past, present, and future—indelibly written on our skin. Outside, the world appeared to have been unwritten by the snow. Staring out the bedroom window past William's bare shoulder as he slept, I entertained the hope that the world had vanished. Ballydoon, Castle Coldclough, Fairwick . . . I would have traded it all for a few more hours here in this room with William, watching the glow of dawn climb up his legs, gild the ridges of his ribs, wash up the curving muscles of his arms, and limn the planes of his face. But when the glow reached his face, he stirred and opened his eyes. He met my gaze and smiled.

"So you're not a dream," he said, reaching out for me.

Halfway to my face, his hand turned deep red. He twirled it in the light, a puzzled look on his face, then turned toward the window. Streams of crimson, yellow, and blue were pouring between the curtains and through the unglazed window. As William rose to his feet, his skin was bathed in light, as if he'd already put on his battle tartan. I watched him walk to the window, feeling as if I was watching him walk across a battle-field.

"They're here," he said, turning back to me, every bit of the boy washed out of his face. I'd lost that boy forever. Today would tell me if I would lose the man, as well.

We quickly dressed without speaking and went down to meet the brigade. There were more men than yesterday—at least two dozen—and they all wore the glowing tartan over their homespun breeks and shirts.

"Did Nan give the rest of you the tartan?" I asked.

Jamie McPhee stepped forward and shook his head. "Nay, we passed it one to the other. The witch hunters came this morning and took Nan and Una. They vow to burn the witches today at sunset. My ma's one of them . . ." Jamie's voice wavered, his brave façade of manhood faltering, but then one of the other men—his brother, I guessed from the family resemblance—clapped his hand on Jamie's shoulder, and the tartan glowed more fiercely. Jamie straightened up, the tears on his face reflecting the blue and crimson glow.

"We'll get her back," Jamie's brother said.

"Aye," William said, "we will not let these monsters take our women. We'll march against the bastards today!"

He pumped his fist in the air, and the two dozen men let out a deafening cheer. Their faces were all streaked with red and crimson now, like the war paint and blue woad tattoos their ancestors the Picts had worn when they went up against the Romans. I had no doubt that they would have stormed Castle Coldclough right this minute, but, remembering the fate of those warriors—and several other doomed Scottish campaigns—I had another thought.

"What say you all come inside and we talk strategy over breakfast?"

Making breakfast for two dozen Scotsmen pretty much exhausted our meager stores, but as I scooped out the last bit of oatmeal from the bin, I realized that if our plan worked I might not be coming back to the cottage. William and I had convinced the men that it made no sense to storm the castle walls, since the whole village had been summoned to the castle for the burning. We would simply join the procession from the village. Once inside the castle walls, the men would form a cordon around the witch hunters. At my signal, they would isolate the other witch hunters and I would take the angel stone from Endicott. Once I had it, I would be able to destroy the nephilim.

"Are you sure you can get the stone off that monster?" William asked when the men left. "The last time you looked at the stone, you fell into a fit. I . . ." His voice faltered. "I thought I was going to lose you then."

The look in his eyes told me the distance we had traveled from then to now—only seven weeks, but it felt as if we had known each other for a lifetime. *For many lifetimes.*

"I'll get it," I said, making myself sound surer than I was. "The stone draws on loss and regret, but I know now that everything I did has led to being here with you, and I wouldn't trade that for anything." *Even if I can't stay.* The unsaid words echoed in the air between us. I knew from the shimmer in William's eyes that he was thinking them, too, but he only nodded and withdrew a soft leather pouch from his pocket. He handed it to me. "I had this made for you—an early Christmas present, since we may not have a chance to exchange presents later."

"I was making something for you," I said, "only it's not done." I went to the basket by the hearth and retrieved the scarf I'd been knitting. It was long enough, but I'd delayed finishing it because I'd somehow felt that, once it was done, I'd really be ready to go. Well, there was no point delaying now. I hurriedly cast off the stitches and tore the undyed yarn with my hands. As I broke the thread, I felt something break inside my chest. I gulped back the sob that had risen in my throat. *You have to be strong for him,* I told myself, as I wove the broken thread back into the scarf with the knitting needles. They were the wooden needles that William had carved for me, and I suddenly couldn't bear to leave them behind. I tucked them into my knotted hair and turned to William to give him his Christmas present—a scarf that had turned as crimson as heart's blood when I'd torn off the last thread.

"Ah, with this on I'll feel like a knight wearing his lady's favor into battle," he said, wrapping the scarf around his neck. "I hope my present to you protects you, as well."

I opened the leather pouch and slid a heavy piece of silver out of it—the Luckenbooth brooch, the two halves made whole.

"I had a traveling silversmith repair it when he passed through town a few weeks ago, so it would keep ye safe when you face that monster."

Bound together, the two hearts formed a tear-shaped loop for the angel stone. I had guessed that the brooch was made as a receptacle for the stone, but I'd wondered why its maker chose the double-heart design. Now, as William pinned the brooch to my cloak just over my heart, I felt a warmth spreading through my chest and I understood. It took two hearts, linked as one, to contain and overcome the grief inside the angel stone.

"Are ye ready?" William asked.

"Yes," I told him. "As long as you're by my side, I'm ready for anything."

An hour before sunset, the village seemed as quiet as it had on the first day I passed through it, when everyone was hiding from the witch hunters. But I soon saw there was a difference. In almost every window hung a small scrap of tartan. The brightly colored bits of cloth waved in the wind like battle flags. Each family that would send one of their sons to carry the tartan to the castle had hung the banner, just as someday British families might hang a Union Jack in the window when their sons went to war. As we passed each house, the door would open and a young man would come out and fall into step behind us. Their mothers and sisters came, too. I even saw Jeannie MacDougal and Aileen join the crowd, their arms linked. By the time we reached the town gate, we had assembled a crowd. When I turned around and saw all their faces bathed in the glow of the setting sun and the tartan, I thought of what Nan Stewart had told me—or *would* tell me in the twenty-first century: *You'll need a village.*

Well, we certainly had one.

The road to the gloomy castle plunged into a deep ravine and then climbed back up the steep, rocky ascent. As soon as I stepped into the abyss called Coldclough, I felt a deathly chill travel from the soles of my feet up my spine and understood why the place had been so named. Strangely, though, the snow that had fallen last night and blanketed the surrounding countryside did not cover the ravine. It had either melted or—I felt with a queasy certainty—dissolved in midair, as if even the snow refused to touch this tainted ground. Certainly nothing grew from the black rocky soil on either side of the cobblestone path. The land looked as if it had been blasted by an atomic bomb. No bird or animal stirred through the wasteland. The only sounds were the footsteps of the villagers following me, but even those were muffled. Halfway down, I was seized by the fear that the entire population of Ballydoon had been swallowed by the gaping mouth of the ravine and I had been left alone.

I spun around and saw that William and the other men had spread their plaid over the crowd to shield them from the unnatural cold. William stepped toward me to envelop me in the tartan mantle, but I held up my hand to stop him and shook my head. Before I faced Endymion, I had to know all I could about the nephilim, and I understood now, as I turned and continued walking into the gorge, that this place held the key to who they were. The cold told a story. It was the cold of expulsion, of being cast out. It was the cold a baby would feel left naked on a mountaintop to die. It was the cold a lover would feel seeing love die in a beloved's eyes. It was the cold I'd felt seeing Bill die. When I reached the bottom of the ravine, my teeth were chattering. The ground was covered with blackened and twisted vines. I knelt and touched one and found it was hard, cold stone. As I stared at them, I realized that the petrified vines had once been honeysuckle vines, like those that grew behind my house in Fairwick, surrounding the door to Faerie.

There had once been a door to Faerie here.

I wrapped my hand around the petrified vine and closed my eyes, searching for a remnant of the connection to Faerie but finding none. This door hadn't just been shut, it had been blasted out of existence, destroyed with a ravaging anger. Images flitted through my brain of beautiful golden creatures—elves—who came through the door and fell in love with humans. But when they lay with human women, the children they produced were horrid leathery-skinned monsters with distorted faces and bat's wings and long claws. The elves took their disgust for their offspring out on the women, destroying whole villages for sport and then abandoning the monsters they had sired. They tried to return to Faerie but were cast out for the crimes they had committed against humans. Trapped, the elves were attacked by their own children, who hated them for making them feel like monsters. The last elf left shed a tear that encompassed all the grief and shame and regret of his entire race—and that tear turned to stone as the door to Faerie was obliterated. The stone was entrusted to a fairy—a doorkeeper fairy—because it was the only weapon that could destroy the nephilim, as they now called themselves. But even a fairy couldn't control the power of the stone unless it was contained. The fey crafted a receptacle made of two linked hearts to corral its power, but then the doorkeeper fairy split the brooch in half to protect the human she had fallen in love with. When she faced the nephilim again, she could not use the stone's power, and the nephilim took it away from her.

That was the stone that Endymion Endicott wore and that I would have to face and seize. The weight of it was so heavy on me that I thought I might not be able to stand up—but then one more vision flickered though my brain and I saw what I must do. I rose slowly to my feet. I was cold all the way through now, down to the bone, but it was the steely cold of resolve. Without looking back, I started climbing toward the castle.

CHAPTER TWENTY-FIVE

The castle was actually a ruin. Fire-blackened walls jutted like broken teeth from the blasted rock. Fragments of statues lay in heaps about the walls, as if they had been pitched from the battlements and they were the petrified remains of the last invading army. The drawbridge was lowered, the portcullis raised, the doors wide open. I walked through into a wide courtyard lit by flickering torches. An enormous pyre stood at the center of the courtyard. Three women were tied to the stake. I recognized Nan and Una and assumed the third woman was Mordag. In front of the pyre, a long scaffold had been erected. More than a dozen more women stood on it, with ropes around their necks. Three cloaked witch hunters stood in front of the scaffold, their faces concealed by beaked masks. The firelight caught a glimmer at the throat of the middle figure. I felt the chill of the angel stone from across the courtyard.

He strode toward me, crossing the space in less time than should have been possible. I heard the flutter of wings behind him and saw their shadows loom on the walls behind the torches. When he was a few feet away he stopped abruptly, the eyes behind the mask riveted on the Luckenbooth brooch. I touched my hand to it to reassure myself it was firmly pinned to my cloak. A spark of static electricity flew off it toward the angel stone. The nephilim tilted his head, like a crow considering a tasty bit of carrion.

"Ah," Endymion crooned, with a smile that set my teeth on edge because he wasn't smiling at me. He was smiling at the villagers behind me. "I see you've brought me another witch."

"They haven't brought me," I said. "They've come with me to save their women and banish you from their village."

Endymion turned his smile on me. "Are you sure, witch? I promised them that if they delivered you to me, I would spare the rest of their womenfolk. And they have delivered you."

I began to tell him he was wrong, but then I recalled how the villagers had waited for me to pass their houses and fallen into step behind me. I had thought they were coming to fight the nephilim, but did I really know that they weren't bringing me as a sacrifice?

I turned to face them. William stood closest to me. He moved toward me, but a woman took a step forward and grabbed his arm. I recognized Jeannie.

"Don't you see," she cried. "William, you've been enchanted by her. Once she's burnt at the stake, you'll be free!"

William shook off Jeannie and faced the crowd, enraged. "You fools!" he shouted. "Do ye think these are men who will honor their word? These are monsters. And how do you think they became monsters? By betraying their own and feeding off the betrayal of others!"

Had they? Had William picked something up in the ravine that I had missed?

I turned back to Endymion, and before his gloating smile could fade I reached out and laid my fingers on the angel stone, reciting as I did a spell I'd learned from Wheelock to ward off regret and grief. *"Abi dolorem! Paenitentiam apage!"* Instead of regret and grief, I felt a swelling of warmth—the love the nephilim had felt for their fathers, a love so strong that when their fathers turned on them, the nephilim offered up sacrifices, first humans and then their own children, in a desperate bid to win back their fathers' love. Those bloody sacrifices had turned them into the monsters they were now.

"And do you believe you are any different, witch?" Endymion sneered. "Wouldn't you sacrifice this whole village for your beloved? And why not? They have turned on you. Sacrifice them, and I will make the Fairy Queen grant you and William safe passage through Faerie."

"You can do that?" The words were out of my mouth before I realized that just asking the question meant I wanted to do it. He smiled, and the angel stone grew warmer under my hand.

"Of course. Every seven years we demand a tithe from the fey in exchange for not slaughtering all the fey in this world. But this year the Fairy Queen planned to renege on our deal and keep William for herself."

"But you took Mordag *before* Halloween night," I pointed out.

"Ah, she was a hostage. We always take one when the tithe is due. The queen knew the price of keeping William. But if we offer to spare her kind until the next tithe is due, then she'll let you and William pass through Faerie. You can take him back to your own time."

I thought of the old stories, like Tam Lin, in which the fairies paid a tithe to hell with a human sacrifice to the devil. But it wasn't to the devil, I saw now; it was to the nephilim, a bribe to keep them from killing their own. It made sense. And if the Fairy Queen had already bargained with the nephilim, perhaps she would again. William could travel back to Fairwick with me . . .

"But Callie will not do that."

It was William, at my side, his hand in mine. I knew without looking at him that if he let me sacrifice his village for his life, he wouldn't be the man I loved, just as he knew that if I sacrificed Fairwick to stay with him, I wouldn't be the woman he loved. I realized in that moment both how much I loved him and that we could not be together. I felt the brooch pulse once over my breast, and the spell echoed in my head. *Abi dolorem! Paenitentiam apage!* As I heard the words, the angel stone dropped into my hand like a ripe apple falling off the bough. Endymion Endicott's eyes grew as wide as apples. Before he could react, I slapped the stone into the brooch. It slid into the space between the two hearts as though it was meant to go there. Energy pulsed through me—a wild, elemental force so powerful I wasn't sure I'd be able to channel it, but then William squeezed my hand and called behind him. "Now, lads!"

At a signal from William, the Stewards raised the plaid field to enclose the circle, trapping the three nephilim in the courtyard. The monsters opened their mouths and made a terrible sound like crows cawing. In answer came the beating of wings above our heads. I looked up and saw the shadow of black wings against the moon. Hundreds of nephilim. So many they soon blocked out the moon. Another signal from William triggered the Stewards to raise their arms. The tartan arced over the courtyard, forming a dome that protected us from the nephilim in the air. We had only to deal with these three.

Facing Endymion, I felt the energy of the tartan thrumming through me. It could be channeled through the stone. I held up the stone and aimed it at Endymion, but at the same moment Endymion gave a signal to the two other nephilim and they dropped their torches on the bonfires. I heard Nan and Una and Mordag screaming. I aimed the stone instead at the nephilim closest to Una. A beam of white light shot out of the stone and struck him. He burst into flame, his screams like the caws of a crow. The second nephilim was running toward me, but I aimed the stone and struck him a glancing blow that set his cloak and hood on fire. He clawed at his burning mask with gloved hands. As the mask burned off, it revealed a face beneath with the same long black beak and glowing red eyes, only now the beak snapped angrily, revealing rows of razor-sharp teeth. The burned-away gloves uncovered long yellow talons, which reached out and grabbed me by the throat, pulling us both into the burning pyre. Searing pain scorched my back, and the stench of the monster's breath—a smell like rotting meat and burning flesh—filled my lungs. He opened his mouth wide as if to swallow me . . . Instead, he seemed to swallow himself, dissolving into black ash that coated me with a sticky resinous film. I blinked in the black rain and saw above me another figure cleaving the flames, but this was not a nephilim. I had seen this creature before—a dark-cloaked man riding a wave of white moonlight, just as my demon lover had come to me. William strode through the fire and lifted me in his arms, his tartan cloak shielding us. I looked back only long enough to see two Stewards wade through the flames, their cloaks protecting them as they rescued Nan, Una, and Mordag.

When I turned back, Endymion stood before us. The fire had burned away his cloak and gloves, revealing eerie white flesh that glowed with a bluish light. Unlike the other two nephilim, Endymion's face was beautiful—the face of an angel. His unfurled wings were golden in the firelight. *How cruel,* I thought, *to be granted such beauty but still be a monster in your parents' eyes.*

I felt William's muscles tense. He slowly lowered me to the ground, placing me beside him. I clenched the stone in one hand, William's hand in the other. Endymion smiled.

"What a worthy opponent you've turned out to be," he crooned, his voice gentle as a lover's. "I look forward to meeting you again."

Then, before I could aim the stone at him, he rose straight into the sky, his great wings beating the air into a maelstrom of ash and sparks. The tartan dome, weakened by the breaks in the line as the Stewards tended to the accused witches, shattered. A rain of multicolored sparks drifted to the ground. I stared up, waiting for another attack, but nothing came. The sky above was clear, the full moon pouring white light into the courtyard like cool water to bathe our burns and clean away the ash. I looked at William. His hair, singed from the fire, stood up in wild peaks, his face blackened with ash and streaked with blood. He resembled one of the wild blue-painted Picts that had defended Scotland from the Romans centuries ago. Like a warrior. I glanced around the courtyard and saw that the Stewards and the villagers were all stained with ash and blood. Una and Nan were tending to them. The glow of the tartan was still on them, and Nan was using it to bind wounds and heal burns. She looked up from treating a gash on Jamie McPhee's forehead and caught my eye. She administered a quick stitch in glowing blue thread, told Jamie he was a "braw lad," and came toward us.

As she approached, her eyes were on my hand that held the stone. I still held William's hand in the other. She reached out her hand for mine, and I laid it in hers. She gently unpried my fingers from the brooch. I heard William gasp. As

I'd used the stone, the silver of the brooch had heated up and burned my skin. The silver was embedded in my flesh. Nan lifted the brooch as gently as she could but not so gently that it didn't hurt like hell. William squeezed my hand as I bit back a scream. Seared into my palm was the pattern of the two interlocked hearts. Nan laid her hand over mine and emitted a healing green light, which smelled like mint and felt like a balm. When she moved her hand, the pain was gone, but the mark was still there.

"Aye," Nan said, "some marks are worth keeping." She lifted her eyes from my hand to my face. "Remember us when you look on that. The Stewards of Ballydoon will always remember you. You've given us a way to protect our village. And now that ye have the stone, you can save yours."

She squeezed my hand again, bathing it once more in her healing green light, then nodded, her eyes shining, and turned to go back to tend her village. *As I must do now.* The green balm could do nothing to ease the ache I felt in my heart knowing that. I turned to William.

"I know ye must go," he said. "Do you have to leave from a particular place?"

"No," I said. "I'm the door, so I can open a passage anywhere. But I don't want it to be here. I have an idea of where it should be. Will you come with me?"

William smiled and touched my face. A bit of the red from the tartan warmed my cheek. "Whither thou goest, I goest."

We walked out of Castle Coldclough and down into the blasted ravine.

"You still have to get past the Fairy Queen," William said as we walked. "She cursed you, too, remember."

"Yes," I said. I hadn't let myself think about that until I had the stone, but now I did. "I think I can convince her to remove the curse. I understand now that the tithes she's been paying have been to save her people from the nephilim. But when she sees that I have the stone and that I can protect her people in the future, she'll have to see reason."

William made a skeptical noise—he knew the Fairy Queen better than I did—but he didn't argue. He seemed to be working something out in his head. I was, too. If the Fairy Queen was willing to bargain to let me through Faerie, mightn't she be convinced to let William through, too? But if I brought him with me to Faerie and she didn't let him into my time, then he'd be trapped in Faerie again. I couldn't take that chance. It was better to leave him here in Ballydoon, where he was safe. Perhaps he had also figured out the same thing in his head. We walked in silence to the bottom of the ravine, where the petrified vines twisted together like a nest of snakes.

"Here?" William asked. "It isna a verra pretty place."

"No," I admitted, "but it once was. And it can be again." I let William's hand go and took a step back. I closed my eyes and uttered the words I'd used when I first tied myself to the door. *Cor mea aperit, tam ianua aperit. As my heart opens, let the door open.* I felt a swelling in my chest . . . and an ache. It felt different than when I'd last done the spell. It hurt—as if to open the door I had to break my heart open.

Because you're leaving him.

I opened my eyes. A small white light was glowing amid the blackened and petrified vines.

"I don't want to leave you," I said. The light wavered like a candle in the wind.

"I know you must go back," he said, taking my hand. The light grew into a pillar and then swelled into an arched doorway. As its light touched the petrified vines, they turned green and flowers bloomed. The air was heavy with the scent of honeysuckle, the scent that had first brought him to me.

"I love you," I said.

William smiled and shook his head. "You love the man I will become . . ." He bent his head to mine and kissed me on the cheek, whispering in my ear, ". . . And so I must become that man." Then he wrapped his arms around me and stepped us both through the door.

CHAPTER TWENTY-SIX

We went straight into Faerie, finding ourselves in a flower-bedecked meadow under a lilac sky. Lambent gold light lapped over everything, but there was no visible source for it—no sun, no moon. It may have been dawn or twilight. It was peaceful and beautiful, but I knew that appearances here could deceive.

"William, what were you thinking? The Fairy Queen said she'd kill you if you came through Faerie again." I anxiously looked around for Fiona, wondering if I could get William through Faerie and into Fairwick. The last time I'd gone through the door, I hadn't paused in Faerie. That hope was destroyed, though, when I saw a procession climbing the hill toward us. It was too late.

The procession was led by Fiona the Fairy Queen and King Fionn on horseback. Behind them was a host made up of myriad creatures: satyrs and centaurs; winged blond Valkyries; a great stag with gold-tipped horns, a herd of deer in his wake; women with feathered legs and the faces of owls; short white-bearded men with red caps, looking like an army of garden gnomes. Even more frightening creatures lurked on the edges of the crowd and in the woods bordering the meadow. Rat-faced goblins and pointy-eared imps chattered and hissed but scared me less than the Fairy Queen, whose emerald-green eyes were fastened on William. I moved to stand in front of him, but he tightened his grip on my arm and held me back. "It's all right, lass," he hissed under his breath. "I know what I'm doing."

But no whisper was low enough to escape the Fairy Queen's ears. In an instant she was upon us, swooping down from her horse and over the grass with the preternatural speed of a hawk, a long sharp-nailed finger an inch from William's throat.

"Didn't I tell you, *boy*, that if you came back to Faerie I'd pluck out your eyes and heart?"

"Fiona," I said, the anger pulsing in my voice with the same force as the blue vein that throbbed beneath William's skin just where the Fairy Queen's nail was poised. "Let him go."

Her green eyes slid toward me with the malevolent stealth of a snake. I'd known the Fairy Queen in Fairwick and had found her formidable, but I'd never thought she was evil. Perhaps she'd gained civility in her long years living among mortals. This Fairy Queen, though, looked very much as if she would pluck out William's eyes, eat his heart, and then happily dine on my spleen.

"Who are you to address me by my name and make demands of *me*? I cursed you, too!"

"I'm the doorkeeper," I said, "and I have *this*." I held up the Luckenbooth brooch.

The green eyes widened as they took in the angel stone. She took her finger away from William's throat and made a grab for it, but I swept it out of her grasp, stepping back to get her farther from William. Instead of running away, though, he

254 · JULIET DARK

moved to my side and addressed the Fairy Queen. "Aye, Cailleach found a way to destroy those bastards."

254 · JULIET DARK

moved to my side and addressed the Fairy Queen. "Aye, Cailleach found a way to destroy those bastards."

While William's pride in me was heartening, I hoped he wouldn't make the Fairy Queen even angrier.

"And did she destroy them all?" Fiona asked nastily.

"No," I admitted. "Some got away. But the rest are in Fairwick, back in my time. Let William pass and we'll destroy them there. You won't ever have to pay a tithe again. I'll restore the door. You'll be able to pass between the worlds . . ." I hesitated, not entirely sure that I wanted to let Fiona back into my world after what I'd learned she'd done to William and other unfortunate young men before him.

"You think to dictate terms to *me*?" she thundered.

"Are you so reluctant to give up your human boys?" The question came from golden-haired King Fionn. He stood even taller than Fiona and had the same fiercely green eyes.

Fiona turned to him, her emerald eyes sparking. "As if you haven't had your own human lovers!" Although she snarled the words, they lacked the conviction she'd had when addressing William and me. She was either afraid of the king or in love with him, I couldn't tell which. Either way, I didn't want to be in the middle of their lovers' spat.

"We want to return to my time and get rid of the nephilim. Surely that is in your interest, as well."

"But it's not his time," Fionn pointed out, glaring at William. "We can't let humans use Faerie to move through time. It frays the fabric of both worlds."

I looked at William, who was glaring at Fionn. "Then let him go back to his time," I said, my voice cracking. It didn't seem fair that I'd have to make this sacrifice twice, but I had to return to Fairwick and I couldn't bear to see William trapped again by the Fairy Queen.

"*No!*"

At first I thought the word came from King Fionn, it was so loud and authoritative. But it was William who had bellowed it. I turned to him, confused.

"No," he said more softly, returning my look with a sad but level gaze. "I won't go back. If I do, then I'll never become your incubus, or Liam, or Bill, the man you fell in love with."

I stared at him, desperately trying to untangle the threads of time and refute his logic. "We don't know that's how time works," I said finally. "The Stewarts had the plaid in my time, but I still hadn't gone back to give it to them."

"As doorkeeper, you are not bound by the rules of time," Fionn said. "But William is. Unless he stays in Faerie and becomes the incubus, you will never meet him and never fall in love with him."

The thought of never meeting Liam or Bill made me feel faint, as if I were standing at the edge of a vertiginous drop. I *was*. The maw of time was opening up to swallow me. It was one thing to give up William and another to give up ever having known him. But if it meant sparing him hundreds of years in slavery, I would have to make that sacrifice. I opened my mouth to tell him so, but he placed a finger on my lips.

"No," he said again, with the same firmness as before but a shade more gentleness. "No, Callie. This is why I came with you. I knew what it meant. I had to come back so I could become the man you fall in love with. Knowing that you're waiting for me at the end, it will be worth it." He slid his fingers from my lips to my cheek and placed his lips where his fingers had been. His kiss tasted like heather and honeysuckle. Like the first breath of summer that had brought Liam to me and the last smoky sigh of fall. It tasted like eternity, but it was over too soon. He pulled back from me and looked into my eyes. "I will see you again," he said. Then he looked past me and strode toward Fiona and Fionn.

I watched as he stopped before the king and queen of Faerie. He straightened his back, legs apart in a stance I'd seen him take when faced with a balky ram. "If I stay, you'll let Callie pass through Faerie," he said—not a question but a demand. The queen glared at me, but at a look from King Fionn she agreed to William's terms.

"I have one more condition," William said. Then he crooked his finger to indicate they should bend their heads to hear what he had to say.

I watched in awe as the royal couple inclined their heads as one to listen to William's whisper. What could his condition be? I wondered, jealously hoping it involved *not* having to have sex with Fiona. But that couldn't be it, because both Fiona and Fionn nodded. Fiona looked up and smiled.

"Very well," Fiona said.

"It will be so," King Fionn proclaimed with all the majesty of royalty.

"We've agreed to your lover's terms, doorkeeper," Fiona said. "You are free to return to your time. You have only to walk over that hill and you will find yourself back in your time among your Fairwick friends."

She pointed behind me, but I didn't turn. I was waiting for one last glimpse of William, but as he turned my way he began to fade. Fiona and Fionn were dissolving, too, but I kept my eyes on William. I heard voices behind me, some that I recognized, but still I didn't turn. I held William's eyes until their green-gold had dissolved into the green flower-filled meadows of Faerie. *I will see you again,* he'd said. And he would. But would I ever see him again?

"Callie? Cailleach McFay?" The voices came closer and called my name. Wiping the tears from my eyes, I turned to face my friends—and a future without William.

All my dear friends who had gone back to Faerie when the door was closing last summer were coming over the hill. I saw Brock Olsen and Dory Browne walking hand in hand with a troop of brownies, Elizabeth Book and Diana Hart among a herd of deer—and one bear, whom I recognized as Liz's familiar, Ursuline—Casper Van der Aart and his partner, Oliver, with a contingent of gnomes, and many other townspeople whom I recognized and who now crowded around me, clapping me on the back and hugging me. I let the tears that had been brimming in my eyes fall, the loss of William mingling with the joy of this reunion.

"You found a way to open the door!" Liz cried. The dean had changed since I'd seen her last. Her gray hair had turned into a shimmering silver. Her skin was unlined and glowed like rose-tinted porcelain. She wore a long gown of glittering material that changed color as she moved from mauve to violet and she looked at least ten years younger than when I'd seen her last. Even Ursuline looked sleeker and shinier. Dwelling in Faerie agreed with them.

"It turns out I *am* the door," I said. "Forging a blood bond to the door last summer was the first step in becoming the door."

"I knew Callie would figure out a way!" Diana crowed, hugging both Liz and me at the same time. Diana had also been transformed during her time in Faerie. The demure innkeeper who had collected animal figurines and run the Fairwick Spinning Circle and Knitting Club had reverted to a wilder self. Her chestnut hair stood up in spikes around a wreath of twisted rowan branches and russet leaves. Her freckles had bred and multiplied, turning her skin into the dappled hide of a young fawn. She wore a skimpy green tunic over coltish brindled legs, looking a bit like a feral Peter Pan. I found it difficult to imagine her and Liz fitting back into their respective innkeeping and administrative roles. But apparently they didn't.

"So we can return now?" Liz asked.

"She's been worried about the college," Diana told me.

"No more than you've been worried about your inn," Liz countered. "How are they? The inn and the college, I mean. And Fairwick, of course. Did you drive out the nephilim?"

I stared at Liz and Diana, wondering how I could describe the awful changes the nephilim had wrought—Diana's inn turned into a frat house, the college ruled by nephilim and patrolled by trows . . .

"Things are pretty bad back there," I admitted. "I came to Faerie to get this"—I held out the angel-stone brooch—"but I had to go back in time to get it." I blinked away tears, thinking of William. Liz and Diana gave each other a worried look, then I felt a sympathetic hand on my shoulder. I turned to find Brock Olsen, my old handyman and Norse divinity, towering over me. Was it possible he had gotten taller in Faerie? He'd certainly grown more imposing. He was dressed in a leather tunic and boots and a fur cloak, his scarred but handsome face both graver and stronger. Beside him was Dory Browne, in a homespun dress and peaked cap, looking tiny but no less fierce. Brock cradled my hand in his and looked at the angel stone. "You had to give up William to get it, didn't you?" he said softly.

"How did you know?"

"It was a story Dolly told me once." Dolly was Dahlia LaMotte, the romance novelist who'd lived in Honeysuckle House and drawn her inspiration from my incubus. "She said it was the one story she couldn't write down, because it hadn't happened yet." He smiled. "I never quite understood that."

"Dolly could be a little cryptic," Dory said, with just a hint of jealousy for the woman Brock had once been sweet on.

Brock squeezed my shoulder before lifting my arm, displaying for all to see the hand that held the angel stone. The crowd gasped at the sight. The golden light of Faerie was filling the stone, making it glow like a beacon.

"Callie has sacrificed much to get this stone," Brock roared. "Are you ready to fight by her side to take back our town?"

A great shout swelled from the crowd. I looked around at the faces of my friends and felt a corresponding swelling in my heart. This was what William had given me. I couldn't let that sacrifice be in vain. As my heart swelled, I felt the door opening within and around me.

"Let's go," I said.

CHAPTER TWENTY-SEVEN

From Faerie we stepped straight into a firestorm. For a moment I thought I'd gone back to Castle Coldclough and was fated to be burned at the stake. The sky above was a roiling mass of red sparked with blue and yellow, the air filled with smoke and shouting. Great black shapes bulged through sheets of flame, roaring like fire-breathing dragons. Through the smoke I glimpsed dark-robed figures shooting bolts of light at the swooping monsters. The monsters responded as if stung by mosquitoes—annoyed but undeterred. One dived down and landed on a black-robed figure, who screamed and flailed at the creature. The figure's hood fell away and I recognized Jen Davies. I ran to help her, but before I could reach her, a large woman stepped between the monster and me, aimed a shotgun at the creature, and fired.

"Touched by an angel, my ass!" roared the woman, whom I recognized despite the ash covering her face: Moondance. "I'll touch you, asshole!" She fired again. The nephilim fell off Jen and hissed at Moondance with a mouth full of sharp teeth. It dug its claws into the ground and tensed its leg muscles to spring. I aimed the angel stone at it, directed my will, and unleashed my ire. A white beam shot from the stone with so much force that I staggered backward, but I stayed on my feet long enough to watch the nephilim explode in a burst of black ash.

"Holy shit!" Moondance swung around, her face now streaked with the ashy remains of the nephilim, her eyes wide at the sight of me. "Callie's back, and she brought a laser gun!"

"Sort of," I admitted. "I've got recruits, too."

Diana knelt beside Jen, healing a gash on her arm. Liz was hugging Ann Chase. All around the circle, the people I'd brought back from Faerie were greeting their friends. "How many have you got in the circle?" I asked Moondance.

"Nine, including myself. Two recruits joined us, and there are the Stewarts outside still holding back the nephilim, but the bastards have been picking off the Stewarts to weaken the field—"

"Is that McFay?" a hoarse voice croaked behind me. I turned and found myself crushed in a bear hug by a man in tattered burned clothing and a blackened face. Only by his voice did I recognize him as Frank. "Damn it, McFay, where'd ya get the light saber? Have you got an army of Wookiees, too?"

"Sorry, just me," I told Frank, holding him at arm's length. His face was covered with soot, and it appeared as if his eyebrows and half his hair had burned off. Blood trickled down from a cut over his eye, and when he stepped back I saw he moved with a limp. But otherwise he seemed okay, nearly recovered from his run-in with Duncan Laird. "How many nephilim are there?" I asked, looking up. I saw now that the roiling red dome was made up of the Stewarts' tartan field. They must have thrown the tartan around the glade to protect me when I came back through the door, but they were being attacked mercilessly.

"Soheila counted thirteen before she went back up there," said Frank.

"Soheila's up there?"

"She assumed her bird shape. She's like this super-owl!" Frank grinned. "It's awesome, but I don't think she can kill them, just distract them. If we don't get rid of them soon—"

A hair-raising shriek cut off his words. Above us, silhouetted black against the tartan field, two winged creatures fought like shadow puppets in a play. An enormous owl creature dug its talons into the neck of a nephilim. It was the nephilim who had shrieked. I raised the angel stone and tried to aim it at the nephilim but couldn't get a fix on it without the risk of hitting Soheila.

"Can I see that thing for a minute?"

I handed the angel stone over to Frank. He turned it over, held it up to the light, then closed his eyes and stroked its surface with his fingertips.

"Are you going to taste it next?" I asked.

He opened his eyes and grinned. "This is a very powerful gewgaw you've got here, McFay, but essentially it's a focusing device, a kind of prism that collects magical power and concentrates it."

"That's what I did with the Stewards in Ballydoon," I said. "If I use the energy of our Stewarts now, the field will collapse."

"We can add the power of the witches' circle, but we'll have to time it just right," Frank said, handing the stone back to me, "and get Soheila out of the sky first. You stay here and fend off any of the bastards who get through the field. I'm going to have a word with Mac about sending up a flare to Soheila."

Frank was gone only a minute before a nephilim forced his way through the field and landed on Phoenix. I aimed the angel stone and blasted the creature into dust. Brock appeared to help Phoenix up from the ground, and she preened and fawned over him as if he'd been the one to save her from the attack. I swung around in the circle, keeping an eye out for any breaches. I was startled to see Adam Sinclair, but before I could aim at him, I watched him and Leon Botwin repel a nephilim trying to wedge through a crack in the plaid. When they were successful, the boys high-fived and grunted, *"Oo-rah!"* So my speech to the Alphas had an effect. Heartened, I continued my patrol until Frank returned.

"Okay, here's the plan," he shouted, grabbing my hand. "We're gonna join hands, but not to sing 'Kumbaya.'"

A circle was hastily formed. When Brock Olsen grabbed my other hand, I felt a jolt of power. The angel stone in my right hand pulsed and burned like a hot coal.

"Hot damn!" Frank shouted. "That baby's ready to blow! On the count of three, the Stewarts will drop the plaid and we'll blow them out of the sky. Ready?"

The circle cheered as one. Frank squeezed my hand. "One . . ."

"Frank," I whispered, "what about Soheila?"

"She knows to get out of the way," he said between gritted teeth. "Two . . ."

I looked up and saw the owl creature winging upward, then one nephilim detached itself from the throng to pursue it. I was going to tell Frank, but it was too late.

"Three!" he shouted. The plaid field melted to the ground in a shower of red, green, yellow, and blue streamers. Frank raised my hand and I concentrated all my power—and all the power of the circle—through the angel stone. A wide beam of white light shot into the sky. Inside the beam, winged shapes writhed and tumbled toward the ground, their delicate wing bones briefly etched against the surrounding glare. I smelled

incense and heard a screaming inside my head. I momentarily felt the nephilims' pain—not just their dying but all the hurt of their long lives, the horror of their fathers, the expulsion from their love, their love of humans twisted into hate because it was their human side that had turned them into monsters. For the briefest moment, I wanted to lower the angel stone and save them—surely there was some way for us to live in peace—but it was too late. Ash fell through the sky like black snow. My arm felt as if it weighed a hundred pounds. I dropped to my knees, dragging Frank down with me. I saw his lips shouting my name, but I couldn't hear him. The nephilim's dying screams had deafened me. Then I saw Frank look up and his eyes filled with terror. The sky darkened, and a great winged creature swept down through the ash. It slammed straight into me, claws raking my throat, wings beating my face. The angel stone dropped from my hand. Bright-blue eyes glared at me out of a blackened face. It was Duncan Laird.

You have destroyed my brothers, I heard his voice say inside my head. *But after I've destroyed you, there will be no one to open the door between the worlds. All your friends will die.* His claws dug into my throat, and my vision blackened. In that darkness, I glimpsed William's face as I'd last seen him in Faerie. He'd sacrificed himself so that I could return. I couldn't let his sacrifice be in vain. I summoned all the strength I had and pulled myself out of the darkness, shoving Laird away. I felt his surprise at my power—and then felt something else: Frank pressing the brooch into my hand.

"Hold on, McFay, and use the damned stone." Over Frank's shoulder, I saw Duncan grappling with another winged creature, but this second creature had the body and face of a woman. *Soheila.* She fought him with all her strength, but one wing hung broken by her side, and her face was slashed. Duncan lifted one wing bristling with razor barbs, just about to bring it down on Soheila. I raised the angel stone and aimed. The white-hot light struck the razored wing, lighting each feather tip with flame and illuminating the bony structure beneath the skin. Veins of fire ran through the wing toward Duncan's heart. I could see his entire skeleton light up like an X-ray, but before the power could dissolve him, he twisted into a knot. His hands tore at his own flesh. There was a horrible rending sound and a scream that vibrated in my own bones. Sparks flew into the air along with a flurry of feathers that rose, flaming, to the sky before drifting down to the ground as ash. When the blizzard cleared, Duncan stood at its center, one soot-stained wing arched over his head like a mantle. He had torn the other wing off to survive the attack. I was so shocked by his self-mutilation that it took me a moment to aim the stone again. Too late. He had already bolted from the circle and vanished into the woods.

CHAPTER TWENTY-EIGHT

"He can't go far with only one wing," Soheila said, limping over to me, her own wing dragging in the dust. "I'll go after him."

"Nothing doing," Frank said. He reached out and gingerly stroked Soheila's wounded wing, his gruff face utterly transformed by wonder and awe, which he spoiled the next moment by asking, "Should we, like, take you to a vet?"

Soheila swatted him with her good wing. "I'm fine," she said, "but I can't transform back as long as this wing's broken."

"I can mend it," Diana said, running her fingers gently over Soheila's broken wing. A golden glow flowed from her fingers—Aelvesgold. Diana was using the magical elixir of Faerie to heal Soheila's bones. Soheila's face relaxed, and she let out a long sigh that blew through the glade. I looked around and saw that all the folk who'd returned with me from Faerie were using the stores of Aelvesgold they'd amassed there to heal those who'd remained in Fairwick. Liz Book was tending a gash on my grandmother's face, Brock was setting Leon Botwin's broken arm, and Dory Browne and her troop of brownies flitted among the Stewarts, tending the many burns they'd incurred holding the plaid against the forest fire—a fire that still smoked beyond the glade.

"How long was I gone?" I asked Frank.

"A couple of hours," he answered. "But it was a fucking long couple of hours."

His answer made me so dizzy I had to sit down. I'd spent almost two months in Ballydoon, but only a few hours had passed here in Fairwick. I supposed I should feel lucky. Fairy lore was full of travelers to Faerie who spent a night dancing with the fairies, only to come back and find they'd been gone a hundred years, all their family and friends long dead, and when they set foot back on the ground, they turned to dust and bones. Instead, I felt as if the last eight weeks I'd spent with William had turned to dust.

"You look like you've been sucker punched, McFay," Frank said. "I have a feeling you had to pay dearly for that stone."

I looked at the angel stone in my hand, which was still glowing. "Yes," I answered. "And I'm not the only one who paid for it."

"Well, then," Frank said. "We shouldn't let it go to waste. Let's go track down that bastard Laird and make him pay."

Healed and recharged by Aelvesgold, the Stewarts and the witches' circle joined the new recruits from Faerie to march back to the campus, where we all thought it likely Duncan would go.

"He's been running this show out of the dean's office," my grandmother told me as we walked toward campus. "He'll go there to destroy records of other nephilim nests around the world, to make it harder for us to track them down."

"Other nests?" I asked, unsnagging a vine from Adelaide's

sleeve. I noticed as my arm brushed against hers that she was trembling. Although I'd seen Liz tending Adelaide's wounds with Aelvesgold, my grandmother looked older and frailer than I'd ever seen her before. She still had the power to make me quake when she scolded me, though.

"Yes, did you think this was the nephilim's only one? Fairwick was to be the center of their dominion, but they've nests in a dozen locations around the world. It will take a lot of work to root them out . . ." Her voice shook. "We should never have allowed them to get a stronghold here."

I took my grandmother's hand. Startled, she looked up at me. When had she grown so small that she had to look *up* at me? "If the Grove and people of Fairwick work together, we'll find them," I told her. "I think there might be hope that we can reform the younger ones. Look at the Alphas. Who'd have thought they'd come to our side tonight?"

"That's your doing," Adelaide said. "You have a knack for bringing people together. Your mother did, too . . ." Adelaide paused, her chin trembling. "When she married your father, she told me that the only hope the witches and the fey had in this world was to unite."

It was the first time I'd ever heard my grandmother speak of my mother without criticizing her—or lamenting her marriage to my father.

"I lost her because I wouldn't see how right she was—or how much in love with your father she was. I hope I'm not too late with you."

"You're not," I said, squeezing her hand.

We came out of the woods behind my house. All the lights were on and I found my students on the back porch, drinking cocoa.

"There you are, Prof!" Nicky cried, jumping up from the porch when she saw me, her face flushed with excitement. "We didn't want to leave the house until you came back, what with the forest fire. We hosed down your roof and yard to keep it from catching fire."

"That was considerate of you—" I began.

"It was the Alphas' idea," Ruby Day broke in. "They saw the fire first and called the fire department. Atticus here"—she dragged a young man, whose Alpha House shirt was torn and covered with soot, off his lawn chair—"formed a hose brigade to protect all the houses on Elm Street. He even rescued Mrs. Sprague's Siamese cat from a burning tree and found this guy." She gestured toward a table loaded with Halloween treats. It took me a moment to notice that Ralph was curled up inside a plastic jack-o'-lantern. One of his ears had been chewed off and he was sleeping deeply, but then I recalled that he often went into a sort of hibernation state in order to heal. I stroked his back as I listened to the rest of Ruby's story, which had shifted locale now to Shady Pines.

"One of the Alphas who works there called to tell us the fire was threatening the home, and some of us went down there," Ruby said.

"We thought we'd gotten everyone out," Atticus said, "but then I noticed that Mrs. Goldstein wasn't there, and Ruby ran back in to get her." He grinned proudly at Ruby, who blushed and breathlessly continued the story of their exploits.

"We helped the fire department downtown. We managed to save most of the stores, but a couple of abandoned store-fronts went up and the tattoo shop, like, exploded."

"That's right next to Fair Grounds," Adam Sinclair shouted, pushing through the crowd. I wondered why Adam would care about the town's coffee shop, but then I saw Leon Bot-win trailing close behind him and understood that the two boys had forged a bond fighting together. "Is Fair Grounds okay?"

"The awning went up, but we hosed it down," Atticus answered, and then added with a sly grin, "Hey, we know how much you like your macchiatos, bro." The Alphas then reverted to teasing each other. There was a lot of arm punching while the girls rolled their eyes.

"What about the campus?" I asked.

The question immediately sobered the students. Scott Wilder, who had remained unusually quiet and wide-eyed throughout his classmates' stories, answered. "We tried to get onto campus to help, but all the gates were locked. So we went through the woods and reached the field house just as it caught fire."

"We knew the security guard was probably asleep inside," Flonia continued, looking proudly at Scott, "so Scott went in to rescue him. He dragged him out, but we weren't able to resuscitate him." Flonia squeezed Scott's arm, and a tear carved a path down his soot-stained face. I saw now that his eyes looked so wide because his eyebrows had been singed off. "The EMTs said he must have had a weak heart."

"Trows are very sensitive to smoke," Liz whispered as she came to stand beside me. Then, raising her voice, she told Scott, "It was brave that you tried to save him. You've all been very brave," she told the whole group. "I am so proud of all of you."

"Dean Book!" Nicky exclaimed. "You're back! Are you taking back the college?"

"Well . . ." Liz began.

"Because you're an awesome dean," Scott said. The rest of the students echoed Scott's sentiments, even though some, like the Alphas, hadn't gone to Fairwick when Liz Book was dean.

"Yes," Liz said, her face glowing. "I am here to take back the college."

The students greeted her announcement with hoots and shouts, which were echoed by the witches, fairies, and humans who had fought in the glade and who had been lingering on the edges of the woods while we talked to the students. They came forward now, though, and I saw the students' eyes widen at the sight of pointy-eared brownies, a winged Soheila, and club-wielding gnomes.

"Wow!" Scott exclaimed. "I always suspected you teachers got up to some crazy-ass shenanigans when we weren't around. Is this, like, some kind of faculty costume party?"

I began to assure Scott that, yes, that's what we'd all been doing, but then I saw how some of the other students were looking at the creatures who had come out of the woods. I exchanged a look with Frank and Soheila and then turned to Liz. "I think the time has come to be honest with our students."

Liz nodded. "I agree. They've proved their valor and their loyalty to Fairwick tonight." Then, turning to the students, she raised her voice. "There are things about this college that we've kept from you—" she began.

"Like the ingredients of the cafeteria's tuna noodle surprise?" someone joked.

"I'm afraid it goes deeper than that," Liz tried again. "Fairwick College is not exactly like other schools."

"Duh," Nicky said. "Don't you think we've noticed that? Look, we know things are different here; you'd have to be blind not to." A murmur of assent moved through the students. "And we think it's about time you trusted us to take a bigger part in what's going on, but you don't have to do it now. We know the college is better off in your hands than in

Duncan Laird's. So we'll march with you to take back the campus."

"Do you think that's a good idea?" I asked. "It could be dangerous."

"We'll make sure the students are protected," Soheila said, spreading her wing over Nicky and Scott, "but I think Nicky's right. Just as the observance of Halloween strengthened the witches' circle, so the active participation of the students will help us to take back the campus—after all, it's their school."

"Hell yeah!" Frank cheered, holding out his fist to Scott Wilder. "The power of student unrest can move mountains. We could call the movement . . . Inhabit Fairwick."

"Cool idea, man," Scott said, returning Frank's fist bump, "but lame name. We'll come up with something better. Let's go take back our college!"

We marched to the southeast gate in the first light of dawn, a motley crew of fairies, witches, Alphas, Stewarts, students, and college professors. We found the gate chained, padlocked, and warded with a spell I recognized as Duncan's. I aimed the angel stone at the padlock and blew it off. As the gates swung open, three trows moved out of the shadows and blocked our way.

"I don't want to hurt you," I said, holding up the brooch, "but this is our college and we're taking it back."

The students behind me cheered. One of the trows turned his massive head slowly, small eyes scanning the students' faces from beneath his heavy, overhanging brow. I was beginning to think it had been a bad idea to bring the students when he grunted and pointed to Scott Wilder.

Liz stepped forward and grunted back at him, and there followed a short colloquy in guttural monosyllables. Then Liz turned to Scott. "He says that you are an honored hero among the trows for trying to save their comrade," Liz told Scott. "You will forever have a place at the great hearth fire of their ancestors, and your cup of mead will be as bottomless as the cauldron of Hymir, which Thor used to brew beer for the Aegisdrekka—Aegir's drinking party, that is."

"Sweet!" Scott exclaimed, then he bowed to the trow and in a sober voice said, "I'm sorry I was too late to save your bro. May his spirit be . . . er . . . carried by a great long ship to the most awesome kegger in the sky."

Liz translated, and the three trows grunted appreciatively and returned Scott's bow. When they raised their heads, they said something else to Liz.

"Scott's heroic act has convinced them to transfer their loyalty to us from the nephilim, who did nothing to help save their friend. We're free to pass and they will march with us to Main Hall, where Duncan Laird and the last of the nephilim have gathered."

"Way to get the trows on our side, Scott!" Frank said, clamping Scott on his shoulder.

"Epic!" Scott agreed, and for once I thought the word was completely fitting.

CHAPTER TWENTY-NINE

The trows wordlessly fell into step with us as we marched through the campus, as if they'd already been informed of the decision to join their ranks to ours. Perhaps they shared a telepathic bond, or the death of their comrade had simultaneously inspired within all of them a desire to overthrow their masters. Whatever the reason, I was glad to have them on our side. Their solid, funereal bearing added gravitas to our procession—and they looked like they could crush a man with one swing of the clubs they wielded, though I was hoping it wouldn't come to that. The angel stone still glowed with a steady, warm light in my hand. Any nephilim guarding Duncan would already know of its power.

We passed Fraser Hall and entered the quad. The grassy rectangle—where students sunned and tossed Frisbees in good weather or hurried across to their classes in bad—was deserted. Neon-hued scraps of paper—all the flyers posted by the nephilim administration—blew across the empty space like fallout from a nuclear holocaust. Stately Main Hall stood at the far end of the quad, looking as forbidding and unassailable as Castle Coldclough, with its gray Gothic exterior and gruesome gargoyles.

Gargoyles?

"Holy Hunchback of Notre Dame," Frank swore. "Where did those ugly bastards come from?"

Crouched on every window ledge and cornice were hundreds of vile creatures. They looked nothing like the beautiful, angelic Duncan Laird. Their skin was gray and leathery, their batlike wings veined in black, their faces pinched and shriveled, with pointy ears. At the sight of us, they opened their mouths as one, revealing long yellow fangs. They cawed like crows, a sound that, along with the leathery rustling of their wings, made my skin crawl.

"What are they?" I asked.

"The first generation," Soheila answered. "When the elves first bred with humans, this is what they produced. These are the monsters rejected by their fathers and reviled by their sons, who have grown more human-looking with each successive generation. We believed these creatures had been banished to an underground tomb, but Duncan Laird must have summoned them to defend him. I wonder if he was keeping them nearby."

"In the tunnels." Anton Volkov had stepped up next to me. "Remember I said there were creatures slaughtering animals and draining their blood? I can smell the blood on them." His nostrils flared.

"There must be hundreds of them," I said. "Too many for me to pick off with the angel stone. Do you think it's possible we can reason with them and convince them to hand over Duncan?"

"We can try," Soheila said. "If Duncan's been holding them as prisoners underground, their loyalty to him might not be as strong as he thinks. I know a bit of their language."

"I don't like you getting that close to those monsters," Frank said.

Soheila smiled at him. "Those *monsters* aren't so different from my own ancestors. And, besides, I won't have to get that close. The wind will carry my voice to them. It's worth a try. Callie's right. She'd never be able to kill them all at once."

"Yeah, but if they do attack, I'm going after them." Frank patted the sword at his side.

"I, too, will join in the attack," Volkov said. "While we hold them off, Cailleach should make a run for it and endeavor to reach Duncan Laird's office."

"Yeah, get that bastard Laird." Frank seconded Volkov by slapping him on the back.

"Happily," I said.

Stepping a few feet in front of the crowd, Soheila flexed her wings, spreading them out in a brilliant fan that caught the rays of the early-morning sun. I'd never seen her winged before—never imagined that our beautiful and elegant Middle-Eastern Studies professor had the ability to become this otherworldly creature. Her wings comprised every color of the desert, from pale sand to burnt umber to deep violet, and when they moved they released a warm breeze redolent of spices and night-blooming jasmine. That wind carried a song on it. Although I couldn't understand its words—I wasn't even sure it had words—it conjured up windswept dunes and sand-scoured rocks carved into graven images. I envisioned great temples where people worshipped the old gods—gods with wings and claws and fangs and tails, gods as grotesque, yet awesome, as the gargoyles, who rustled their bat wings and perked their pointy ears as they listened to Soheila's song. *We were once gods,* she told them, *as you were, too, and we, too, were overthrown for newer gods.* The song changed, and the images in my head were replaced with ones of violence and chaos—statues torn down, cave paintings defaced, women with Soheila's particular beauty reviled and stoned to death.

Unsurprisingly, the gargoyles became agitated at these horrific scenes. They beat their wings and raised a great raucous howl that tore away the fabric of Soheila's vision like claws shredding silk, replacing her desert scenes with a wintry waste where gargoyles wandered cold and naked, expelled by their beautiful fathers. *This is what* we *have suffered,* their cries told us. I felt the angel stone pulsing at my throat in sympathy with their grief. I touched the stone, wanting to communicate to them that I heard their cries and felt their suffering, but as soon as my hand was on the stone, I plunged deeper into their twisted psyches, finding myself in a wasteland colder and bleaker than the arctic tundra. The gargoyles were insane, their minds rent by centuries of captivity in dark caves with only hatred for company—hatred for their fathers for turning their backs on them, hatred for their sons for sealing them beneath the earth, but, most of all, hatred for humans, whose DNA had turned them into monsters. Our smell was inciting them now into a lather of bloodlust. Amid that seething maelstrom was a calm voice directing their rage: Duncan's voice. He had tapped into the gargoyles' minds and was controlling them, funneling their inchoate rage into a pungent stream.

"They're going to attack," I told Frank the second before a hundred pairs of talons pushed off their stone perches and a hundred pairs of leathery wings beat the air.

"Go!" Frank screamed. "We'll hold them back. Get Duncan."

Silver flashed in the air as Frank unsheathed his sword, and he leapt to attack the flying gargoyle heading for Soheila. A trow got it first with his club. I aimed the angel stone at another winged beast headed for Frank. It exploded in a shower of ash that rained down over me. Then I was running toward Main Hall under a swarm of gargoyles sweeping through the air like huge bats. Whenever one came close to me, I shot it with the angel stone. When I reached the front door of Main, I hesitated. Should I stay and fight with my friends? But Frank was right. If Duncan was controlling the gargoyles, I had to get to him.

I pulled at the door . . . and found it locked. *"Sprengja ianuam!"* I hissed the spell under my breath, and the door swung open. As I crossed the threshold, though, I felt a sizzle of energy that made my hair stand on end. A ward. I passed through the electric shock, wondering if this was how dogs felt when they hit an invisible fence. The jolt fried my nerve endings and made my heart miss a beat, but I made it through into the empty lobby, where I stood panting, heart palpitating. I swept my eyes over the marble floor, worn from the tread of generations of students. I scanned the walls, with their portraits of past deans and bulletin boards announcing student events. Looking for guards, I was overcome by the ordinariness of the academic setting and a longing for that world, where students walked these halls on their way to class to discuss literature and art. Instead, my students were outside, battling gargoyles. A surge of anger swept over me and I strode across the marble floor toward the stairs—and into a second ward.

This one knocked me off my feet. Sprawled on the hard floor, I looked up at a shimmering wall. Runes and sigils flashed in the air and then melted in a shower of sparks, like fireworks fading in a night sky. The wards were hastily created. Duncan must have hurriedly put them up as he retreated to the dean's office. I just needed to see the runes and sigils again. I searched the floor for something I could toss at the field, but other than a crumpled Cheetos bag and scraps of paper, which were too light, there was nothing. All I had was the angel stone. I held it up to the field and the sigils and runes lit up like a computer screen. I scanned the symbols, looking for one that glowed brighter—a trick Duncan himself had taught me, to unlock wards—and saw it just before the field melted into a shower of sparks: a sigil shaped like a half-moon with a squiggle on top, located in the lower left-hand corner of the ward field. I crouched low on the floor, positioned my left hand in front of where I thought it had been, and, with my right hand, held the angel stone against the ward. When the sigil flared, I placed my hand on it. Electric bolts shot up my arm, but I kept my hand on the sigil and turned. The ward field vanished and I rolled through where it had been. I scrambled to my feet and charged up the stairs. Two more wards were at the top of the stairs and one was midway down the hall. I figured out how to disarm each one using the angel stone, but the process was wearying. By the time I reached the dean's office, I felt like a drained battery.

The office door was open. And Duncan sat behind the desk, leaning back in the sleek ergonomic chair, his feet up on Dean Book's lovely Louis XVI desk.

"Ah, Callie," he said, smiling at me as if I'd come to discuss my tenure review. "I'm so glad you made it. It's always gratifying to see a student using the skills you've taught them. But, then, I always suspected you would be good at disarming wards. You are a doorkeeper, after all. Please have a seat. As you can see, I've made a fire. Winter comes early to these mountains."

I glanced at the fireplace and saw a roaring fire in the hearth. A thick manila envelope succumbed to the flames.

"So you're destroying all evidence of your plans?" I said. "Do you imagine that will save you?"

"I was hoping it would save the nests of gargoyles and

nephilim that remain. That way, you won't know where I've gone."

"What makes you think I'm going to let you leave?" I asked, stepping closer to the desk and holding up the angel stone. "You'd only come back again—or victimize humans and witches somewhere else."

"The latter, actually. We can usually find some war-torn corner of your world where women are so victimized that we can continue our breeding program unnoticed." His eyes sparkled as he saw me wince. "I don't think I'll try for Fairwick again so soon. Not while you're still here. But in a couple hundred years when we've built up our strength again . . ." He shrugged, one shoulder lifting higher than the other. "Who knows? And as for why you will let me go . . ." He took his feet off the desk and leaned forward. I saw now that, where his wing had been torn from his back, a new one was growing. I gripped the angel stone in my hand and extended my right arm, using my left to steady it. "You'll let me go because you no longer have the power to stop me."

I directed my power through the stone and aimed for the middle of his chest. Nothing happened. I looked down at the stone, which lay cold and inert in my hand.

Duncan laughed. "The wards," he said, almost gently. "They drained the stone. It's only temporary, but"—he looked down at the gleaming gold Rolex on his wrist—"it should give me enough time to get far away from here."

He stepped over to the window, his wings unfurling. Outside, the sun was climbing higher over the eastern mountains. The light touched the tips of the feathers and limned his wings with gold, like the gilding on a Renaissance painting. He *was* as beautiful as an angel. A few more generations and, who knew, perhaps the nephilim would create a race of exquisite creatures—but they would subjugate human women to do it, and the race would be as heartless as it was beautiful. I couldn't let him go. I bowed my head . . . and felt a tug at the nape of my neck. My hair, twisted hurriedly into a knot when I'd left the croft, pulled at my scalp. I touched my hand to the back of my head and felt among the tangles. There, still clinging despite all the battles I'd fought in the last twenty-four hours, was one of the knitting needles William had made for me.

I drew the needle from my hair, a thread of glowing red wool still clinging to it, and leapt over Dean Book's Louis XVI desk and plunged it into Duncan's back, just below his left rib cage. He wheeled around to face me, his fingers flailing to grab the knitting needle. He pulled it out, trailing a long red thread.

His lip curled in a sneer. "Did you really think you could kill me with a knitting needle?"

"No, but I thought this might work." I touched my hand to his chest and pulled the thread lodged beneath his ribs up and forward. Straight through his heart. His eyes widened and his mouth fell open. I yanked harder and he gasped, black gore rising from his throat and dribbling over his lips. He fell to one knee, his wings sagging behind him. He would have fallen flat on his face if I hadn't held him up by the thread. His eyes rolled back in his head, staring up at me.

"That's for killing Bill," I said, tying the knot that cut off his heart.

CHAPTER THIRTY

Frank told me later that as soon as I killed Duncan, it was as if the strings holding the gargoyles up in the air were cut. The monstrous creatures tumbled out of the air, slack and dead-eyed. A few were killed in this passive state, but once Soheila realized what had happened, she ordered a cease-fire, organizing the trows to form a cordon around the gargoyles. A few, coming to their senses, took wing and escaped, flying into the Catskills, but the rest seemed resigned to being prisoners. From the window above, I stood watching Duncan's ashes scatter in the wind until the last speck of him vanished. By then the sun had risen high over the mountains and bathed the village of Fairwick in a rose-gold glow. Smoke still wafted from Main Street and the woods, but the fires had all been extinguished, and already the townspeople were out putting the town to rights and helping one another. Fairwick and Fairwick College would survive and, with the nephilim banished, prosper again. As long as I lived, I could serve as the door between Faerie and Fairwick and so the fey would be free to come and go, bringing the balm of Aelvesgold into this world to heal the wounds we had suffered.

But not all wounds. As I walked out of Main Hall, I felt a tug in my chest. It was as if I'd wrapped the magic thread around my own heart and pulled until I cut off the flow of blood, leaving a lifeless stone in my chest instead of a living, pumping organ. That weight grew heavier as I saw the devastation wrought by the battle. The trows, spurred by the death of their comrade, had rushed headlong into battle and suffered the worst casualties. The survivors stood around their fallen comrades, singing haunting dirges. Brownies and witches, gnomes and Fairwick students sang with them. Scott Wilder stood arm in arm with two trows, swaying as they sang. I searched the crowds for the rest of my students: I spotted Nicky and Flonia administering first aid to a wounded gnome, and Ruby Day and two other girls I recognized from the fairy-tales class were helping Ann and Jessica Chase set up a triage center. I felt a lightening of the weight in my chest when I saw that all my students had survived, and I began to look for my friends. I spotted Frank, Soheila, and Diana crouching on the ground beneath the four red maples that marked the center of the quad. As I approached, I saw that Liz was there, too, as well as Brock, Dory, Phoenix, and Jen. I put my hand over my heart and told myself that all these people were alive because William had sacrificed himself. I was lucky, I told myself, but then Soheila lifted her head and met my gaze and I felt a sirocco of grief pour off her. I hurried toward the four maples, scared to see who was at the center of the circle.

It was my grandmother. She lay on the ground on a blanket of red, which at first I thought were the leaves of the Japanese maples but then realized was her blood. Her head was cradled in Jen Davies's lap. Liz, Diana, and Dory had spread their arms over her, forming a triangle of Aelvesgold that poured over the wound in her chest, but the color of Adelaide's face told me that the Aelvesgold wasn't penetrating her skin. As I knelt beside her, Adelaide's pale-gray eyes fastened on mine, and her hand fluttered weakly in the air. I took it, alarmed at how cold she was.

"What happened?" I cried.

"A gargoyle was headed straight for Nicky Ballard," Frank answered. "Adelaide threw a repulsion spell at him, but it wasn't strong enough. She took the blow that would have killed Nicky."

A garbled sound came from Adelaide's lips. I leaned closer to hear her better.

" . . . make up . . . curse . . ." she gasped.

"You were making up for the curse you put on the Ballards?" I asked.

She nodded and I squeezed her hand. "Thank you," I said, and then, turning to Diana, "Can't you help her?"

Diana lifted her doe eyes to me and shook her head. "She isn't absorbing the Aelvesgold. It sometimes happens when a witch has used too much Aelvesgold in her lifetime."

Adelaide squeezed my hand and made a sound. I leaned my ear down to her lips again and heard her say, "It's my time. I'm so glad you're here and all . . . right." Her eyes scanned the faces surrounding her—all my friends who had rushed to Adelaide's aid, even though she had once been their enemy, because she was *my* grandmother. She mouthed two more words, and then her eyes fluttered closed and her hand went slack in mine. I held on to her hand while my friends, one by one, got up, touching my back and murmuring soft words of condolence, then leaving me alone with Adelaide under the red maples. I sat, looking at her face, red leaves falling over her broken body like a gentle blanket. My grandmother had shown me little kindness in the years when I had needed it the most, but she had taken me in, and I was glad that we had patched up our differences before she died. Still, I wished I could feel more. Her last words, I thought, had been meant as a consolation for leaving me.

Good neighbors, she had said, meaning the family I'd found in Fairwick.

She had also meant to say, I was sure, that she had put away the anger she'd felt when my mother fell in love with one of the fey. Looking at her face, I watched the years of anger and resentment falling away, leaving her far more peaceful and younger than I'd ever known her. Most powerfully, more than I'd ever known, she resembled my mother. For a moment the likeness was so strong that I thought my mother was here with me. I felt her presence as strongly as I had the time I went on a spirit quest and met her inside the spiral labyrinth. My mother's features were momentarily laid over Adelaide's, like a thin, gauzy cloth. Like a benediction. I felt tears well in my eyes and cried for both of them. Together now.

In the coming weeks, as autumn turned toward winter, I saw what good neighbors the townspeople of Fairwick—human and fey—truly were. Although Honeysuckle House had been spared from the fire, others were not so lucky. The Lindisfarnes' house was badly damaged, and the Goodnoughs' animal clinic had burned to the ground. Luckily, Nicky Ballard's mother had noticed the fire in the animal clinic as she was coming home from an A.A. meeting. She'd run back to the church, where half a dozen participants were still chatting over coffee and donuts, and organized them into a rescue team and saved all the animals. The Goodnoughs were so grateful that they gave her a job at the clinic, and she had enrolled in the vet tech program at the community college. In the weeks following the fire, I heard a lot of stories that reconfirmed my faith in the resilience of the community. Newly returned from Faerie, the Esta family reopened their pizzeria and organized a Meals On Wheels for people who had lost their homes. While Shady Pines was being rebuilt, families volunteered to take in residents. I heard that Mrs. Goldstein was staying with the Chases and that she and Jessica played cards every afternoon.

I was most heartened by how active my students were in helping the town. I'd been worried that the sudden revelation that their college was inhabited by witches and fairies would be too much for them, but they seemed to adjust almost effortlessly. Scott Wilder and Ruby Day started a student–fey liaison club called Students for a More United and Reintegrated Fairwick—SMURF—and asked me to be the faculty sponsor. At the first meeting, they invited Dean Book and lobbied for classes on magic and fairy history. The dean informed them she'd long been thinking of doing just that.

"Mightn't that be dangerous?" I asked Liz after the meeting.

"We'll have to go slow and make sure that only students who are responsible enough learn the higher levels of magic. We'll get Soheila to vet students for emotional stability. But I think it's a good idea. I've often thought that Fairwick could have a wider mission in this world. We've focused so long on mere survival, hiding out here in our secluded valley, but look at where that got us. The evils of this world sought us out. There *are* real evils in the world—fey and human—and real suffering. We should be doing more to train our students to relieve suffering and uproot evil. It's a troubled world out there. Fairwick can be a beacon of hope. I hope you'll be involved, Callie."

I told her I would be. Besides, I needed a mission— something on which to focus my attention. It wasn't that my classes weren't going well. In fact, they were going so well they practically taught themselves. My students eagerly prepared oral reports and group presentations on the assigned readings and engaged in animated discussions that filled up the entire class period. Having learned that fairies and monsters were real, they read the fairy tales with a new urgency. They debated and argued about them as though Little Red Riding Hood and Beauty and the Beast contained the secrets of the universe—and perhaps they did. Appearances are deceiving. Trust in yourself. Be kind to the old and the weak. Follow your heart. As valid a set of precepts for leading a good life as you would find anywhere. *But what if you did all that and you defeated the evil monster, but at the end Prince Charming was dead and the evil queen had pulled your heart out of your chest?* Those were the questions that I itched to scrawl across my students' papers.

Instead, I corrected their faulty grammar and misspellings but not their hopeful illusions. Even if I no longer believed in happy endings, I wanted them to. But when I put down my red pen, Honeysuckle House loomed around me like a haunted house. Floorboards creaked, windowpanes rattled, cold drafts stalked the hallways, and shadows lurked in corners. With Ralph curled in my sweater pocket as he continued to recuperate from his attack, I paced the halls, trying to pin down the fleeting shadows, listening to the rustle and murmur of the old house settling on its foundation, watching for a glimpse of its ghost. But the house wasn't haunted by a ghost; it was haunted by *time*. Something in its walls had made itself into a home for the incubus and still retained the impression of his incarnations. The pebbles and bits of wood that Liam used to bring home in his pockets migrated along the window ledges and shelves. I heard Bill's hammer in the pound of branches on the roof, and I smelled William's heather in the roving pockets of cold air. Each of them had left an impression on the house—even William, who had never been inside it.

Or had he? When he returned to Faerie, he said it was to become the man I would someday fall in love with. So William had become Liam and then Bill . . . but when I tried to sort that out, I tied myself into a knot that further tightened around my heart. What did any of it matter? I had lost all three of them, and I didn't need to be a scholar of fairy tales to know that was all the chances I would get.

I kept busy. I joined the curriculum committee charged with creating the new classes to teach students magic and volunteered for Meals On Wheels. I delivered two dozen turkey dinners on Thanksgiving—the last one to Nan Stewart in the hospital. She'd been one of the Shady Pines residents too ill to go into a private residence. Mac had told me she'd asked to see me, but I'd shamefully put off the visit, afraid it would be too painful to be reminded of Ballydoon and William. On Thanksgiving, though, after seeing the faces of the old people light up when Dory and I delivered their turkey, I decided that was a poor reason for not visiting an old woman who might not have much time left. So I went home and made a special plate for her. I found her sitting up in her bed, a plaid shawl around her shoulders, refusing the tray of hospital food the nurse was pushing on her.

"I thought you might come," Nan said, gratefully accepting the plate of hot buttered bannocks I'd baked. "Ah, I see you learned how to make them properly on your trip."

I was about to ask her what trip she meant, but then I realized by the mischievous gleam in her eye that she knew exactly where I'd been. I looked at her more closely. She didn't just *resemble* the seventeenth-century Nan Stewart—she was identical.

"It *was* you."

"I ken what ye mean, lass, and, aye, I'm the same Nan you first met in Ballydoon."

"First met? But didn't we meet first here in Fairwick this fall?"

"First for you, but not for me," she said, dunking a bag of the PG Tips tea I'd brought into a mug of hot water. "I met ye first in the Ballydoon market square the morning after All Hallows' Eve, 1659, when ye brought my nephew William back from Faerie."

"But I hadn't done that yet when I met you here this fall. I hadn't gone back yet."

"Aye, but ye had. I know it's confusing." Nan patted my hand kindly. I looked down at her hand and saw the deep scars around her wrists where the witch hunters' manacles had bit into her skin. "Everything about ye was a bit blurry when ye came to visit me, but after Halloween it all came clear—or most of it. I remember now your coming to Bally-doon and the time you spent there, how ye showed me to use the tartan—"

"That makes *no* sense," I objected. "I saw the Stewarts use the tartan *before* I went back. How can I be the one who taught them how to use it?"

Nan shrugged and bit into her bannock. "Sense or no, that's how I remember it. Just as I remember ye defeating the nephilim at Castle Coldclough."

"And what happened after that?" I asked.

"Why, the village went back to normal, except that then we had a group of young men who could protect us from harm with the tartan. I taught new ones to use it over the years. Eventually they became known as the Stewarts instead of the Stewards. I discovered that I aged slowly and never died—an effect of the tartan, mayhap—and so I became the Stewarts' ancient granny." She leaned back in her hospital bed and plucked a corner of her plaid shawl over her shoulders. "But last year I began to feel a bit tired of looking after generation after generation of great clod-heided boys. I began to feel my time was finally coming on me, so I came to Shady Pines and then here. I think that I've been waiting all these years to meet ye again, to send you back. And now that I have . . ." She smiled, but wistfully. "Well, I think it might finally be my time."

I started to object, but Nan squeezed my hand. "Dinna fash yerself, lass. I can rest easy knowing those monsters are well and truly gone. Since you came to see me, I've found myself half-living in those auld days, and I have an inkling that when I go, I'll go back to those sweet-smelling hills . . ."

Her voice trailed off, and her eyes fluttered. I thought she might be *going* right now, but she was only falling asleep.

"She drops off like that these days after her tea," the nurse said, coming quietly into the room on her rubber-soled shoes and tucking the shawl around Nan. "She always smiles like that, too. I wonder what's she's dreaming of."

Heather-covered hills, I thought, *and violet skies.*

I got up to go, more confused than when I came, and bent down to give Nan a kiss on her weathered cheek. Her eyes flickered open. "I saw him one more time," she said.

"Who?" I asked, although I knew who she meant.

"William. He came to me in the Greenwood and told me a story. I told it to Mairi—you remember Mairi, don't you? The lass you saved from the pest . . . She married a fellow from Edinburgh . . ."

"Yes," I told Nan, trying not to sound impatient but wanting to hear William's story more than whom Mairi married. "What was the story?"

"It was about—" Nan began to cough. I poured a glass of

water and held it up to her lips. "It was about a lad taken by the Fairy Queen. He's saved by his true love but then must sacrifice himself to save her."

I sighed. "I know that story."

"Do you know the part where the lad makes a deal with the Fairy Queen?" Nan asked anxiously, her voice weak and fretful.

"Yes," I told her, patting her hand and tucking her shawl around her shoulders again. "I know that part."

"Ah," Nan sighed. "That's all right, then. That was the part I was meant to tell ye . . ." Her eyes closed and she fell asleep.

I left, feeling sadder than ever as I walked home. William had appeared to Nan to tell her why he had vanished. Even if I went back in time to Ballydoon, he wouldn't be there. I now realized I'd been considering that as a possibility. Surely I wouldn't have gone back, leaving my friends and the life I'd made in Fairwick, even if he had been waiting for me. But knowing that it wasn't a possibility made me feel as though one more of the threads that bound us had been broken.

CHAPTER THIRTY-ONE

The next morning, Mac Stewart showed up at my door. From his red puffy eyes I knew immediately what had happened.

"My nan died in her sleep," he said, sniffling. "She looked fine when I stopped by last night. Everybody's saying it's a good way to go, but I . . ." His voice wobbled, and I invited him in for tea and leftover bannocks.

"Just like Nan's," he sniffed, wiping his nose on the cuff of his flannel shirt and smearing butter over his chin. Ralph, who'd woken up from his long nap, jumped up on the table and offered a napkin to Mac. "She liked you," Mac said, taking the napkin and dabbing at his face. "She told me last night that she wanted to give this to you." Mac reached into a shopping bag and pulled out the tartan shawl Nan had been wearing the last time I saw her.

"Oh, no, Mac, I couldn't take this. It's a family heirloom."

"She said that you *are* family. She said you were married to her nephew . . . or would be married . . ." Mac scrunched up his face, confused. "I'm afraid Nan was wandering a bit in her mind . . . You don't have a fiancé, do you?"

"I haven't even got a boyfriend," I replied.

Mac started to smile but then remembered about his nan and sniffled. I gave him a handkerchief to blow his nose and drew Nan's shawl into my lap, my eyes filling as I stroked the soft wool. I noticed that there were threads of purple in the weave that reminded me of Ballydoon, and I recalled what Nan had said—that she thought that's where she would go when she died. Picturing her walking over the heather-covered hills of Ballydoon made me a bit less sad.

Nan's death released something in me. Who was I to sit around feeling sorry for myself while people had real reason to grieve? I roused myself to finish the semester with more spirit and energy. I even accepted an invitation to Fairwick's annual solstice party, which this year was to be held at the new Alpha house.

Although Diana could have reclaimed her inn from the Alphas, she had opted instead to move in as their den mother—a role that seemed to suit her perfectly. From my windows I'd watched the restoration of the house—the ratty couches and empty beer cans banished from the porch and replaced with rocking chairs and wicker settees, the shrubbery and rosebushes trimmed, bird feeders filled regularly, garden gnomes and statuary mended and restored, Christmas lights strung up and menorah lit—but I hadn't been inside. I was surprised to find an oddly cheerful combination of the old twee inn décor and frat-boy paraphernalia: a wide-screen TV decorated with pine swag, a foosball table in the sunflower porch, and a basketball hoop outside in the rose garden. The Alphas themselves were dressed in elfin costumes and carried trays of mini-quiches and non-alcoholic punch. I found Frank drinking a Heineken and having a spirited conversation with Adam Sinclair and Ruby Day on the Jets' chances in the playoffs. They all greeted me enthusiastically, and after a few minutes

Adam and Ruby exchanged a meaningful look and excused themselves to help Diana in the kitchen. Warily, I watched them go.

"Do you think Ruby's okay with him?" I asked. "I mean, Adam is—"

"A perfectly normal college guy," said Frank, "so, within reason, yeah, I think Ruby can take care of herself. Diana gives a talk to the boys once a week on respecting women. She's got them volunteering at the battered women's shelter and doing yoga and meditation for anger management."

"But aren't they . . ." I couldn't think what word to use. *Evil? Doomed? Tainted?* ". . . like their fathers?"

Frank grimaced. "The nephilim were created because the elves forced themselves on human women and produced sons who were monsters in their eyes. And because they were monstrous to their fathers, they became *monsters*. Generation after generation repeated that awful cycle for . . . no one knows for how long. They're not immortal but long-lived. Soheila thinks they stopped breeding for hundreds of years but then started again when they hatched this plan to close the doors to Faerie in revenge against the fey. These boys are more human than not. Some will grow wings, claws, and perhaps an overweening sense of entitlement, but Diana, Liz, and Soheila think that they can be managed with the right nurturing."

"And what do you think?"

Frank took a swig of his beer and shrugged. "I think if anyone can civilize a bunch of brute males, it's those three. And, just in case, I've got the Stewarts keeping an eye on them."

I looked around the room. Interspersed among the college students were a dozen plaid-wearing townspeople, including Mac Stewart, who was now captivating Flonia Rugova with a story. "I hope they're salvageable," I said, glancing around the room at all the couples—Diana and Liz, Adam and Ruby, Nicky and Scott. Soheila was standing alone in a corner, looking over at Frank and me. Turning back to Frank, I intercepted a look between them.

"How about you, McFay?" Frank asked.

"Am I salvageable?" I asked, trying to make a joke of it, but Frank didn't smile. "I honestly don't know, Frank. You know, I found him."

"No, I didn't know," Frank said. "Other than telling us about your run-in with the nephilim witch hunters, you've been pretty quiet about your whole Scottish adventure. I guessed, though, that you found Liam."

"William," I corrected automatically. "William Duffy. That's who he was before he became an incubus."

"Ah," Frank said, "and were you in love with him?"

"Not at first," I said, "but then . . ." My eyes filled with tears and I closed them. I saw what I always saw when I closed my eyes: William silhouetted against a hill covered with purple heather, making his way home to the cottage. "He told me that I didn't love him, that I loved the man he would become, but—" I broke off, unable to finish the thought.

"Idiot," Frank said, but with a fond smile. "Didn't he know that women always love us for the men we will become? If they didn't, we'd still be living in caves and conking them over the head with clubs." He waved his beer bottle at the room and began what would, I'm sure, have been a colorful lecture on the civilizing influences of women, but Soheila came over and informed him that some of the boys had organized a touch-football game in the back that was threatening to destroy Diana's arbor.

"I'll go have a talk with them," he said, with a gleam in his eyes that suggested to me that he'd get in a pass or two before corralling the game. "That is, if you're okay, McFay?"

"Go," I told him. "I'll be fine."

Soheila began to say something to me but was summoned to the kitchen to save a burned casserole.

I stood awkwardly by myself for a few minutes after she left, wondering how soon I could politely slip out, but then Nicky, Flonia, and Ruby surrounded me and regaled me with their plans for the winter break. Dean Book had gotten them invited to an IMP conference as student delegates.

"We're spearheading a campaign for student representatives at the institute," Nicky said. "We call it Occupy Narnia."

"And we're also getting to attend panels on magic and fairies," Flonia said. "I'm going to one on Romanian folklore with Anton Volkov. It is so exciting. All my life I have listened to the old stories my nana told me, and I thought they were nonsense. Now I know they were true. After I graduate, I am going to work with nocturnals who are having difficulty assimilating into modern society."

A vampire social worker? It wasn't the career path I had imagined for my student, but after all Anton Volkov had done in the fight to save Fairwick, I didn't doubt that the nocturnals were worth helping. And who knew what other opportunities the new Fairwick would present to my students? It *was* exciting, and for the half hour I stood in my students' company, listening to their bright, enthusiastic chatter, I felt a little of the gloom lifting off me. When Flonia and Ruby drifted away toward a game of beer pong, I thought I'd be going. Nicky, though, lingered behind, clearly with a question on her mind.

"What is it, Nicky?"

"I just wanted to say . . ." She blushed and looked awkward. "I just wanted to thank you for lifting the curse off my family. Dean Book told me about it."

I blushed as red as the punch in my cup. "You don't have to thank me, Nicky. It was my great-great-grandfather who cursed the Ballards in the first place."

"But that wasn't your fault, and Dean Book said you went to a lot of trouble to lift the curse, so I wanted to thank you and to tell you it's working. My mom is getting herself together, and I feel . . . Well, it's like in the William Duffy story, when he says at the end that everyone deserves not just a second chance but a third. You've given that to my mom."

"You're welcome, Nicky," I said, trying to keep the tears from my eyes at the mention of William. "He was right." I paused. "But I don't remember that part in the story."

"You know," Nicky said, tilting her head, "neither did I. But when I reread the story, there it was, right at the end. In fact, the whole ending was different from how I remembered it. I wrote about it in my paper."

"Which I haven't read yet," I said guiltily. "I'm going to go home right now and do that."

Nicky looked embarrassed all over again. "Oh, Dr. McFay, I didn't mention the paper because I thought you'd read it already, although I am anxious to know what you think about it. I followed your advice and wrote to the Center for the Book about the folklorist Mary Brodie McGowan—"

"Did you say Mary *Brodie* McGowan?" I asked.

"Yes, Brodie was her maiden name. You were right about her being related to the publisher. She married Alisdair McGowan and published under that name. But here's another funny thing about her name. Later the family changed its name because of Mary's fairy stories and because she claimed that she was saved from the plague by a good fairy who spread a magic blanket on her and an old woman in the village told her fairy stories. You'll never guess what she changed it to . . ."

"McFay," I said as if the name was written on the air between us.

"Yes! Your name! Maybe you were related. Is anything wrong, Dr. McFay? You've turned white as a ghost."

I felt as if I'd just encountered one. The Mary Brodie McGowan she was describing must have been Mairi, and the old woman who told her fairy stories must have been Nan.

"You said the ending of William Duffy was different from how you remembered it?" I asked urgently.

Nicky shrugged. "I must have misremembered it. I wasn't getting a lot of sleep at that point in the semester, what with all those bells ringing all the time. Maybe I confused it with another story, although I don't know how. I've never read a fairy story that reads quite like this one. Are you sure you're all right, Dr. McFay? Maybe you should sit down?"

"I'm perfectly fine, I just have to go home *right now*. Thanks for telling me about the story . . . and giving me the book . . . and writing your paper on it . . . and just—thank you!" I gave Nicky an impetuous hug and fled the room, dodging colleagues and students wishing me a Happy Solstice and a Merry Christmas.

"Merry Christmas!" I shouted back at them as I escaped out into the frigid air. It had started snowing. "Merry Christmas!" I shouted as I ran across the street, like Jimmy Stewart in *It's a Wonderful Life,* running down the main street of Bedford Falls, greeting his restored world. I felt the same excitement bubbling in my chest, fizzing around my heart, which I'd thought would never fizz again.

William appeared to Nan after he'd gone back to Faerie, and he told her a story. Nan had told that story to Mairi—Mary Brodie McGowan—and she'd written it down in a book that Nicky had found in Edinburgh. That story had changed from the story I'd read before Halloween. Maybe William had only sent a final goodbye across time, but even that—one more word from him—would be better than nothing.

I ran up my porch steps, slipping on a light coating of snow and dropping the keys onto the floor. As I bent to retrieve them, I found myself looking into emerald-green eyes. I had forgotten to leave the outside light on, but the light from my foyer shone through the fanlight, casting a reflection of the stained-glass face on the porch floorboards. Liam's face, then Bill's, then William's, looking at me as though across an ocean of time. *Hurry*, those eyes said, *I am waiting for you.*

I retrieved my keys and opened the door. Without taking my coat off or closing the door behind me, I crossed the foyer into the library. I went to find the book on the shelves, but where I'd last seen it there was an empty slot—or not exactly empty. Ralph was curled up napping where the book had been. I looked down and saw the book lying open on the floor. I knelt and picked it up. It was open to the story of William Duffy. Still kneeling, melting snow dripping from my hair, I read.

It was the same story I remembered, until I got to the part where the Fairy Queen rides out with her captive. Now a girl named Katy (which I remembered was what the villagers had called the first Cailleach) is waiting at the crossroads to pull William from his horse. He changes into a lion, a snake, and a burning brand, but she holds on to him until he's human again. The Fairy Queen tells them that if either of them steps into Faerie again, she will pluck out their eyes and hearts and replace them with eyes and heart of wood—the same curse the Fairy Queen had placed on William and me! The story in the book had changed because I had gone back in time. The page shimmered in my hands like moving water, as if it were caught in the flow of time and it might vanish at any moment, but then I saw it was only because my hands were shaking and my vision was blurred by tears. I wiped them away and read on.

Unlike Tam Lin, the story didn't end with the hero and heroine reunited. Monsters descend on William Duffy's village, and he and Katy defeat them with a magic plaid. But they still can't be together, because Katy must return to her own village to fight their enemies. To buy her passage through Faerie, William sacrifices himself to the Fairy Queen.

My hands were shaking so badly, the tears flowing so freely by this part of the story, that I was forced to sit on the floor and lean on the bookshelf. I let the book fall in my lap and my head drop into my hands. My poor William! What really broke my heart was that he must have come back to Nan to tell her this story, as if he'd had to explain it to someone to justify the choice he'd made—to willingly become a monster so his beloved could become a heroine. Or perhaps William had told it to Nan so I would understand.

I looked back down at the book. William says his farewell to Katy, but before he goes, he whispers something in the Fairy Queen's ear, a condition of his deal. *His beloved could not hear what he asked and mayhap she would never know, but I heard this tale from my gran, who heard it from Old Nan Stewart of Ballydoon, who said she had it from . . .*

"For the love of Mike, Mary Brodie McGowan, spit it out!" I cried, turning the last page so fast I nearly ripped it from its binding.

. . . from William himself, who appeared to her in the Greenwood and told her that the boon he asked of the Fairy Queen was this: to give his beloved three chances to gain him back.

The book nearly slipped out of my benumbed fingers. *Three chances?* I stared at the words. The rule of three was the most common fairytale device of all. Cinderella goes to the ball three times; Jack climbs his beanstalk three times; Snow White receives three visits from her evil stepmother. Mary McGowan might have added it just to give her story a more satisfying rhythm.

Or perhaps William really had asked the Fairy Queen to give me three chances to get him back.

Once for Liam, who I didn't love enough.

Twice for Bill, who I loved and saw die.

Thrice . . .

I looked up from the book to the clock on the mantel. It was ten minutes to midnight on the winter solstice: A time, like Halloween, when the fabric between the worlds grew thin. Was William waiting for me in that gauzy membrane between the worlds, waiting for me to pluck him out of limbo as I had dragged him from his fairy steed? Did I really have one more chance to save him? Could I dawdle here a moment longer if I did?

I ran out the back door, not pausing to change into boots. The snow seeped through my thin party shoes, but I didn't feel the cold. My heart was knocking against my chest, unbound for the first time since I'd returned from Ballydoon, pounding out a three-beat rhythm. Once for Liam, twice for Bill, thrice for . . . for whom? William? But hadn't I already had my chance with William and lost him, too? What if I'd already used up all my chances?

I skidded to a halt, my heart juddering as if it had gone ahead without me, and looked around at the bare limbs and vines, first blasted when the door was destroyed last summer and then scorched by the Halloween fire. The door wasn't in these woods anymore. I was the door. I was William's way back into this world—but how? I could open a door to Faerie, but would he be there?

I started to walk again, instinctively heading for the glade in the center of the honeysuckle thicket where the door had once been, where Liam and I had stood together a year ago, where Bill had died. Where I'd come back after leaving William. If there was any place where I could make him whole again, this would be it.

Walking slower now, I noticed something happening to the woods. Draped in snow, the vines looked almost as if they were in bloom, and the dark places between the trees were full of the glint of snow sifting down from the pine boughs. The whole forest was starred with floating orbs of light, like Christmas lights or . . .

Looking closer, I saw that the floating lights were tiny winged creatures no larger than fireflies. They flocked around me, gaining in numbers as I walked—a host of tiny fairies accompanying me. As they touched the honeysuckle vines, flowers burst into bloom, filling the snowy woods with a summery scent but also with the smoky peat smell of autumn on the Scottish moors and the wild-heather scent of spring. All of time surrounded me, as if it were happening at once: my time with Liam and then Bill and then William. They were *all* with me now as I walked through the snow and blossom-laden woods.

As I remembered the first moonlit, honeysuckle-scented air that had brought Liam to me, the vines around me erupted into bloom. I remembered Bill humming the lullaby his mother had once sung, and the wind in the trees sighed the tune. I remembered the wild heather William had brought me, and the purple blooms broke though the snow-covered ground. My memories brought each time to life because I *was* the door between those times. I had the power to bring each moment back to life, and if I could do that, I could bring my incubus back—not just one of his incarnations, but all of them. I wanted the wild lover who'd come to me in moonlight and shadow, the kind man who'd fixed my broken heart, *and* the boy who'd given away his youth so he could become those men. I said their names as I walked through the woods. William, Liam, Bill. William, Liam, Bill. The same name, really. *William,* I had read once, meant *desire.* Their last names— Duffy, Doyle, Carey—all meant *dark.* My dark desire. *Come into the light.*

As I stepped into the glade, the moon rose above the trees on the other side. When its light touched the ground, a gust stirred up the snow into a whirlwind. I stood transfixed, barely daring to breathe as the snowflakes moved faster and faster, coalescing into the shape of a man made of moonlight and shadow, of desire and dreams, of joy and pain. He took shape in front of me, but he was still insubstantial. A moment's errant breeze would blow him out of my life forever. How did I make him flesh . . . what spark . . . ?

I felt something tingling in my hand. Looking down, I saw that the scar the Luckenbooth brooch had left in my hand was glowing, the two hearts pulsing as one. *This* was the spark.

I reached into the swirling chaos and grabbed his hand, the blood that pumped beneath my flesh igniting his atoms into life. His hand clasped mine. He turned in a flurry of snow, becoming flesh in my arms, green eyes still carrying the primordial spark of the ether from which I'd plucked him.

"I knew you'd find me," he said, pulling me into his arms. For a moment I felt the world spinning, but then I looked into his eyes and knew where I wanted it to stop. He crushed his mouth to mine, my flesh to his warm *human* flesh.

"You're really here," I cried, trying to touch and see all of him at one time. "You're really . . ." I stopped, unsure what to call him.

"Will," he said, smiling. "Call me Will."

ABOUT THE AUTHOR

JULIET DARK is the pseudonym of bestselling author Carol Goodman, whose novels include *The Lake of Dead Languages*, *The Seduction of Water*, and *Arcadia Falls*. Her novels have won the Hammett Prize and have been nominated for the Dublin/IMPAC Award and the Mary Higgins Clark Award. Her fiction has been translated into thirteen languages. She lives in New York's Hudson Valley with her family.

OCT -- 2013

STAINS NOTED 5/17/16